To Mom, Dad, and Lynne

# *The Cygnet*

## Caryl C. Block

ISBN 978-1-63575-941-9 (Paperback)
ISBN 978-1-63575-942-6 (Digital)

Christian Faith Publishing, Inc.
296 Chestnut Street
Meadville, PA 16335
www.christianfaithpublishing.com

Printed in the United States of America

# *Acknowledgments*

---

Barry Sheinkopf, Director of Services of the Writing Center, Englewood Cliffs, NJ. Thank you, Barry, for helping me turn my writings into a book all those years ago. I have become a better writer because of what you taught me.

\* \* \*

My friends who have read the manuscript: in New Jersey, Erin DeCanio and Kelly Mancini; in Colorado, Marcia Baldon, Paula Carlson, Mary Clifton, Virginia Morris, Gisela Sutton, and Cathy Taylor. Thank you, ladies, for loving my story and for your suggestions for making it even better.

# Prologue

---

## Monday, April 9, 1855

Jack Matthias sat in his study, a frown beginning to crease his forehead. He reread the single sheet of paper, then, stretching back in his maroon leather chair, handed it across the cluttered desk to the younger man opposite.

"What's wrong?" Arthur Jamison asked his friend and mentor.

"He's coming, Arthur. After everything I have written him about the State Department's position on such matters these past two years, the king of Ahrweiler insists on discussing his internal problems in person."

"If President Pierce will see him." Arthur scanned the letter. "Have you thought about writing again?"

"I doubt it would do any good. He'll be here in early summer. If I wrote, my letter would miss him." Jack watched the sun motes streaming from the windows. "We'll have to tell Marcy."

"He'll just give it back to you. You *are* the expert on the lesser German states."

"At least I'll have help entertaining them." Jack glanced at the portrait of a girl on the wall, and his face relaxed. "Clarinda's coming home next month."

Arthur, his blue eyes twinkling, matched Jack's smile. "For good this time?"

"She's eighteen in November. Too old to be a schoolgirl, eh, Arthur?" Jack laughed as his companion blushed.

"Will she be joining you here?" Arthur managed to ask.

"No, I'll be opening Landfield. It's the only home she knows, and, for the summer anyway, healthier than Washington."

"And when summer's over?"

A knock on the door stopped conversation. Following Jack's acknowledgment, a tall, thin woman let herself in. Her eyes traveled around the wood-paneled room, and clearing her throat, she announced, "The Royces have arrived, Mr. Matthias."

Jack looked up. "Well, Bernice, I assume you have met with them. Do you think they will suit?"

The somber housekeeper ignored the chair vacated by Arthur. "They are not exactly what I pictured from Mr. Armitage's letter, although their references are excellent."

"Meaning?"

Her narrow lips tightened, and she inhaled sharply. "I thought, after reading the letter, Mr. and Mrs. Royce would be able to replace Mattie and Jacob. Mrs. Royce might do, but Mr. Royce . . . *he'll* never be more than a menial." She dropped her voice. "And they have children."

"I know. Three girls and a boy. Perhaps *they* will do."

Catching the irritation in his voice, she continued, "I left them downstairs."

"In the kitchen?"

"Housekeeper's room. You will see them?"

"In a few minutes."

As Bernice prepared to leave, she asked, "Will you be dining here, Mr. Matthias?"

"I'll be eating at the club." Jack watched the retreating figure in the black silk dress. "Make sure the Royces get settled. If they can't be of use here, we can certainly use them at Landfield."

"Of course." She bustled out of the room.

Arthur, who had been studying the portrait of Jack's niece, returned to his seat. "I don't see why you keep Bernice on. She acts like she owns the place."

"She does an excellent job, both here and at Landfield. Besides, she has nowhere else to go."

"Indeed?"

"She worked for Ralph and Jane before Jane died. When Ralph moved to Landfield with Clarinda and I took over this house, I asked Bernice to stay on."

"I didn't know."

"Well, it is old news." Jack paused for a moment. "That's about all for today."

"Same time tomorrow?"

"Fine. I'll walk you down."

The two men descended from the third floor, Jack thinking about Arthur and his reaction to the mention of Clarinda. "It wouldn't be such a bad match," Jack said to himself. "They're fond of each other, and I know he would take care of her." It was difficult to think of his little Clarinda as a young woman, and Jack sighed.

"Something the matter?"

"Oh no. Just reflecting on how quickly time passes." They came to the door, and Jack let the other man out, spotting the unfamiliar carriage with two excited faces pressed against the window. He smiled, shut the door, and headed for the service door.

The Royces were standing in the center of the room, a little out of place amid the elaborate upholstery and carefully draped table, which represented Bernice's taste. A cursory review by Jack revealed they were of average height and typical Germanic coloring—fair, light-eyed. *Rather ordinary*, he thought. He also sensed an uneasiness about them, which he attributed to nervousness. Offering them a seat, he settled into a divan. "Mr. and Mrs. Royce, I am Jack Matthias. Mr. Armitage wrote me, saying you needed work."

"Yes, Mr. Matthias," the woman replied in a clipped accent. "We felt it was time to move on."

"How long did you work for him?"

"A year and a half."

"And before that?"

"Three years in Philadelphia. The lady asked us this before."

Her directness caught Jack off guard. Hoping to move into less sensitive territory, he remarked, "I understand you are Swiss."

Adele Royce's eyes darted around the pale-green flocked wallpaper, finally discerning her husband's sidelong glance. "Yes, Swiss," she answered. "But we have been in United States for eighteen years. Our girls were born here."

Jack grinned at the mention of the children. "And your son?"

"He was . . . he was born in old country. He is twenty-one."

"If he is capable, I would like to use him here as my manservant — valet, butler, that sort of thing."

"My boy helps me. All he is good for."

A surprised Jack stared at the heretofore silent Joseph Royce, who — with his scrawny physique, his weasel-like face screwed up in anger — resembled a fighting bantam. "Mr. Royce, I shall decide for myself what your boy is or is not good for as well as the rest of you." He turned his attention back to Adele. "Have Miss Lycoming bring your son to my study, then speak to her about the particulars of your employment. She'll get you settled here until we move on to my home in the country."

"We are hired?"

"Yes." Excusing himself, Jack left the room and, after speaking briefly to Bernice, returned to his study.

* * *

Ten minutes later, Bernice entered once more, followed by a young man. Tall and dark, with a haunting sadness in his nearly black eyes, he attempted to hide behind the housekeeper, but she pulled him forward. "Mr. Matthias, this is the Royce boy."

"Thank you, Bernice. Please sit down," Jack added as the door closed behind her.

The young man chose a leather wing chair, which stood by the door. Staring down at his shoes, he mumbled, "She said you wanted to see me, sir."

"That's right." Jack looked through the box of letters on the mahogany desk, finally finding the one he wanted. Quickly reading it, he asked, "You are Richard?"

The other man looked up in surprise. "How did you know?"

"Your last employer wrote me, and he mentions you in particular, if you are Richard."

The sadness immediately became fear. "It wasn't my fault. Mr. Armitage said it wasn't my fault."

"What wasn't your fault?"

"The accident to Master Peter." Richard's head dropped.

Jack sat a moment, recalling the near-tragedy in his friend's life. Walter Armitage's son had been severely injured in a riding accident, and, apparently, this young man believed himself responsible, though it had been purely an accident.

"Richard" — the boy started — "Mr. Armitage didn't mention his son's accident. He said he felt you are an exceptionally able worker, and he was sorry to see you go."

"He said that about me?"

"Here's the letter. You can read it if you would like."

Richard shook his head. "He wouldn't lie to you, sir."

Walking around the small room, Jack studied the young man. He certainly was honest; the way his emotions showed in his eyes told Jack that. He could also see a fair degree of intelligence, and though he hated to admit it, Jack knew the handsome servant with the soft baritone would definitely be an asset at dinner parties. Jack returned to his seat behind the desk and asked, "Have you ever been a house servant, Richard?"

"A couple of times when I was little. Helping her in the kitchen, mostly." He ran his fingers through his hair. "The people we worked for in Boston started to have me trained in the dining room before we moved on."

Jack smiled. "I need a male house servant, especially here in Washington, and I believe you will do nicely."

"I haven't done that since I was twelve. After we left Boston, all he's let me be is a gardener or stableboy. It's all I'm good for," Richard added, almost inaudibly.

"Why do you say that?" Jack probed, recalling Joseph had made the same comment earlier about the boy.

"He tells me I'm clumsy and stupid; that I can't do anything except what he lets me do."

"Wouldn't you like to better yourself, prove your father wrong?" The haunted look returned to Richard's face. "I believe you're old enough to decide what you want to do."

"What did he say?"

"That you help him."

Richard began glancing around the room, his long fingers lacing and unlacing. His gaze fixed on the portrait of Jack's father, which hung between the two windows. Staring at the steely-eyed old gentleman, his back stiffened and, focusing beyond Jack to the books that lined the wall behind him, said flatly, "I'll do what he wants."

Taken back a little, Jack questioned, "You're certain? If your father is the problem, I can arrange for you to stay here permanently instead of moving to the country with the rest of the household."

"I-I can't. He won't let me. If I do what he wants, he won't be mad at me."

"All right, then, but if you should ever change your mind, my offer stands. I hate having potential wasted."

Richard took a few deep breaths, then stood. "May I go now?"

"Certainly." After Richard left, his employer, still surprised by the turn of events, lit a cigar and wondered if Bernice's evaluation of the Royces had indeed been the correct one.

Joseph was waiting when Richard came out to the carriage. "What did the new master want?"

"He asked me to be his house servant."

"And what did you tell him?"

"I said no."

Joseph sneered. As he did, Richard cringed inwardly. "Perhaps you're not so stupid after all. You know what your place is."

*You've showed me often enough,* Richard thought. "What do you want me to do?"

"Take them boxes inside. That Miss Lycomin' tell you where to put 'em."

"I thought she said we'd be working in the country."

Joseph cuffed him hard across the face. "I don't tell you to think, and I don't like your smart-mouthin'. I don't need you to lose us *this* job, like you always do." The tirade having its desired effect, he continued, "When you finish that, take this horse and carriage back to the livery." His gray eyes narrowed, and he hissed, "And don't be slow about it. You're already too lazy as it is."

\* \* \*

Late that night, Richard turned away from the wall, his back aching where Joseph had switched him earlier. It wasn't his fault he became lost in the city and the new master had found him and brought him back, but, Richard thought resignedly, it didn't matter anyway. *He'd* have found something to hit me for.

The voices in the adjacent room faded. So many years Richard had forced himself to stay awake, listening to their conversations, but he learned nothing because they spoke about him in German, a language he no longer understood. He lay quietly a few moments more. Certain everyone was asleep, he got the blanket.

He found it in her trunk when he was almost five. When she discovered him with it, she'd become angry and taken it from him, but someone found it and gave it to him, making it his greatest possession.

Time had taken its toll on the soft wool blanket; it had begun to fray around the edges and was quite soiled. Putting it on the bed, he carefully fingered it, then as a distant clock chimed eleven, he lay down and, cradling the blanket against his cheek, fell asleep.

# *Chapter* 1

---

Monday, May 21, 1855

Clarinda Matthias looked out the window of the train as it pulled into the B&O New Jersey Street Depot in Washington. She was coming home after completing her formal education, and, she had written to her uncle, she felt free, anticipating nothing but good times ahead. Finally spotting the face she had been searching for, she waved enthusiastically before drawing back into the coach.

Jack felt his heart lurch when he saw his niece wave to him. A lifelong bachelor, he had never realized how much he'd missed until she went away to school. She had been home summers and on holidays, but now that she was back to stay, he paced the platform, waiting for the train to rumble to a stop.

The reunion between them was an emotional one. He lifted her off the step and held her like a small child while she wrapped her arms around his neck, planting kisses on his cheeks. Putting her down, he stood back to look at her.

"Well, Clarinda. You certainly appear grown up."

"I am so happy to be home, Uncle Jack. I've missed you, and Landfield, so much this year."

"You say that every time you come back."

"And I mean it every time I say it." She glanced around the platform. "Where is Jacob?"

"He and Mattie left two months ago. They finally decided to move West."

"What for? Surely things were better for them here. Out West there's nothing."

"Jacob's wanted to go West for years."

"Why didn't you write me?"

"I thought I did, but I've had important things on my mind."

"Official?"

"Official." He took her chin in his hand and chuckled. "How was your trip?"

"Wonderful. Thank you for arranging for Mrs. Armitage to meet me in Philadelphia. I don't think I could listen to Grandmother Franklin plan my future one second more, and having to hear Bernice complain from Philadelphia to Washington would have been impossible." She twisted a strand of Jack's graying brown hair and pouted. "Why didn't you come?"

"I've been very busy, honey. In addition to my job, I've had to break in new staff and get Landfield ready for you."

"What are they like, the new help?"

"Hardworking but secretive. They keep to themselves."

"What's wrong with that?"

"Nothing, really. I guess I'm too used to Mattie and Jacob. I'm sure we'll become accustomed to the Royces."

"Of course we will. So Mrs. Royce is the new upstairs maid and Mr. Royce is our butler."

"Not quite," Jack laughed. "Mrs. Royce is indeed the upstairs maid, but Joseph — Mr. Royce — is the caretaker at Landfield. Their children help too."

"Children?"

"They're not that little. The youngest girls are twelve."

"What do they do?"

"The twins work in the kitchen and downstairs, and the older girl, Patsy, helps her mother. Then there's Richard."

"Their son."

"He's our stableboy, when he's not helping Joseph." Glancing over his shoulder, Jack saw the luggage being unloaded from the baggage car, a fact confirmed by the approaching stationmaster. Jack thanked the man, then, drawing Clarinda's arm through his, led her to where his carriage waited.

Upon their arrival, the shorter of the two men by the carriage came over. "Clarinda," Jack said, "this is Joseph Royce. Joseph, my niece, Miss Clarinda Matthias."

"Mornin', miss." Joseph touched the brim of his tweed cap and bowed slightly.

"Good morning, Joseph, or do I call you Mr. Royce?"

Frowning, he answered, "Joseph is fine, miss." She noticed the other man still waited by the carriage, staring at her. When he caught her looking back, his eyes quickly fell to the ground.

"The luggage is off the train," Jack was saying. "Go get it. I want to leave for Landfield as soon as possible."

"I'll have my boy get 'em, Mr. Matthias." Joseph swaggered back to the open landau and, after a loud monologue punctuated by several shoves, returned to his employer while the younger man ran to the platform.

"Was that necessary, Joseph?" Jack demanded.

"That boy of mine. Thinks he's too high and mighty to do real work."

"You're much too hard on Richard."

"Aren't you going to help him, Mr. Royce?" Clarinda interjected.

Joseph glared at the girl. "He don't need my help. He do what I tell him." He walked past her, muttering, "That boy has always been more trouble than he's worth."

She turned to Jack, eyebrows knit together, green eyes indignant. "Can't you do something?"

"Clarinda, it's best we stay out of it. Getting involved will only make trouble." Jack had learned in the six weeks of the Royces' employment the less he became involved in their domestic problems, the better it was all around.

"Well, if you won't do anything . . ." She stormed over to the carriage. "Joseph, there is too much luggage for Richard to handle alone. You will help him with it."

He sneered at her. "Very well, miss," he grumbled and walked off toward the station, his face scarlet, thinking that if the boy knew what was good for him, he'd keep away from the new mistress.

Joseph returned ten minutes later carrying a half dozen boxes, which Clarinda recognized as the lightest of the twenty pieces she brought with her. Watching angrily while he slowly loaded the carriage, the sound of loud laughter caught her attention. Turning, she saw Jack in conversation with Sally Armitage, so she followed the noise.

At first, all she could see was the circle of onlookers. A couple walked past her commenting, "I never saw anything like it. How that boy thought he could carry all those bags at one time . . ." The woman began to laugh again, and her companion wiped his eyes.

Clarinda pushed her way through the crowd, finding her luggage and Richard in the center, the tall, well-built servant gathering together the scattered boxes and picking up the assorted pieces of clothing which had fallen out. His task almost completed, his foot slipped on one of her petticoats, and he went sprawling on the platform amid another roar of laughter. Clarinda laughed too until she caught the embarrassment and shame on the young man's face. She walked over and knelt down. "Hello. Are you all right?"

He looked up in shock. The crowd began dispersing since, apparently, nothing more was going to happen and she started to pick up her white-sewing. "I didn't mean to surprise you, Richard, and I'm sorry I laughed with the others. But you looked so funny when you slid on my petticoat, the laugh just came out."

Noticing for the first time the rose traveling dress and the chestnut hair peeking out from under her white straw bonnet, the embarrassment on Richard's face quickly turned to fear. "I'm sorry, miss. I didn't mean to drop the boxes. Now he'll tell me how clumsy and stupid I am. I really do try hard, miss."

She put her hand on his shoulder; he recoiled from it. "Please, wait a minute. I understand you're trying your best, but there is too much luggage for one trip. If you'll finish picking up the boxes, I'll go get Joseph."

"No, please, miss, don't get him. I'll manage."

"I'll see Mr. Parker, then. Perhaps he has a wagon you can use."

"You really want to help?" he asked incredulously. "I thought you were making fun of me."

"Why would I want to do that?"

He didn't answer; he just began to collect the assorted pieces of luggage while she went to find the stationmaster. She came back, pulling a small handcart. With quiet efficiency he loaded it, impressing the girl with his strength for he lifted her large steamer trunk onto the cart like a stevedore. Finishing, he gave her the offending petticoat and other odd items of clothing, then took hold of the cart handle.

They started out together, but despite her lighter load, Clarinda lagged behind the taller Richard. He slowed a bit, and as she panted up to him, she gave him a grateful smile. "I just wanted to ask you —"

"What, miss?"

"How were you carrying all this? You don't have enough hands."

"I tied the little ones together, and some of the others I fastened to the trunk handles."

"That must have been so heavy."

"It wasn't too bad, once I got started."

"Then why did you stop?"

"I stumbled on something and lost my footing. Before I knew it, I'd dropped everything."

"Why didn't you make two trips?"

A shadow crossed his eyes. "I heard Mr. Matthias. He wants to get back." Unconsciously, Richard picked up his pace. "Besides, he told me not to be slow." Clarinda was surprised, for she had not seen Jack speak to Richard. Then she realized he was referring to Joseph.

"I think Joseph's wrong about you. You're neither clumsy nor stupid. You're clever and resourceful, and I'm quite impressed with your abilities."

The deep sadness in his dark eyes lifted a little. "Thank you, miss. I'll try not to disappoint you."

She smiled and then, with maximum effort, attempted to keep up with him the remaining fifty yards to the carriage. Seeing Richard had returned, Joseph came over.

"So you finally came back." He looked at Clarinda and, spotting the bundle of clothing, commented, "I see you found help with your job. You too lazy to do it yourself?"

"I told you earlier, Mr. Royce, there was too much luggage. If you had been of more help, or a little more understanding of Richard, he wouldn't have believed it necessary to try and carry everything in one trip."

"He still have to make a second trip." Joseph said nothing more but loaded the carriage while Richard returned the handcart to the depot. When he reappeared, Richard took over for the older man, and soon, all the luggage was secured. He notified Jack, who nodded, then turned to his niece.

"Well, honey, are you ready to go home?"

"Home," she sighed. "Sounds wonderful, Uncle Jack."

Settling in the carriage, she looked at Richard. He slid the rope through the frayed belt loops on his trousers, and for the first time, she saw the briefest of smiles. The men took their seats, and they began the trip to Landfield.

* * *

An hour later, the carriage turned a corner on a narrow country lane and stopped in front of a large gray brick building. Rising two and a half stories, Landfield House occupied three hundred acres in a secluded valley near Oak Store, Maryland, close enough to Washington for Jack to travel to work, yet far enough away to offer a quiet haven from the city. Jack looked at Clarinda, who grabbed his hand, for she had been lost in memories as they made their way up the maple-lined drive, the air filled with the fragrance of early roses and the twittering of cardinals and blue jays. Her eyes traveled over the house, noting the changes that had been made since her last visit home: the fresh paint on the eight Ionic columns supporting the white neoclassical pediment and on the shutters flanking the long windows, the neatly trimmed lawns and boxwood hedges. A profusion of daisies and tiger lilies spilled out of the thick underbrush into the gravel path leading to the white stable and paddock, while on the porch, large baskets of wisteria and fuchsia swayed in the warm breeze.

The front door opened. Bernice walked out onto the wide portico, followed by the rest of the staff. Clarinda peered at the unfamiliar faces, and Joseph said proudly, "That's my family, miss. *They'll* work hard for you, you'll see."

Clarinda caught the emphasis and started to say something, but Jack leaned over. "Later," he whispered, then he exited the carriage and handed her down.

She rushed up the steps, her bonnet sliding onto the back of her neck, stopping in front of the stern housekeeper. Bernice's disapproving eyes scanned the girl, then, managing a small smile, she said, "Good morning, Clarinda. Welcome home."

"Thank you, Bernice. I'm glad to be home." The relative coolness with which Clarinda greeted the housekeeper evaporated when she saw the two white-haired ladies behind Bernice. "Mary! Laura!" she squealed, then ran into Mary Fergussen's outstretched arms.

"Well, just look at you, Miss Clarinda, all grown up." Mary took the girl's hands and displayed her to the other woman. "Hasn't our young miss become quite the lady, Laura? The image of her mother."

Clarinda laughed. "Mary, you know I don't look anything like my mother."

"But you do resemble her, more than you know."

"Mary is right, Miss Clarinda," Laura Minton concurred. "Maybe not so much in the way you look, but in the way you act." Clarinda blushed as the elderly cook added, "I can recall many times when Mrs. Matthias would come running from one place or another, her eyes dancing and twinkling, just like yours are now."

Jack joined them on the porch and led Clarinda over to the new staff. "Honey, this is Adele Royce and her daughters Patsy, Iris, and Lily. Adele, this is my niece Clarinda."

The woman curtseyed, and the three girls followed suit. "Good day, miss," Adele said. "Your uncle has often spoken of you, as have Mary and Laura."

A giggle drew Clarinda's attention from Adele to the trio of girls beside their mother. Unsure of what to say, she smiled at them until Joseph climbed the stairs and kissed first his wife, then his daughters, astounding Clarinda with his obvious affection. They went into the house after that, but not before Clarinda glanced back, seeing Richard busily unloading the carriage.

With Patsy close on her heels, she sped up the graceful staircase to her rooms. Delight spread on Clarinda's face when she saw the cleaned and aired suite, fresh flowers set out in both the sitting room and bedroom. The younger girl danced around, pleased by her new mistress's approval.

"I'm so glad you like what I did. Mama let me clean your rooms all by myself, and I fixed the flowers too. Mrs. Fergussen said you liked flowers."

"I do and thank you. Everything looks very nice."

"Mama says I can watch Mrs. Fergussen. Perhaps I'll be your maid someday."

"Have you had any training as a lady's maid?"

"At our last place, Mama was Mrs. Armitage's maid, and she let me help her. Papa says we should try to make ourselves better."

"How old are you, Patsy?"

"Sixteen, Miss Clarinda. Papa says the day I was born was the happiest day in Mama's life."

"And when your sisters were born?"

"The second happiest day," she giggled.

"What about when Richard was born?"

"Papa doesn't talk about that."

A knock on the door interrupted them, and Mary entered, followed by Richard. He appeared uncomfortable in the rose-colored room with its light oak furniture and apple green satin chair covers, but he relaxed a little when Clarinda smiled at him. Mary led him into the bedroom with the luggage he carried, Patsy behind them. Two minutes later, he came out alone.

"All finished?" Clarinda asked.

"I have to make a second trip. I didn't have help this time." It was said without rancor, and she smiled again. "Patsy's helping Mrs. Fergussen. They'll have your things unpacked in no time."

"Patsy seems nice."

"I'll get the rest of your cases," he stammered, then left.

Almost immediately afterward, Jack came in with a large box. "Just a little something to welcome you home."

She opened it, shrieking when she saw the contents. "Oh, Uncle Jack, it's magnificent! How did you know I needed a new riding habit?"

"I read between the lines of those letters you sent," he chuckled.

"Can I wear it today?"

"Absolutely. I'm taking you on a picnic at the oak stand."

"I'll be ready in fifteen minutes." She picked up the box and raced into the bedroom.

True to her word, fifteen minutes later she was changed and was waiting for Jack in the parlor. The new habit fit like a glove, the dark hunter green complementing her hair and eyes perfectly. Studying her reflection in the ormolu mirror over the marble mantle, her head tilted slightly to the right, she adjusted the sable derby and tugged on the veiling, hoping her uncle would approve of her appearance.

The uneasy feeling that she was being watched caused her to turn toward the half-open door. Expecting Jack, she was surprised to see Richard staring at her, his brown eyes nearly black.

"Did you want something, Richard?"

He edged into the room. "I just wanted to tell you . . . I finished bringing your luggage in."

"Thank you."

"I also wanted to-to thank you for your help before. He didn't like it at all, but I don't care. I liked it."

"Oh, here you are, Clarinda." Jack strode into the parlor and spotted the young man standing against the wall. "Richard, will you get our horses ready? We'll be out in a few minutes."

"Yes, Mr. Matthias." He started to sidle out of the room, then stopped. "I didn't mean to stare at you before, miss. You look so beautiful . . . I couldn't help it." He bowed and left.

"Richard certainly explains a lot, doesn't he?"

"Only with you. With me, it's 'Yes, Mr. Matthias,' or 'Right away, Mr. Matthias.'"

"What about, 'No, Mr. Matthias?'"

"Richard never disobeys an order."

"Perhaps he should."

"We'll discuss him at the oak stand. Iris and Lily have very sharp ears."

"All right, Uncle Jack." They went to the big homey kitchen where Clarinda chatted with Laura while Jack checked the contents of the wicker basket on the oak table. Shortly afterward, they headed for the stable.

* * *

The oak stand, private and secluded, to which they rode was a particular favorite of both uncle and niece. Jack maintained the tiny clearing surrounded by a circle of eight ancient trees on the outskirts of his property as a sanctuary where he and Clarinda could be alone with each other or their thoughts. Laying out a blanket, he helped her from her horse and set out the picnic lunch before embarking on the subject of the Royces.

"Now that you've met them, what do you think of the Royces?"

"They seem all right, I guess, but I'm not sure I'm going to like having them around."

"Anything specific?"

"I don't know. There's just something very odd about them."

"Including Richard?"

"No, he's different from the rest of them." She took a bite from her chicken sandwich. "Uncle Jack, does he always look so sad?"

"I'm afraid so."

"Do you know why?"

"I wish I did, but I think it has to do with the way he is treated. Sally Armitage gave me quite an earful this morning about the Royces."

"What did she say?"

"Sally believes—and I tend to agree with her—that Richard is a bastard or, more precisely, Adele's bastard."

She nodded. "It makes sense. He doesn't look like any of them. Besides, Richard's afraid of Joseph."

"And with good reason. Joseph beats him." Clarinda gasped, and Jack took her face in his hands. "Why do you think I told you to keep out of things before? Richard will pay dearly for your interference."

"I'm sorry, Uncle Jack. All I wanted to do was help," she sobbed.

"I understand, sweetheart. But Joseph is irrational where Richard is concerned. Sally told me, about three months ago her daughter Phoebe was sketching the boy while he worked. Joseph caught her and not only tore up the sketch but beat Richard so badly he could barely move for two weeks. In fact, the recommendation to me that I hire the Royces was an attempt by the Armitages to separate Richard from them."

"How?"

"Walter hoped Richard would stay in Baltimore. Unfortunately, Joseph persuaded the boy otherwise."

"But if Richard isn't Joseph's son, and he gets treated so poorly, why does he stay with them?"

"Perhaps he has nowhere else to go."

They ate more of the picnic lunch, but Jack knew Clarinda was thinking about something. "Uncle Jack, Richard is so much better than just carrying boxes and saddling horses. Can't we do something for him?"

"I originally wanted him as Jacob's replacement, but he declined my offer. Apparently, he doesn't want any more."

"He doesn't, or Joseph doesn't?"

"Joseph doesn't," Jack answered, flabbergasted by his niece's insight, "and what Joseph wants, Richard wants. Please, Clarinda, don't encourage him to do something he will end up regretting."

"Why can't we help him?"

"I'm not telling you not to be friendly toward him or not to build his self-confidence because Richard certainly needs both. Just don't push him faster than he's ready to go."

"All right, Uncle Jack."

"Now" — he took her hand — "have you made any plans for your future?"

"Oh, you sound just like Grandmother. The whole trip from New York to Philadelphia, all I heard was, 'You'll have to spend more time with us, so we can introduce you to the proper sort of people.' I want to have fun before I get married."

He laughed. "So what do you want to do?"

"This is fine, thank you."

"Have you forgotten I have a job? I can't spend all my time with you as much as I would like to."

"Could Richard accompany me when you're not able to?"

"Bernice or Mary would be more proper choices."

"But Aunt Mary hates to ride, and Bernice is worse than Grandmother about acting like a lady."

Jack smiled and shook his head. "It's because you so easily forget, just like your mother. But . . . Richard was Peter Armitage's groom, and Sally informed me he is completely trustworthy. I think it can be arranged."

"Good. Then perhaps you can ask him again about being a house servant."

"What?"

"Perhaps you can—"

"I heard what you said. He'll only turn me down again."

"Because of Joseph?"

"I thought I explained matters, Clarinda. I cannot afford to have Richard laid up, simply because Joseph has beaten him."

"But doesn't he deserve a chance like the rest of them?"

He looked at her sincere face with its determined chin, so much like his own. "All right, honey. I'll ask Richard again, although I'm almost certain he'll refuse."

"Thank you."

"Now if you don't mind, I would like to finish my lunch without any more surprises."

She giggled, and they continued their picnic. But Clarinda could not forget the young man with the sad, dark eyes who — she decided — must look like his father. Later in the afternoon, as she sat in the library watching him work outside, she resolved, *If anyone needs to be shown care and understanding, it's him, and if no one else wants to do it, then I will.*

# *Chapter* 2

The next morning, Richard stood outside Jack's study, palms sweating and mouth dry, certain he would receive a reprimand for the incident at the train station. With a sigh, he knocked timidly on the closed door. Thirty seconds later, Jack opened it.

"You wanted to see me, Mr. Matthias?"

"Yes. Please come in and sit down." Richard did what he was asked and, Jack noticed, again stared at his shoes. "Do you remember what we discussed the first time I spoke with you?"

"Yes, sir. I remember."

"Yesterday, Miss Clarinda and I discussed—"

"Mr. Matthias, it was her idea to help with her things. I didn't ask her to."

Jack looked at the troubled young man and smiled. "You thought I was angry about her helping you?"

"He was." But Richard relaxed a little, so Jack continued.

"Miss Clarinda wanted me to ask you again to be our house servant."

"I'm happy doing what I'm doing, Mr. Matthias."

"Are you?"

"He hasn't said too much about my work, and I like working in the gardens and with the horses."

"We both know you are capable of far more than that. I would like you to reconsider."

"He'll be angry with me."

Shaking his head, Jack probed, "If Joseph wasn't involved in this decision, would you say yes?"

"I think so, Mr. Matthias."

"As far as I'm concerned, Richard, he isn't."

The boy began trembling. "But I can't. He'll . . ." Biting his lip, Richard suppressed a gasp and stood to leave. "He told me to have the rose bushes tied up by lunch."

Jack restrained him. "Do you do everything Joseph tells you to do?"

"I don't know any different."

"And what if he told you to jump in the river and swim upstream? Would you do *that* too?" They turned toward the open study door as Clarinda walked in, eyes flashing.

"What are you doing here, Clarinda?" Jack demanded.

"I was just passing by, Uncle Jack." She faced Richard, who had returned to his seat. "Well, Richard? Would you jump in the river?"

"No, Miss Clarinda."

"Then why won't you accept our offer? Do something for yourself once, instead of because Joseph tells you to do it."

"Clarinda," Jack said angrily, "that will be enough!"

She went on, ignoring her uncle, "You said you liked it when I helped you yesterday. Can't you see all we're trying to do is help you again?"

Richard looked up, and for the first time, Jack saw hope in the young man's eyes. "You really think I can do it, Miss Clarinda?"

"Don't you?"

"I haven't worked in a house in a long time."

"You'll do just fine."

He sat for a minute, thinking. Then a smile grew on his face. "I'll accept your offer, Mr. Matthias, but only if I can continue doing my other jobs too. He can't be angry with me if I do both."

"Very well, but your house duties will take precedence over the other, understood?"

Richard nodded, and Clarinda whispered something to her uncle. "My niece wonders if you would also be interested in being her groom," Jack said.

"Oh yes, sir!" Richard exclaimed, his happiness unmistakable.

"Good. Now you'd better get back to work."

"Yes, Mr. Matthias, and thank you. Thank you, too, Miss Clarinda."

Jack waited until Richard was downstairs before addressing his niece. "I thought I told you not to push him."

"I just wanted him to see how foolish it is to do something because Joseph says to do it."

"This isn't going to change things between them, you realize. In fact, it could make matters worse."

"Maybe Richard will start to become less compliant."

"Maybe." Jack sat on the horsehair divan and patted the seat beside him. "Anyway, now that Richard is going to be your groom and my butler, we're going to have to get him the right clothes. Jacob's would have been too small, if he had left them, and I can't have him serving dinner in what he currently wears."

"It would be a novel idea," she chuckled, curling a lock of hair around her finger. Then she added in all seriousness, "Do you think Daddy's clothes would do in the meantime?"

"Hm. You could try them. Your father was similar in size and build."

"Then he could start today."

"All right, young lady. You take care of outfitting Richard, and I'll speak to Joseph." He sighed, sending the girl into another paroxysm of laughter.

"Yes, Uncle Jack." She kissed him and left the room.

\* \* \*

Clarinda found Richard in the garden. She watched for a minute, then went over, being careful not to startle him.

31

"Richard?"

"Did you need me for something?"

"My uncle asked me to make sure you have proper clothes for your new duties."

He stared at her. "I'm getting new clothes?"

"Yes, but at first, your clothes won't be new. They belonged to my father."

"They'll be new to me, Miss Clarinda."

She smiled and took him up to the attic. Quickly locating the trunk which contained Ralph Matthias's wardrobe, she opened it and, fighting off the overwhelming memories and smell of camphor and cedar, sorted through shirts and trousers until she found the items she wanted. Pulling them out, she gave them to Richard. "Here. Try these on."

He took the offered breeches and shirt and went behind an old Chinese screen to change, fingering the fine twill and cambric for several minutes before putting the clothes on. They fit him well, and he beamed with pride when he came out. "These are too fine for a groom, Miss Clarinda," he said as she nodded her approval, but his eyes dared her to take them back, and she laughed.

"Nonsense. Will you need boots? I think there are a few pairs of Daddy's here somewhere."

"No, Miss Clarinda, I have a pair."

"All right." She went to a clothes press and removed a linen bag. "This was Daddy's evening outfit. If the riding clothes fit, this is bound to." Once again, he took the clothes and returned behind the screen. Finally changed, he came out.

Now it was Clarinda's turn to stare. In the formal attire, he looked magnificent. He caught the glance and started feeling uneasy. "Is something wrong, Miss Clarinda?"

Slowly, she found her tongue. "No, Richard, nothing's wrong. Have you seen yourself?"

"There wasn't a mirror back there."

She found an old cheval glass under a sheet and after uncovering it, brought him over. "There. You look wonderful."

He stared at the gentleman in the mirror. He had not expected to ever look as he did; the black jacket and trousers fit as if they had been made for him, and the white silk shirt accentuated his dark brown hair and eyes. The more he looked, however, the more he felt something wasn't quite right. "Miss Clarinda, I think there should be a tie."

"I'll tell Uncle Jack to get you one."

Suddenly, Richard's whole face radiated with happiness. "I remember my papa would wear a fancy neckcloth with an outfit like this. When I would play with it, he'd say, 'No, no,' then he'd laugh and kiss me." A minute later, he shook himself, the memory gone. "There should be a tie," he repeated sadly.

"And shoes," she replied, recovering from her shock. "Proper ones that won't squeak when you serve. Jacob's wouldn't have fit you. Oh, you need to wear the coat only when we have guests. When it's just family, the vest alone will do."

"I'd better be getting back to work, Miss Clarinda. I still have a lot to do." He took one last look in the mirror as if trying to recapture the flash of memory, then changed back into his work clothes.

After he was gone, she rested on an unopened trunk, reflecting on the transformation of Richard's face when he saw himself in the mirror, and the reference he had made to his papa, a man he could still remember. She sat there, oblivious to everything except her musings, until a sharp knocking beside her brought her back to reality.

"Penny for your thoughts, Miss Clarinda."

She looked up into the light gray eyes and oval face of Patsy Royce. "How did you know I was here?"

"Iris saw you and Richard come up here, and I saw him go back down alone. I figured you stayed here."

"You and your sisters are very observant."

"Papa says we have to be. 'Always stay one step ahead,' he says. 'That's how you get on in the world.'"

"And do you?"

"Stay one step ahead? I guess so. Get on in the world? Not really. Oh, we move to bigger houses and such, but our station never seems to improve. Of course, Papa blames Richard for that."

"Was your family ever well off?"

"You mean rich? No. Papa always tells us what a big man he'd be in his village in Austria or Switzerland because he grew up in a small dirt-floor cottage."

"Austria *or* Switzerland? Doesn't your father remember where he's from?"

"Well, it was Austria in Boston, but it changed to Switzerland by the time we moved to Philadelphia. I think, as Mama and Papa's English got better, their village moved around."

"But your last name is *English*."

"Mama said they changed it when they left their village. Papa doesn't like it much."

"How do you feel about it?"

Patsy giggled. "It's my name."

"And Richard?"

"He doesn't say much about it, but then, he doesn't say much about anything."

"How old is he?"

"He's almost twenty-two. Mama and Papa are married twenty years, and they got Richard when he was nearly two."

"They *got* him?"

"Didn't he tell you? Of course not, he's too embarrassed about it. Richard's a foundling. Mama said someone left him on their doorstep right after she and Papa were married. Papa wasn't too pleased about taking him in, but if it made Mama happy . . . Mama said Richard looked so frightened and alone, like he knew what'd happened. That's why he's always sad."

Wishing to change the subject, Clarinda commented, "You seem very well-educated, Patsy."

"Mama and Papa made sure we all got to school, even Richard. Papa said he didn't want any unlearned children."

"So you can all read and write."

"And do figures too. Richard's real good at book learning. He'd help me and the twins all the time. Oh, Miss Clarinda, I nearly forgot. Your uncle was looking for you. That's why I came up. I'm sorry I talked your ear off."

"It's all right, Patsy. Please tell my uncle I'll be right down."

Patsy scurried off, her light brown hair flying in stringy braids behind her. Clarinda took a final look around the attic, then started downstairs. Almost by accident, she had discovered more about the mysteries surrounding Richard and his relationship with the Royces, but the revelations seemed to ask more questions than they answered, and she shook her head in frustration.

\* \* \*

Jack smiled as she entered the study. "The clothes fit?"

"Almost as if they had been made for Richard and not for Daddy."

"Joseph wasn't too pleased when I told him. He said I'm making a mistake. He also thinks that you, my dear, are a meddler."

"Why?"

"Because you're showing an interest in Richard, I would think. By the way, what took you so long? I sent Patsy for you a quarter-hour ago."

"She was in a talkative mood, so I encouraged her."

"Did you discover anything?"

"She said her parents were from Austria or Switzerland. As their English improved, their village moved around."

"They told me they were Swiss."

"She also told me they changed their name to Royce when they left their Austrian-Swiss village."

"That could happen."

"But Patsy said Joseph doesn't like his name. Why would he use a last name he didn't like?"

"Perhaps it was changed here."

"Perhaps." She walked around the desk, tidying the papers cluttering it. "Patsy said Richard's a foundling, that he was abandoned on the Royces' doorstep twenty years ago. It means he's not a bastard."

"Honey, Adele and Joseph may have told the girls that to shield them from the truth. After all, an illegitimate child is not something you want people to know about."

"But, Uncle Jack, there's so much that doesn't seem to fit."

"Such as?"

"Well, before, Richard remembered —"

Someone knocked on the door. Joseph entered and, ignoring Clarinda, turned to Jack. "Patsy said you wanted to see me?"

"Yes. Tell Richard I need him to ready our horses as well as one for himself. I want to purchase his new clothes today."

"She already took him away from his work once. When he's finished with his jobs, then he can get them."

"I am tired of telling you what Richard's priorities are." Jack turned his steely gaze on Clarinda. "Tell Richard we need the horses."

"Yes, of course, Uncle Jack." She left immediately, for the undertone of Jack's order forbade disobedience. Finding Richard again in the garden, she delivered her message. He was overjoyed to be able to perform his new duties so soon and he told her he would be ready in a flash. His enthusiasm reminded her that she, too, had to change, and she dashed up to her rooms.

\* \* \*

The ride into Oak Store was all too brief for Richard, reminding him of the times when he and Peter Armitage had ridden together. He watched Clarinda, who was deep in conversation with her uncle, and longed for the day when he would be able to ride alone with her because there was so much he wanted to tell her. Clarinda, meanwhile, spent most of the twenty-minute journey laughing, for Jack insisted on describing the busy last days Jacob had worked for him. One particular anecdote had both of them in hysterics, although all Richard heard was something about an old

THE CYGNET

rooster and a pair of brooding hens. Suddenly, the ride was over, and they were dismounting in front of the bootmaker's shop.

Once inside, Clarinda took charge. "Mr. Perkins, this is Richard Royce. He and his family work for us, and he'll be our butler. He needs a pair of shoes—proper ones that won't squeak."

"Certainly, Miss Matthias. Come with me, Mr. Royce. I have just the pair."

Richard glanced warily at the bootmaker. Catching the look, Clarinda went over to him. "It's all right, Richard. Mr. Perkins won't bite."

He smiled back at her, then followed the cobbler into the back of the shop.

A half hour later, Richard returned, carrying two pairs of black leather shoes. "Mr. Perkins said I should have a second pair, so they'll last longer."

"Quite right," Jack commented. "After all, I can't be buying 'proper shoes that don't squeak' every year."

"Oh. If they're too expensive, I'll put a pair back. I don't want to impose on your generosity."

"Richard, you are not imposing on anything," Jack said, trying to reassure him, "and you will not put anything back. I was merely trying to make a little joke. Obviously, I did not succeed."

"I'm sorry. I thought you meant it."

"There is nothing to be sorry for. Now what do I owe you, Tom?" While Jack settled his account with Mr. Perkins, Richard went out and tied the bundle to his saddle as Clarinda stood at the store window, a small grin beginning to form. Jack finished with the bootmaker, and they moved on to the tailor.

Once more, Richard was taken into a small back room where he was measured and fitted while Jack placed the order with the short, slight tailor, for the clothes, unlike the shoes, would not be ready to take with them. After he finished, Jack joined his niece, who was sorting through a large flat box on the counter.

"Oh, Uncle Jack," she exclaimed, holding up a patterned strip of silk. "Do you think Richard will like this?"

"For what?" he said, chuckling.

"A tie, of course."

"If he was a dandy. He's going to need something practical." Jack asked the clerk for the tray of black ties. "This is more suitable."

"But black's so ordinary."

He just shook his head, then addressed the boy behind the counter. "Have Mr. Warner add three black and two white stocks to my order, Andy, and several pairs of white cotton gloves. Make sure the gloves fit the young man in the back."

"Yes sir, Mr. Matthias."

Clarinda reluctantly put back the pale blue brocade. "I still think . . ." she murmured, then turned as Richard rejoined them, a quiet happiness in his eyes.

The final stop was at the barber shop. The barber worked quickly, the shapeless bowl haircut Richard had had since Boston replaced by a style, which, if not the height of fashion, was perfect for the dark-haired servant. When he finished, the two men left the shop, and while Richard checked the horses, Jack located Clarinda. He actually looks more capable, she found herself thinking, amazed at the difference the new haircut made in Richard. Satisfied all was well, Richard put Clarinda on her horse and held Jack's stallion while he mounted, before mounting himself.

The return trip started off sedately enough until, quite unexpectedly, Clarinda took off at a hard gallop. Richard, who had been riding a respectful distance behind the Matthiases, immediately went after her, but she was already sixty yards ahead of him, the gap between them beginning to widen. He dug harder into Brandy's sides with his heels. The roan gelding reared slightly then bolted forward in a dead run.

On and on they went, Richard urging his mount with his legs and hands while the scenery blurred by them. After what seemed hours, he began to gain ground on Clarinda, first inches, then feet. Finally, he drew alongside her and, with one final kick, sent Brandy slightly ahead. Clarinda was stunned when she saw him, her shock changing to anger as he grabbed her reins and forced her gray mare to a walk.

"Why did you stop me? Let go of my horse!"

"What happened? I didn't see anything that would startle the horses."

"Nothing happened," she snapped. "Now will you let go? I want to continue my ride."

"*Nothing* happened? Do you always ride like that?"

"Well, not always, but when it's a fine day, and the road isn't too rocky or rutted, I like to give Moonbeam her head."

"I'm sorry I annoyed you, Miss Clarinda. I didn't mean—"

"You were really worried, weren't you?"

"I don't want anything to happen to you."

"Is that why you checked the horses before we left?"

"Mr. Brown, he was the coachman at our last place, he said you can never be too careful. Sometimes, careful isn't enough," he added, almost in a whisper.

She put a gloved hand on top of his bare one. "I truly am sorry I worried you, Richard, and I thank you for coming to my rescue. I won't let it happen again."

"Coming to your rescue?"

"No, worrying you. I liked having you rescue me." She chuckled, and they started forward slowly. Through sidelong glances, she found herself admiring the muscles rippling under the shirt and breeches of the rider beside her, and she tilted her head slightly to catch more of his thick, wavy hair and straight-nosed profile. "You ride very well, Richard. Jacob was never able to keep up with me."

"Mr. Brown said I had a real aptitude for handling horses. I used to worry about that until he explained that meant I had a natural ability. I felt better after that."

She laughed, and he smiled back, then he let go of Moonbeam's reins and urged his horse into a gallop, defying her to catch him. She took up the challenge at once, and they thundered down the road, disappearing in the billow of dust the horses raised, the stillness punctuated by her laughter. Jack grinned as he watched them, but he decided he'd better tell her what had happened in Baltimore, recalling the panic in Richard's face when he went after her.

* * *

They arrived at Landfield at a trot for Richard and Clarinda had stopped their race in order for their mounts to cool a bit after their workout. She was disappointed for she found herself wishing she could continue riding with him. Riding with Jacob had never been as exhilarating as this. Richard seemed so much more at ease away from the house, away from Joseph. She couldn't wait for the next time they could be together because there were so many questions she wanted to ask him. Dismounting at the paddock, Jack loosened the horses' saddles while the two young people went to the house, a seething Joseph watching from behind the bowered garden gate.

Richard returned a few minutes later, wearing his old clothes. Inside the fenced enclosure, Joseph had begun to circle with the horses; the boy went over to him.

"I'll cool them."

"Mr. Matthias tell me to do it. Guess he feels you be too good now for *this* kind of work."

Refusing to answer, Richard took the horses from Joseph and started around. Joseph, however, wasn't finished. He followed, his short bowed legs trying to keep up with the longer-strided young man. "I think you think you're too good."

"You know that's not true."

"Then you remember that Miss Clarinda's better 'n you, even if she do buy you presents and give you fancy clothes."

"Miss Clarinda said I needed them for my work."

"So they want you to pay for what you got."

"They never said anything about paying. Miss Clarinda . . . she said the clothes were mine."

"You really think folks like them would just give things to you?" Joseph left then, knowing he had stripped the boy of the happiness he felt.

Finishing his task, Richard removed the horses' tack and, while he rubbed them down, thought about what Joseph had said. It was true the Matthiases had never mentioned payment, but they hadn't said he didn't have to pay them either. As soon as he finished, Richard decided he would talk to Mr. Matthias.

* * *

Jack and Clarinda sat in the parlor, drinking some of Laura's ginger beer after their excursion. He could tell she had enjoyed the outing for her eyes sparkled like emeralds. "So you had fun, honey?"

"It was wonderful, Uncle Jack. And didn't Richard look splendid? He rides so well too."

"You gave him quite a scare."

"I didn't mean to, and I apologized afterward."

"Please, don't do anything like that again."

"Why not? You know I always ride that way."

"I wrote you about Peter Armitage's accident, didn't I?"

"His horse threw a shoe, if I remember your last letter."

"The horse had to be destroyed, and Peter . . . it was days before Walter and Sally knew he would recover from his injuries."

"But what has that got to do with today?" She drew her knees up to her chest, her bootless feet resting on the Louis Quinze divan.

Jack told her.

"Is that why Richard is so extra careful?"

"I would think so, and that's why I'm telling you about it. I don't want him to have anything like that on his conscience again."

"Could it have been his fault?"

"No, it was purely an accident. But Richard feels things very deeply as I'm sure you've noticed, and guilt, whether real or imagined, could destroy him. Don't add to whatever remorse he still has about Peter's mishap."

"I won't, Uncle Jack."

There was a quick knock on the door. "Come in," Jack answered. "It's open."

"I'm sorry to bother you," Richard began, taking a deep breath. "I've come to arrange payment."

"For what?"

"The clothes and the shoes."

"You need the clothes for your job, and I don't expect my staff to pay for what they need."

"But he said—"

"Richard, I've paid for more butler's outfits than I care to recall.Jacob wore out several suits a year."

The young man managed a smile but said, "He always says we should never take anything for nothing. He did that once and has regretted it ever since."

Jack sighed for he knew the boy was talking about himself. "If Joseph should ask, and I doubt he will, you are working off the cost of the things you got today by being Miss Clarinda's groom and my butler. Fair enough?"

"Yes, Mr. Matthias. Thank you," Richard replied, relieved.

"I suggest you finish outside. You are serving tonight, and dinner is at seven."

"Yes, sir." With the matter settled, Richard left.

Clarinda pressed her knuckles to her lips and sniffed indignantly. "I have a good mind to talk to Joseph."

"I told you, honey, it's best we don't interfere."

"But—"

"If anything needs to be done, I shall take care of it. Richard will never gain confidence in himself if you fight his battles for him."

"I see."

"Now get along with you. I have things to do before dinner."

"Yes, Uncle Jack." She untangled herself and went out.

He watched her leave the room, finding himself agreeing with Joseph's evaluation of her earlier. Her outspokenness and impulsiveness might someday land her in trouble, but, he thought, that was what made her so remarkable. He only hoped that where Richard was concerned, her frankness would not backfire.

# Chapter 3

At six that evening, Richard entered his room to change for dinner. He dressed slowly, still not quite believing he was getting the opportunity to prove himself, just like anyone else. He wrapped one of the black ties around his neck, knotted it, and after putting on his new shoes, climbed the back stairs to the attic as a pair of gray eyes watched.

Inside the hot, musty room, he began pacing, deliberately shuffling his feet to roughen the smooth soles, trying to remember everything Mr. Jervis had taught him about waiting on the table. His travels brought him near the mirror; stopping, he stared again at his reflection in the glass.

"Well, don't we look pretty."

He turned and saw Iris, the older of the twins, ogling him. Of the three girls, she was the most like her father in looks and attitude and as a result, she despised Richard, and he liked her the least of the Royces' daughters.

"What are you doing here?" he asked.

"I saw you come up. I wanted to see what you were doing."

"I don't like being spied on."

She came over and fingered his shirt sleeve. "I think Miss Clarinda's sweet on you, giving you such fancy clothes."

"I need them for work, and if you will excuse me, I don't want to be late." He pushed her hand off his arm.

"Oh, you don't want to be late. How come you came up here, then?"

"None of your business."

"I know. Miss Clarinda don't know where your room is. Why, I'll bet she's up here right now." Iris ran around the attic, looking under sheets and calling for Clarinda.

"Doesn't she need you?"

"Mama don't need me. Lily's helping her." Suddenly, she came back to him, her small eyes wicked. "You still can't call her 'mother,' can you, Richard? But then, you never could."

"She isn't my mother. My mama—"

"Dumped you on *my* mama's doorstep when you were two. Your mama didn't love you any more than my mama and papa do."

"I have to go downstairs," he stammered. Then he half-walked, half-ran from the attic.

Iris sat on a trunk, laughing. "You're a big nobody, Richard," she sneered. "Papa knows it, I know it, and soon, Miss Clarinda will know it too. Then it'll be my turn." She glanced around at the collected history of the Matthiases, her gaze caught by a flash of white near one of the windows. Walking over to where an old dress of Clarinda's hung, she muttered, "Well, if she can give him fancy clothes . . ." and took the garment.

* * *

In the parlor, Clarinda fidgeted. "Uncle Jack, what time is it?"

For the third time in the past half hour, he withdrew his watch from his vest pocket. "Five minutes to seven. Why are you so nervous?" he added as she wiped her hands down the skirt of her peacock blue silk gown.

"It's Richard's first night serving, and I do so want him to do well."

"You have nothing to worry about. He wants very much to please you."

The knock on the door stopped her wriggling. She turned, and the approving smile she gave Richard did much to restore his confidence. "Excuse me, Mr. Matthias, Miss Clarinda. Dinner is served."

"Thank you, Richard." Jack stood and took Clarinda's hand while the servant removed himself to the dining room.

"Doesn't he look splendid?" she crowed, her face aglow.

"You said that earlier. But you are right." He drew her arm through his, and they left the parlor.

"I was just thinking about Jacob. He always looked like a butler, no matter how formally he was dressed."

"What are you getting at?"

"Something happens to Richard when he puts on Daddy's clothes. He looks like he was born to wear them."

"They say clothes make the man. Being gentleman's attire, perhaps they make him appear to be a gentleman."

"But Richard said something, remembered something, that implied his father was wealthy."

"You started to tell me earlier. What did he say?"

"That his father used to wear those fancy neckcloths."

"Perhaps the man was Joseph, and the Royces were well off once and fell on hard times."

"Patsy said they were never rich. Besides, Richard was talking about his papa. He never refers to Joseph as his father. It's always 'he' or 'him.'"

"Honey, feelings can change as quickly as circumstances."

"Uncle Jack, can you honestly believe that Richard has *ever* thought of Joseph as his papa?" The open door of the dining room made further conversation on the topic impossible, but they both knew it was one that would be continued at a later time.

They entered the spacious room, the last streaks of daylight shimmering on the highly polished mahogany table, two places set at one end. Jack seated Clarinda before nodding to Richard to begin serving the spring soup. It was quickly apparent Richard had been well taught for the little training he had for he performed his duties efficiently and was around only when needed. Clarinda was overjoyed watching him circulate, and she intended to thank her uncle for taking her suggestion and increasing Richard's responsibilities.

Conversation during dinner was light and general. All too soon, Richard was removing the remains of the roast leg of lamb and curried veal and setting out dishes for dessert. Jack asked him to bring over the port decanter, waiting until he had done so to dismiss him for the night and to tell him to have the twins come in an hour to clear the table. When the service door was closed and Richard well out of earshot, Jack began to laugh. "Clarinda, please get the port for me. The dear boy brought me Madeira by mistake."

Exchanging the bottles, she asked, "Why didn't you correct him?"

"He did so well this evening. I didn't want him to feel he had failed on his first night. If it happens again, however—"

"You'll firmly say, 'No, Richard, not Madeira. Port."

"Will you show him the wines tomorrow?"

"Of course." A grin spread across her face. "You really thought he did well?"

"Yes. It's been ten years since he's done anything like this, and, after Joseph's 'glowing' recommendation, I wasn't sure what to expect. It seems Richard was trained thoroughly, and he remembers what he learned."

"Except for the wines."

"He was only twelve. That's a little young to be instructed on spirits."

They were halfway through the gooseberry trifle when she asked, "Uncle Jack, do you like the Royces?"

"They do a good job, and Bernice hasn't said anything concerning their performance, but I'm not comfortable with the way they're always around."

"So were Mattie and Jacob."

"It's true, they were, but I was never aware of them. With the Royces, I always have the feeling there is one or another of them standing behind a door or in a hallway, particularly Iris."

She nodded, recalling the conversation with Patsy earlier in the day.

"Be careful what you say around them, honey."

"I will." They continued eating, and while Jack lit up a cigar, Clarinda thought about the secretive Royces, especially Richard, whose secrets were not of his own making.

"Clarinda?"

"Yes, Uncle Jack?"

"I just asked you if you wanted to play some whist."

"For pennies or points?"

"Points, you little minx."

"Oh, and I was feeling lucky tonight." They left the dining room laughing, returning to the parlor for an evening of cards.

* * *

In the kitchen, Richard found a dish of food waiting for him on the hot plate. He sat at the table while Laura got his supper and began eating.

"Are you eating late every night, Richard?" Lily asked, a little awed by his appearance.

Swallowing a mouthful of mashed potatoes, Richard nodded as Patsy piped up, "I heard Miss Clarinda telling Mrs. Fergussen that Mr. Matthias wants Richard to serve dinner, just like he did in Boston." She leaned on Richard's shoulder and whispered in his ear, "I still think you look like the picture in my storybook, no matter what Papa says."

"He didn't need you before Miss Clarinda came home," Iris taunted.

"I turned him down before," Richard answered.

"Then how come you said yes now?" Iris started to laugh. "I told you, didn't I, Lily? Richard's Miss Clarinda's pet. He'll do anything *she* asks him to."

"That's not funny," Patsy rebutted.

"Maybe you're her pet, too, Patsy. That's why you're always hanging around her room."

"You're just jealous, Iris, 'cause I might get to be her maid, and you won't. You're too young, anyhow."

"Who says older's better? Richard's way older than you, and he's not better than anybody."

"Iris, that will be enough!" Adele snapped.

"Why, Mama? That's how Papa feels about him."

"How your papa feels is not important. Richard's still your brother."

"Let Iris be, Adele," Joseph broke in. "The girl's entitled to her opinion."

"Because it agrees with yours."

Despite the sick, gnawing feeling in his stomach, Richard continued eating. He glanced up briefly; Adele was looking at him with what appeared to be tears in her eyes. *Maybe she's afraid of* him, *too*, Richard thought, and focused again on his plate.

Bernice was speaking. "And to avoid any further problems, Richard will have his supper in the housekeeper's room when he finishes upstairs."

"He don't need no special treatment, Miss Lycoming."

"Make up your mind, Mr. Royce. Either he eats here or in the housekeeper's room. Which will upset you the least?"

Joseph thought for a minute, only his furiously tapping foot indicating his irritation. His eyes narrowed, and he replied, "Oh all right. He can eat in the housekeeper's room."

"Thank you for your cooperation, Mr. Royce," Bernice said sarcastically, then turned her attention to Laura. "I think we'll have the lamb cold for luncheon tomorrow, and perhaps a chicken for dinner."

"Excuse me, Bernice, but shouldn't Miss Clarinda select the menu, now that she's home?"

"Yes, of course, Laura, but you know Clarinda. She'll just tell me, 'Oh, you choose, Bernice.'"

"It's still her decision."

Bernice began rubbing her forehead. "I seem to be getting another headache. I'm going to lie down. Mary, tell Clarinda I will discuss the menu with her tomorrow morning. Good night."

After she left, Mary looked at the cook. "I think Bernice is jealous of Miss Clarinda."

"She's afraid of losing her position, and with her having been in charge for all these years, I'm not sure I blame her. I certainly wouldn't want to be something less all of a sudden, even with a mistress as understanding as Miss Clarinda."

Richard finished his supper. Rising to leave, he turned to Adele. "Mr. Matthias wants Iris and Lily to clear the table when he and Miss Clarinda are finished in the dining room. Thank you for saving my supper, Mrs. Minton."

He was barely out of the kitchen when Iris mounted her protest. "Why do Lily and I have to clean up? Richard's the high-class butler now. Why don't he do it?"

"Because he'll dirty his clothes," Joseph mocked. "You girls better be gettin' started, and Patsy, you go upstairs."

They left, and Mary and Laura went to their private parlor. As Adele prepared to wash the dishes, Joseph came over to her.

"Why couldn't I have had a boy?"

"We have a son, Joseph — Richard."

"You know what I mean." He waited a minute, then continued, "He would have had the chances then, not that stupid brat."

"And what chances has he had? You've taken them away from him."

"What do you call this that the Matthiases are doin'?"

"Because they need a butler, and he happens to be qualified? Would you complain if one of the girls received a better position?"

The service door opened. "All Miss Clarinda cares about is Richard. That's why she spent the whole day with him."

"What are you doing back, Iris?" Adele demanded.

"Bringing in the dishes. For two people, they sure use a lot of plates to eat dinner."

"They're rich," Joseph explained. "Rich people always do things up big."

Iris put her load down on the counter near the sink. "I'd better be getting back. Lily'll probably break something."

"Don't pick on your sister," Adele chided. "She's a good girl. You're all good girls."

"Besides, we have Richard to pick on." The girl left the kitchen laughing.

Adele looked at her husband; he could see the pain in her eyes. "Joseph, why don't we just let him go? Maybe he could make something of himself."

"I want him here," Joseph answered, his voice tense.

"Why? You hate him, and he's miserable."

They lapsed into German. "What did our little job cost you, Adele? I lost everything of value to me, and to have it thrown back in my face day after day . . . I told you it would be better—"

"And in New York, when you had the chance to be rid of him, you said no. All you had to do was agree, and you'd have had everything you wanted."

"I knew what it was doing to you when Mrs. Anderson mentioned searching for the boy's parents. Oh, her friend would have found them all right, and the day you knew that brat was dead for real, you'd have died too."

"So I am supposed to continue to let you abuse him out of gratitude for saving his life?"

He answered in English. "I like havin' him under my thumb." He pressed his thumb on the scrubbed wooden table as if he were squashing an insect. "A boy like him, under my thumb."

* * *

Richard sat in the dark attic, his mind in torment. He hated how they treated him as nothing more than an object for ridicule. Perhaps the Matthiases were laughing at him too. He thought about his parents, those shadows in his memory who, he believed, had loved him, but then why? The echo of Iris's laughter was his only answer. Trying not to cry, he picked up the blanket and clutched it tightly. The old fabric gave in his hands, and spreading

50

it out on a trunk, he found the three tears. As he tried to figure out what he was going to do, the attic door creaked open and a light intruded into the darkness.

"Is someone up here?"

He stood. "It's only me, Miss Clarinda."

"Do you realize what time it is? It's nearly eleven."

"How did you know I was here?"

"I heard someone walking around. My bedroom's right under this part of the attic."

He noticed the dark blue dressing gown, her hair tumbling in tangled curls down her back and over her shoulder to the waist. "I'm sorry I disturbed you, Miss Clarinda. I'll leave now." While he picked up his shoes, she came over to the trunk, the light from her candle falling on the blanket.

"I don't remember seeing this up here before."

"It's my blanket," he said so low she barely heard him.

"What?"

"My blanket," he repeated, a little louder. "Well, I think of it as mine."

"Oh, look, it's torn."

"I ripped it by accident this evening. But it's so old . . ."

"How did you get it?"

"I found it when I was little. She had it, in a trunk, but when she saw me with it, she took it away from me. I guess she must have thrown it away because somebody found it and gave it back to me." Even in the candlelight, Clarinda could see his embarrassment. "You're the first one since then to see it."

"Why do you hide it?"

"I'm afraid they'll take it away from me again." He looked at her for a long minute. "Miss Clarinda, would you do something for me?"

"If I can."

"Would you fix my blanket for me? I know it's silly to have, but it's the only thing I've ever felt was really mine."

"Of course I will. And I don't think it's silly. Everyone needs something to call their own."

"Thank you, Miss Clarinda." He left the attic. A minute later, she followed with the blanket.

It wasn't until she unfolded it in her room that she saw the embroidery in the center. Soiled though it was, there was still something endearing about it, and she traced it over and over with her fingers. Taking out her sketch pad, she copied it, then, placing the blanket and sketch in her cedar chest, went to bed.

\* \* \*

The following morning, after Jack went into Washington, Clarinda asked Richard into the dining room. He was surprised to see the assorted crystal, wine bottles, and decanters assembled on the table, but he sat in the chair she indicated. "What's all this for, Miss Clarinda?"

"My uncle asked me to compliment you on your excellent service last night."

"But?"

She smiled. "Were you trained in wine service?"

"I was too young." His face clouded. "Did I do something wrong?"

"You brought Uncle Jack Madeira instead of port. He concluded you hadn't been trained, and that's what this is all about."

"I still don't understand."

"Uncle Jack wants me to teach you about the wines and also the correct glasses to use."

"You're younger than I am, Miss Clarinda. How do you know about this?"

"I used to follow Jacob around, and I asked a lot of questions. So I learned."

"All right, Miss Clarinda. Which one is port?"

For the next two hours, she instructed him in the basic wines and spirits. He was a quick learner, and when she asked him for a glass of sherry, he beamed with pride as he handed it to her.

She sipped, then nodded her approval.

"I thought it would be harder."

"It is, once you start with the wines in the cellar. They're mostly French. But Uncle Jack and Bernice know them pretty well, so you won't have to worry too much about it right now."

"Could you teach me anyway?"

"You'd better ask Uncle Jack to teach you the wine cellar. I'm afraid I don't know *Pouilly-Fuisse* from *Châteauneuf-du-Pape*."

"*Pouilly-Fuisse* is the white wine," Bernice remarked, entering the room. "What is the meaning of this, Clarinda?" she continued, spotting the cluttered table. "You know your uncle is very particular about his liquor supply."

Clarinda sighed while the housekeeper seated herself. "Uncle Jack asked me to go over the wines with Richard."

"I see. I have been managing the wine cellar for years, and he asks *you* to train another servant?"

"Miss Lycoming, may I get you something to drink?" Richard asked.

"What? Absolutely not!" Bernice spotted the nearly full sherry glass at Clarinda's hand. "And you, young lady, it is highly improper to be imbibing at this hour of the day." Handing the glass to Richard, the irate woman ordered him to dispose of its contents, sternly warning him not to drink it, "or Mr. Matthias will hear about it." Richard left.

"What did you want, Bernice?"

"I have been waiting in the housekeeper's room the better part of the morning to discuss the luncheon and dinner menu with you."

"Oh, I'm sorry, Bernice. Mary did tell me, but I forgot. I thought you had taken care of it."

"Apparently, it isn't my responsibility anymore," the older woman said icily.

"Could I have a lamb pie for lunch?"

"It's a bit late for that. If Laura had had more time, she might have been able to prepare it."

"That's all right, I'm going riding shortly. I can have luncheon when I return."

"And what about dinner?"

"Anything you decide will be fine."

Bernice pursed her lips, and the hem of her black serge dress fluttered noticeably. "Thank you, Clarinda." Rising from her chair, she swished out of the room. As Clarinda began to collect the crystal, Richard returned.

"May I help you with those?"

"Richard, why don't you change while I finish here, so we can go riding?"

"I'd like to know where everything belongs. Then I won't make another mistake."

"Certainly."

Twenty minutes later, Jack's liquor supply and stemware safely returned to their proper places, Clarinda and Richard prepared to leave. She grabbed the doorknob, but he stopped her.

"Do you want something?"

"Just to thank you for teaching me today." He took her free hand between both of his and held it for a minute, then released it and disappeared through the service door.

She stood there, a flood of emotions racing through her mind. *He's a servant,* she thought. *I've only known him three days.* But no one else had ever caused this odd sensation or sudden warmth inside her. Then came the feeling that, if she told him to jump in a river, he would. She turned and went to her room.

* * *

They rode to the oak stand, but after dismounting, the two young people felt increasingly awkward with each other for Clarinda had told him she wanted to talk to him. Richard loosened the horses' saddles and tethered them to a dead tree while she made herself comfortable on a rustic bench a few feet away. She offered him a seat beside her, but he sat on a fallen oak tree near the horses.

"Miss Clarinda?"

"Yes, Richard?"

"I . . . didn't mean to be so familiar before. I'm sorry."

"You mean when you held my hand? It's all right."

"No, it isn't. I forgot my place again, just like at the station when I let you help me. He hit me good for that."

The matter-of-factness of his statement caught her off guard, and her stomach tightened. "Does Joseph hit the girls too?"

Richard shook his head. "They're his children. I'm not."

"But you grew up with them."

"I was never theirs. She tried in the beginning, but when her own came . . ."

"Her own? I'm sorry if I'm embarrassing you, Richard, but aren't you—"

"I know what people think I am. She's not my mother."

"Patsy told me you were abandoned on the Royces' doorstep."

"I don't believe them. My mama and papa would never abandon me."

"Wouldn't or couldn't? It happens."

"If my parents didn't want me, like they say, why did they wait so long to abandon me? Most foundlings are infants. I was almost two."

"Perhaps they couldn't keep you, or maybe they died. My parents did."

"Then why leave me with poor people? Wouldn't you try to make your child's life better?"

"What if they did? Patsy said Joseph would be a big man in his village."

"Now. Not then."

They sat for a few minutes, Richard picking at loose pieces of bark while Clarinda studied his face. There was such an emptiness when he spoke of the Royces, she knew he must be terribly unhappy with them and she found herself thinking of Richard's parents. He revered them, but they had hurt him too, worse than Joseph ever had. Or perhaps, there were no parents, as Jack had suggested the night before, just Richard's attempt to cope with an unhappy life by creating his own imaginary world. "Is there anything you remember about your early life?" she inquired cautiously.

"You mean, before them?"

"Yes."

"I dream about a big room, with sunshine walls and a soft, furry floor, and a gray-haired lady with a white apron. I see my parents too, sometimes, but usually they're only shadows." His eyes softened and he smiled. "And there are always stars."

"Stars?"

"They glitter and shine, and they sweep down into my mama's eyes when she looks at me. She loves me so much, then she goes away, and they're there." He dropped his head, afraid to let Clarinda see him cry.

She also choked back tears. When she was able to speak, she said haltingly, "Patsy says they talk about you at night."

"If you knew the nights I forced myself to stay awake, just to listen, but they speak German, and I can't understand them."

"Then how do you know they're talking about you?"

"My name gets used often enough, and they never talk about the girls in German."

"But if the Royces are Austrian or Swiss, wouldn't you be too? Then German would be your native tongue."

"Any German I might have known I forgot long ago." Once again, his face became illuminated as if lit by the stars he always saw in his dreams. "Don't you see, Clarinda?" he exclaimed in a husky, emotional voice. "My mama and papa couldn't have abandoned me. They loved me."

"But, Richard, what if—"

"They died? I'd have been raised by relatives or put in an orphanage. I'd never have just been given to them."

She thought about her own life, how her mother's family had fought to raise her after her father died. "Of course you're right," she said, then, to change the subject, asked, "Is Richard your real name, or did the Royces give it to you?"

"It's my name. She wanted to call me Willy, but I wouldn't forget my real name, so they let me use it."

"Do you know when your birthday is?"

"June 22. When's yours?"

"November 4."

Richard opened and closed his mouth a few times, then stared at the ground. Realizing he wanted to say something, Clarinda probed, "Is there something you want to ask me, Richard?"

"I" —he cleared his throat—"Iris said that—"

"What did she say?"

"That the reason you're doing all this is-is because you're sweet on me. Are you?"

She picked up a fallen oak leaf, turning it by the stem and fingering the veins. Uncertain of her own feelings, yet afraid to give him any false hopes, she finally replied, "I like you, Richard. I enjoy being with you, and I'm grateful that you feel you can trust me. But . . . I don't know." His eyes repeated the first part of his question.

"I knew you were better than being just a handyman or stableboy, and I wanted you to have the chance you deserve."

"Others tried before, but he always stopped them."

"The way he tried with Uncle Jack?"

"Sometimes, but mostly, we moved. Ever since we left Boston, I've . . . it was better if I just did what he told me to do."

She twirled the leaf with her thumb and forefinger. "Richard, if I asked you to jump in the river and swim upstream, would you?"

He smiled, then grinned. Suddenly, the quiet was broken by the sound of something rarely heard—Richard's laugh.

"I'm serious. Would you?"

"No, Miss Clarinda. Why would I do such a stupid thing?" He continued laughing, and she joined him, their laughter ringing through the air. When they stopped, he asked, "Why did you ask me that?"

"I wondered if I was replacing Joseph in telling you what to do. I didn't mean it to be funny."

"I know, but I saw a picture in my mind, and it was so ridiculous, I just had to laugh. I don't get too many chances to, and I even forget what it sounds like."

"Well, anytime you feel a laugh coming on, see me. I'll take care of it for you."

"I bet you will." He laughed again, then stood up. "Miss Clarinda, I think we should be getting back. I have a great deal to do."

"I think you're right." She patted her stomach. "I am becoming rather hungry." Walking over to where Richard was busily checking over their mounts, she added, "I'm glad we had a chance to talk."

"I like talking to you too, Clarinda — I mean, Miss Clarinda." He flushed scarlet and mumbled, "I'm sorry."

"No need to be. I feel we've become friends."

"I will be careful around other people, especially him, but when we're alone —"

"Just Clarinda is fine."

"Thank you." He helped her onto Moonbeam, then mounted himself. "Not bad for someone who . . ." he whispered something to her, and beginning to laugh again, they started back to the house.

# *Chapter* 4

---

Two weeks after Clarinda's return, Jack received the official notification he had been expecting . . . and secretly dreading. Coming while he and Clarinda were at breakfast, he sent a return message to the State Department that he would not be in, then went in search of Bernice.

Within the hour, the entire household was gathered in the dining room. It was unusual for Jack to do this, but he felt he needed to speak to them all at once. Removing an envelope from his jacket pocket, he glanced at Bernice and took a seat at the uncleared table. "I've asked you to meet me here this morning because I have something of importance to discuss with you."

Seeing his somewhat grim face, Clarinda asked, "Is something the matter, Uncle Jack?"

He smiled at her. "Not really, honey. It's the problem I've been working on at State, and now it has come here instead of being in Germany. Not that I wasn't expecting the king of Ahrweiler, but I rather hoped he would reconsider and resolve his internal conflict without our government's help."

"Who, Mr. Matthias?"

"King Johann of Ahrweiler, Laura. He is in New York, and he and his entourage will arrive in Washington within the week. What this means is that I shall have to reopen the townhouse."

"For how long?"

"I don't know, Bernice. It could be as long as a month."

"Which means you'll be closing Landfield."

"No, Bernice, it does not. First of all, accommodating the king and queen, plus Ahrweiler's prime minister and their retinue will be difficult enough. I will not have room for all my household as well in Washington. This is the reason I asked you to determine who I would need to care for my guests. Also, if there are too many people, I will need to have Landfield ready for them."

"Who will you be taking, Uncle Jack?"

"Bernice?"

"You'll need Laura, of course, and one of the Royce girls to act as maid of all work." Bernice glanced at the corner of the room, where Richard stood. "Fortunately, Richard can double as butler and coachman."

"Very good. We'll be leaving on Tuesday."

Jack continued explaining the details of the upcoming royal visit while Joseph and Adele stared at each other. He finished and dismissed the staff; as the Royces made their way past Clarinda, she heard Joseph whisper to Adele, "He won't go. I'll make sure of it."

* * *

The hall clock chimed the quarter hour. Drumming his fingers on the chair arm, Jack wondered out loud, "What is keeping Richard this evening?"

"Hm?" Clarinda replied, looking up from her book.

"Richard's late tonight. Usually, he's in here at the stroke of seven to announce dinner."

"Maybe dinner isn't ready."

"When's the last time you can remember Laura not having dinner ready on time?"

"I can't, but there's a first time for everything."

Hearing footsteps in the hall, Jack smiled. "There he is now."

Bernice entered the parlor, a more dour expression than usual on her thin face. "I apologize for the delay, Mr. Matthias, but dinner is ready to be served."

"Where's Richard?" Clarinda asked.

"He isn't feeling well." The housekeeper's lips tightened. "He seemed perfectly fine two hours ago."

"Has someone examined him?" Jack questioned.

"Mrs. Royce says her son is not in need of any medical attention, that it is just a small cold."

"Well, let's have dinner, and I'll check on him later."

"I don't see why you have to bother, Mr. Matthias. If Mrs. Royce says it is nothing—"

"And what if it is cholera or typhus? We could all become infected."

"Cholera? In late spring? I hardly think so. And I happen to know Richard is meticulous about cleanliness. Typhus is out of the question." Sniffing with indignation, she continued, "The soup is cooling," and left the room.

Jack watched her go, then chuckled. "Poor Bernice. She really does dislike serving."

"Do you think Richard is all right?"

"Oh, I'm certain he is, honey. Come on. Let's have dinner." They stood and headed for the dining room.

* * *

Several hours later, Jack knocked on Richard's door. "It's Mr. Matthias, Richard. I understand you're not feeling well." When he received no answer, he tried the knob, surprised that it refused to turn. "Richard, would you unlock the door?"

A long pause before the young man replied, "I can't. He's locked me in."

"I'll be right back." Jack procured a skeleton key and, unlocking the door, entered.

A single candle on the battered chest of drawers illuminated the small room. Richard lay curled on the short, narrow bed, partly to accommodate his six-foot-three frame, staring at the flame. Seeing his employer, he slowly pushed himself up on one elbow.

"No, don't get up. Adele says you have a cold. Do you?"

"I guess so." For a second, their eyes met. Then Richard fixed his gaze once more on the candle.

"Why did Joseph lock you in here?"

"He don't like it when I'm . . . sick." Richard sighed; to Jack it sounded more like a sob. "Mr. Matthias, please don't take me to Washington."

"If it's only a cold —"

"Take him instead. He said he'd hit me again if . . ." The young man turned toward the wall, groaning slightly as he did.

"Joseph's beaten you, hasn't he?"

"No."

"Is that why he locked you in your room? To punish you?"

"He don't want the girls to get sick too."

"All right, then." Jack started to leave. "I'll have the doctor sent for in the morning."

"No, Mr. Matthias, I mean, that won't be necessary. I'll be okay tomorrow. I'm already feeling better." Hiding the pain the best he could, Richard sat up.

"Why are you lying to me, Richard?"

"I'm not."

"I know Joseph beats you because the Armitages told me he does. Now I will ask you again, did he beat you today?" The servant bit his lower lip and nodded. "Do you know why?"

"I think because you're taking me with you. He don't want me to go."

"Joseph has no say in the matter. I need you in Washington."

"Don't make me go, please. He said that" — Richard rubbed his eyes; Jack realized he was wiping away tears — "he said he'd beat me so bad — and this time, he'd make sure it showed — that you wouldn't be able to take me."

Jack thought for a moment. He had to have the help in the city, and Richard's versatility eliminated hiring extra servants. He also resented Joseph Royce's continued interference where the boy was concerned. But if this upcoming visit had so upset Joseph—for Jack suddenly recalled what could only be described as disbelief in the man's face earlier in the day—that he had taken it out on his son, perhaps he should reconsider. "We'll see, Richard."

"Mr. Matthias, please don't tell Miss Clarinda."

"She's concerned about you, you know. But this is something she doesn't have to be aware of."

"Thank you, Mr. Matthias."

Leaving Richard's room after that, Jack saw Joseph coming down the hall, a slight smirk on his face. "Joseph!"

The man stopped, shocked to see the master in the servants' quarters. "Yes, Mr. Matthias?"

"I've just been with Richard."

"What'd that stupid boy of mine do now? I'll—"

"Since Richard is not well, and I cannot risk my guests becoming ill, I'm afraid he will have to stay here at Landfield, and you will be coming to Washington instead."

"Me? But I—"

"I need *someone* to drive my carriage, Joseph." Jack took a few steps toward the kitchen, then turned. "And as for your boy, I think you've done quite enough. Good night, Mr. Royce." He continued down the hall, the door closing angrily behind him.

* * *

Five days later, Jack left Landfield for Washington. Clarinda, a little disappointed that she would not be able to accompany her uncle, watched from the porch while Jack supervised the last-minute loading of the large closed coach. When that was completed, he joined her on the broad steps.

"I wish I could come, Uncle Jack."

"I know, honey, but I'm afraid I won't have the room for you. Their Majesties are traveling with quite an entourage, ten servants and, I understand, a detail of soldiers." He patted her cheek reassuringly.

She smiled back at him, certain they would have to come to Landfield. "If there is room, will you send for me?"

Jack laughed. "You know I will. Besides, someone has been very eager to see you."

"Arthur?"

"He has missed you terribly this past year."

"Why doesn't he come out here?"

"Unfortunately, the State Department and I keep him very busy. But once this Ahrweiler matter is settled, I'll see to it that Mr. Jamison gets a nice long vacation in the Maryland countryside."

"Please give him my—" She was about to say *love*, but the word somehow didn't seem appropriate any more. "Tell Arthur I'm looking forward to seeing him too."

"Of course, honey." Over the girl's head, Jack saw Laura and Lily Royce entering the coach. "It's time, Clarinda."

She threw her arms around his neck, the tears beginning to sting her eyes. "I'm going to miss you."

Jack's eyes also misted as he held her tight, her head resting under his cheek. "Sweetheart," he started, his voice husky with emotion, "I'll be home soon. I promise." Then he released her and, giving her a last kiss on her tear-wet cheek, descended the stairs.

\* \* \*

Clarinda sat in her sitting room, waiting for Patsy to leave for the night. With Jack gone, she had nothing to do during the evening except listen to Bernice discuss the household accounts and dinner menus, things that held little interest for her. Now with Patsy chattering and fussing about, Clarinda longed to get back to what she had nicknamed "the project." But still Patsy puttered on.

She finally finished turning down the bed. "Will you need anything else, Miss Clarinda?"

"Not tonight, Patsy, thank you."

"Good night, then."

"Good night."

The younger girl left and Clarinda picked up a book, but a minute later, she was back. "What time will you be needing me in the morning, Miss Clarinda?"

"Eight o'clock, just as always."

The door closed again, Clarinda knowing from experience Patsy would be back. Nor was she disappointed, for a few minutes passed and there was another knock. "Yes, Patsy," she chuckled, "what is it?"

"Mama wants to know what you want for breakfast."

"Tell her eggs and toast is fine."

"Sorry to have disturbed you, Miss Clarinda. Good night."

Clarinda smiled at the quickly shut door, then returned to her book. Once more the door opened but this time, Bernice entered. Frowning slightly at the title of the book the girl was reading, the older woman reported, "I just wished to inform you that everything is secured, and I am retiring for the night."

"Thank you, Bernice."

After she left, Clarinda read a little longer. Then when it became apparent she would not be disturbed again, she put the book away and took out Richard's blanket. During the time she'd had it, she had, with Mary's help, managed to repair the damage of the years and wash it, for she assumed Richard did not have much opportunity to do so. With the dirt and grime removed, the gray blanket was, in reality, a soft blue, the center design a monogram just a few shades darker, gold thread interwoven with the blue. Running her fingers lightly over the design, a slight squeak above her caused her to look up and smile as she took out her embroidery frame and started to work.

* * *

Three days after his departure, a note arrived from Jack. Bernice quickly scanned the envelope, a little surprised it was addressed to Clarinda and not herself, and brought it up to the girl's room, where Mary was putting the final touches on Clarinda's hair.

"I just hate rainy days, Aunt Mary. Don't you?"

"It's been a very dry spring, and we need the rain."

"I know, but—"

"You're just disappointed because you can't go out riding is all." Mary patted the top of her charge's head. "There. I think those curls should stay put now despite the damp."

"Clarinda"—the girl turned toward Bernice—"this arrived for you a few minutes ago."

"Thank you." Clarinda slit the envelope with her nail file and read the brief message, her face glowing with excitement. "Oh, Aunt Mary, they're coming to Landfield!"

"Your uncle's visitors?"

"Yes. Uncle Jack writes that Count von Bronstein will be here tomorrow, and the king and queen are following on Monday. I'm so happy for Richard."

"Richard?" Bernice questioned.

"Don't you see? He'll get his chance to prove Joseph wrong." Clarinda stood and headed for the door. "I'm going to tell him right now."

"Make sure you take an umbrella, Miss Clarinda," Mary called after her.

"I really don't see what all the fuss is about, Mary. Richard will have plenty of opportunities to serve Mr. Matthias's associates."

"Don't you, Bernice? His success will be hers, and if he fails, she will too."

"Well, I know the child has spent a great deal of time trying to help him."

Mary looked out the rain-spattered window, spotting an unprotected Clarinda running toward the stable. "Our Miss Clarinda isn't a child anymore."

* * *

Clarinda found Richard busily rubbing down Moonbeam. Standing there, she saw the pleasure he took in his work, for he talked quietly to the mare, a smile playing around his lips. She watched for a few minutes before going over and putting her hands on his shoulders.

"Hello, Clarinda."

She giggled. "How did you know it was me?"

"By your touch. Nobody else touches me the way you do: gentle."

Dropping her hands, she withdrew the letter from her pocket. "I got this today from Uncle Jack. There's been a change of plans."

He lay down the currycomb and faced her. "I'm going to Washington, Clarinda?"

"Oh, we'd better be careful, Richard," she chided jestingly. "We wouldn't want Joseph to find out you're becoming so familiar."

Chuckling, he slid an arm around her shoulders. "He's with your uncle."

She smiled back at the handsome young man as he maneuvered her between himself and the horse, and she forgot everything except that she was with him.

"You were saying?"

"My uncle, Uncle Jack, he sent a note today."

"You've already said that."

"Oh yes. They're coming to Landfield, Richard. Count von Bronstein arrives tomorrow, and the king and queen are following Monday."

"I hope I'll be ready to serve them."

"Of course you will, and you know it."

"You're sure?"

"I haven't been wrong yet about you, have I?"

"No." He gazed down at her, then started to reach for the currycomb, but she stopped him.

"You seem happy, Richard, taking care of Moonbeam."

"Working for Mr. Matthias, and you, has made me very happy, and I'd be content just to work for him."

"That should be no problem. Uncle Jack has been pleased with everything you've done so far, and you know how I feel. You're welcome to stay here as long as you'd like."

"That won't be possible," he replied sadly.

"Why not?"

"Because we're always moving on, 'lookin' to get on in the world,' he says. Whenever I think we've finally settled down, something happens, and he's looking for a new position."

"Why don't you leave them?"

"Leave them?"

"Richard, let them move on if they want, but, please, stay here."

"He won't let me." All of Richard's happiness evaporated with his statement, and he looked at his shoes.

"Are we back to that? How can he stop you?"

He lifted his head. "When I was little, it was easy for him. I didn't have a choice in the matter."

"But you're old enough now."

"Don't you think I've tried to escape?" He laughed bitterly. "I joined the army once, when I was eighteen. When I made the mistake of telling him, he made me tell them I had lied about my age, that I was only fifteen. And I was planning to run away from Armitages', but how *he* found out? The day before I was going to leave . . . Master Peter had his accident going to tell his father what he was doing to me."

"Oh, Richard."

He stroked Moonbeam's neck. "Mr. Armitage wanted me to stay on, but I was afraid of what he would do to me if I did. So I thanked him for his offer and came here."

"I'm glad you did."

"Why?"

"Because if you had stayed in Baltimore, we wouldn't have met or become friends."

"Is that all we are, friends?"

"No, I don't think so." She dropped her eyes, afraid to look into his face.

"I-I'm . . ." He was afraid to admit the rest, even to her.

"What is it, Richard? Please, tell me."

"How can I? I'm not supposed to —"

"Fall in love with me?" she whispered, the tremor in her voice betraying her emotions.

"What would your uncle think? Servants aren't supposed to take advantage of their employers, and people like me . . . I'm sorry, Miss Clarinda. I didn't mean to forget my place."

She touched a fingertip to his lips. "Richard, if anyone had told me two months ago that I'd be in love with one of my servants, I'd have laughed in his face."

He stared at her, astounded. Then he drew her to him and kissed her. "I'll never leave you, Clarinda," he groaned.

Tears welled up in her eyes, and she put her arms around him. She returned his kisses, his endearments quieting her heart. They were in a magical, golden world all their own until a sudden move by Moonbeam brought them back to reality, and they saw Iris standing there.

"I wonder what Papa will say when I tell him about this. He'll put you back in your place for certain." Iris turned and left, her laugh echoing wickedly through the stable.

Clarinda looked at Richard. His eyes, which just a moment before had been warm and loving, were lifeless, his body tense.

"I'm sorry, Miss Clarinda. This won't happen again."

"Richard . . . please, it's all right. Joseph can't do anything to you, to us."

"And what if he tells your uncle? Mr. Matthias will never trust me with you again."

"Because you kissed me? We love each other. Uncle Jack will understand."

"He'll make it sound like I did more than that."

"Richard, Uncle Jack knows you, and he certainly knows me. He couldn't possibly believe that you could . . . or that I would permit you to."

"You don't know *him*. Please, Clarinda, leave before anything else can happen." He released her and returned to grooming the mare. Shocked and confused, she stumbled out of the stable and returned to the house, oblivious of the rain.

\* \* \*

Count von Bronstein arrived at Landfield the next afternoon, accompanied by his valet and secretary, the squad of soldiers, and Joseph. Jack had also sent Arthur Jamison to keep an eye on Bronstein. Watching them, Clarinda managed a smile for the young man as the open victoria stopped in front of the porch steps, and he waved to her. She straightened her shoulders and descended to meet her guests.

"Good afternoon, Your Excellency. Welcome to Landfield."

"I am pleased to meet you, Fräulein Matthias. Your uncle has spoken very fondly of you."

"And Arthur, it's always a pleasure to see you."

He smiled at her. "It's been a long time, Clarinda. You've grown into a lovely young woman."

"Thank you. Now please come in. I'll let you get settled, then I'll have tea set out in the parlor."

Joseph came up on the porch, followed by Bronstein's retainers. "Where's His Excellency stayin'?"

"Upstairs, second room on the right." Clarinda saw the two large valises in Joseph's hands. "I am surprised, Joseph," she said pointedly. "I thought only Richard carried the heavy luggage."

He glared angrily at her, then went into the house, followed by the count. Excusing herself to Arthur, she went to the kitchen.

\* \* \*

After speaking to Adele, Clarinda found Richard in the formal garden, trimming a row of boxwood. Her heart lurched, but when she went over to him, she refused to touch him. "Richard," she said, her voice a little shaky, "would you be able to serve tea in a half hour?"

He dared not turn around when he heard her. "Serve tea?"

"Never mind," she snapped. "I can see you're too busy. I'll get Adele or Bernice to do it. I'm sorry I disturbed you." Clarinda started to leave.

"Clarinda, wait." She froze in her steps. "What's happened to us? Don't you like me anymore?"

"What a silly question," she murmured, her eyes filling with tears.

"Then why did you barely speak to me last night at dinner? And this morning, when you didn't want to go riding, I was sure—"

"I've been so miserable, thinking about what happened, and last night, I couldn't sleep at all. Even Bernice noticed something was wrong, and she's thick as mud."

"I promise you. I'll never do anything like that again."

"That isn't the problem. Everything was wonderful, beautiful, until Iris made her presence known."

"Now you're not sure about . . ."

"I thought you weren't sure." She faced him, her breath catching in her throat. He stood there, looking at her, all his love and uncertainty focused in his eyes.

"He's hurt me too often. I don't want him to hurt you too."

"How do you think I felt? I thought you were shutting me out."

"I'm . . . oh, Clarinda." He took her hand. Two seconds later, she was in his arms and he was kissing her, all his doubts disappearing. Finally, he released his hold and smiled at her. "Will you be needing me, Miss Clarinda?"

"Well, it does seem rather silly now to have you change, just to carry a tea tray." She took out her handkerchief and blew her nose. "I'll ask Adele."

"All right." He gazed into her eyes, which still shimmered with her tears. "I'm glad we talked."

"I am too." She kissed him quickly. "I'll see you tonight at dinner." Then she returned to the house in a decidedly better frame of mind then when she came out.

Arthur was waiting in the front hall, running his fingers through a bowl of rose petals on the walnut occasional table when the front door opened. "Clarinda, are you all right?" the slender, auburn-haired man asked, surprised to see her coming in from outside, her hair tousled and her eyes red.

"I'm fine, Arthur. Why do you ask?"

"You look like you've been crying."

"I have, a little. But I really am fine."

"Good. I'd hate for my best girl to be unhappy." He came over and, taking her hands, kissed her cheek. "I wanted to welcome you home properly. I've missed you."

"I-I have to set up for tea, Arthur."

"Of course," he replied, but he refused to release her. "I meant what I said before, Clarinda. You really are beautiful." Kissing her a second time, he dropped her hands.

She smiled and murmured, "Oh, Arthur."

"I'll see you in a few minutes." Arthur strode into the parlor, while Clarinda continued on to the kitchen. The girl could see something was bothering Adele, who was busy preparing the tea tray, and the request to serve did not improve matters.

"I thought Richard was serving."

"He's busy in the garden and won't have time to change."

"Very well, Miss Clarinda." She dried her hands with the huck towel by the sink. "When will you want me to come up?"

"Fifteen minutes and thank you." As Clarinda left, Adele wondered what could possibly be wrong with her for she also noticed the girl's red eyes and blotched face.

\* \* \*

Count von Bronstein entered the parlor ten minutes later, finding Clarinda and Arthur engaged in conversation. The two of them stood when they saw the large man in the doorway; he inclined his head toward his hostess before settling into an easy chair.

"I hope everything meets with your approval, Your Excellency," Clarinda commented, retaking her seat.

"Your staff has done an excellent job on short notice, Fräulein."

"Thank you, Your Excellency."

As she spoke, Adele entered with the tea tray. Suddenly, Clarinda felt uneasy for, while neither Adele's nor Bronstein's expression changed, a sign of recognition seemed to pass between them when their eyes met. Placing the tray in front of Clarinda, the older woman withdrew after exchanging a second brief glance with the count. "Do you know Mrs. Royce, Your Excellency?" she asked, passing the tea cups and a plate of ladyfingers and lemon biscuits.

"What?" Bronstein started at the girl's question. "No, I never met the woman before this afternoon."

"Oh."

"Your Excellency," Arthur interposed, "perhaps Miss Matthias would like to hear about your country."

"Yes, I would. I'm afraid I'm not familiar with Ahrweiler."

Bronstein laughed, a little too heartily. "It is one of many German kingdoms and principalities that are not well known, Fräulein Matthias."

"Where is it located?"

"About fifty miles northwest of Coblenz."

"That isn't very close to Switzerland, is it?"

"I'm afraid not. Switzerland is far to the south." The count rested back against the striped plum satin upholstery and drank some tea. "Why do you ask?"

"The Royces are from Switzerland or Austria, and I thought . . ."

Realizing where the conversation appeared to be headed, Arthur asked, "How *are* the Royces working out, Clarinda?"

"Pretty well, Arthur. I was quite surprised when I came home to find the Royces here and Mattie and Jacob gone."

"But Jacob always had a pioneer nature."

"That's why he and Bernice didn't get along too well. She can't understand why anyone would want to pick up and move into unknown territory. I think Landfield is about as uncivilized as she cares to get." The two young people started laughing.

"What about you, Fräulein? Do you have this pioneer nature?"

"I don't know, Your Excellency. I've just finished school, and I'm glad to be home. What I want to do in a year or two remains to be seen."

Arthur gazed warmly at the girl in the brown and cream silk day dress. "What about marriage?"

"Eventually," she answered, feeling herself blush.

Encouraged by the sudden sparkle of her green eyes, Arthur gently probed further. "Someone special?"

"I think so."

"Does Jack know?"

"Not yet. I'm planning to tell him when he comes back."

Noticing the dry, gray-brown smudges on her back and the surprised look on Arthur's face, Bronstein raised an eyebrow. "Will your uncle approve of this man for you, Fräulein Matthias? It is not wise to be hasty in such a grave decision, to confuse a physical attraction for love."

"I'm hoping he will approve, Your Excellency." She blushed again, then, seeing the gentlemen had finished their tea, rang to have the service removed. A moment later, Iris entered.

"You're finished with the tea, Miss Clarinda?"

Clarinda stared at the younger girl, who was wearing the dress she had taken from the attic. "Yes, Iris, we are," she answered coldly. "And do be careful taking the service to the kitchen. I would hate for you to ruin your dress."

Picking up the tray, Iris left the room. Excusing herself to her guests, Clarinda stormed into the kitchen after the girl.

"I would like to know why you're wearing my dress!" she shouted.

"Oh, I see," Iris returned. "It's all right for you to give Richard clothes, but I'm not good enough for your charity."

"First of all, if you needed clothes, my uncle and I would have provided them for you, you don't have to steal them. And since you mentioned Richard, the only reason he received clothes was that he needs them for his job. Secondly, if you had wanted that particular dress, you should have asked me for it, not just taken it."

"Is that all, Miss Clarinda?"

"No, that is not all. I demand you stop spying on me. I do not appreciate having a shadow everywhere I go around here."

"You just don't want me watching you and Richard 'cause if any of your friends found out" — Iris started to laugh — "the lady of the house and her stableboy. You'd be ruined."

"Why you little! You *know* nothing happened."

"Well, it's still your word against mine."

Clarinda raised her hand to slap the smirking Iris. As she did, the door opened. "Somethin' goin' on here?"

Iris ran over to her father, throwing her skinny arms around his waist. "Papa," she sobbed, "Miss Clarinda's yelling at me."

"Iris do something, Miss Clarinda?"

Clarinda glared at the girl. "Nothing of importance. You may keep the dress, Iris." She turned on her heel and left the kitchen.

Joseph looked down at his daughter. "What did you do, Iris? Miss Clarinda don't yell for no reason."

"Well . . . I saw this dress in the attic. I liked it, so I took it. I didn't think she'd mind since she gave Richard all them clothes."

"That's stealin'. You're lucky she give you the dress after you took it."

He sat on a chair by the table, and she climbed onto his lap. "Miss Clarinda also wants me to stop spying on her and Richard. But I was just doing what you told me to do."

"But you gloat about what you find out. You have to be less obvious about bein' around."

"You mean discreet, Papa?"

"Yes."

She started to laugh. "Papa, you're not gonna believe what I saw them doing," and she whispered it to him.

"You're certain?"

"I don't know what would have happened next if her stupid horse hadn't heard me."

He hugged her. "You done good, *Liebchen.*"

"You'll put him in his place, won't you, Papa?"

"Soon. Not now."

"When?"

"When Mr. Matthias comes home."

* * *

Several hours later, Bronstein waited alone in the parlor. He refrained from pouring a before-dinner brandy, not wishing to infringe upon his absent host's hospitality, but walked around the room, inspecting the various *objets d'art*. As he was taking a seat by the fireplace, mopping his brow with his handkerchief, he heard a man inquire, "Excuse me, Your Excellency. Miss Matthias has asked me to see if you would like anything before dinner."

The hairs on the back of Bronstein's neck rose. Turning, he stared at the tall man before him, amazed when the other bowed.

"Your Excellency? May I get you something?"

"*Ja--ein Kognak, bitte.*"

When Richard failed to move, Bronstein asked for the brandy in English. "A large one."

The count returned to his seat as the young servant went for the drink. A minute later, he was back, a small silver tray in his hand.

"Your brandy, Your Excellency."

"Thank you . . ." Bronstein answered, taking the glass.

"Richard, Your Excellency."

"Of course, Richard."

"Will you require anything else, Your Excellency?"

"No, thank you, Richard." Bronstein downed the brandy as the servant bowed and left the parlor.

"Your Excellency?"

Bronstein jerked his head up to see Clarinda before him. "Ah, Fräulein Matthias. What is it?"

"Dinner is about to be served."

"Thank you, Fräulein. I shall be in momentarily."

"Is something bothering you, Your Excellency? You seem troubled."

"No, Fräulein. Nothing is wrong." Setting his brandy snifter on the tea table, he followed Clarinda into the dining room.

*Chapter* 5

---

That evening, Clarinda found it extremely difficult to perform her duties as hostess. To her surprise, Bronstein appeared focused on Richard, his hooded gray eyes following the young servant's every move. Even Arthur, who had enlivened other formal dinners of Jack's, seemed boring. She turned her attention back to Richard, and while the expression on his face never changed, the warmth of his eyes told her everything he was feeling.

Richard had removed the asparagus soup and begun circulating the boiled beef and chicken cutlets when Bronstein turned to Clarinda and said, "Fräulein Matthias, there are only three of us. Dismiss your butler. We can serve ourselves."

"Excuse me?" she replied, the dish of minted carrots in her hand.

"Your butler is not needed tonight," the count asserted. "I want him dismissed."

"On the contrary, Your Excellency, I think he is needed."

"I am not used to having my requests denied, Fräulein."

"Your Excellency—"

Bronstein pounded the table, rattling the china and silver. "I will not have Richard serving dinner, and that is that."

Leaning over to her, Arthur whispered, "Clarinda, do what the count asks. It is protocol."

"And this is my home, Arthur," she angrily whispered back.

"Do I have to dismiss him myself, Fräulein?"

"No, Your Excellency." Clarinda turned toward the sideboard. "Thank you, Richard, that will be all for this evening. Please have Bernice bring up the dessert."

"Yes, Miss Matthias." Richard bowed and left the dining room.

"There, gentlemen. I hope you both are satisfied." She attacked her chicken viciously.

"Clarinda, dear, I know you're upset, but it's best that you forget about this," Arthur commented *sotto voce*.

"We'll see what my uncle has to say about it."

Dinner continued in a more somber mood for Clarinda as she worried about what Richard was thinking. Finally, it ended, and they retired to the parlor.

While Arthur, at Bronstein's request, poured after-dinner drinks, Clarinda studied the large, heavy count. There was something unsettling about the set of his mouth within the gray beard as if the real man were masquerading behind the mask of the courtier, and his eyes reminded her of a hawk's, right before capturing its prey. He was different from any other person she had previously known, and in spite of herself, she shuddered.

Bronstein's glance drifted toward the rosewood piano in the corner of the room. "Do you play, Fräulein Matthias?"

"A little. I'm not very good, I'm afraid."

"You're too modest, Clarinda," Arthur countered. "Would you play something?"

"Arthur, I—"

The young man leaned over her chair. "For me, please?"

"All right." She crossed the room to the instrument. Running her fingers lightly over the yellowed ivory keys, she sat on the tapestry-covered stool and began.

Her performance was one of skill and feeling, but not brilliance, which her audience did not seem to notice. She started with *Für Elise* and the *Moonlight Sonata*, her particular favorites, adding some short Mozart pieces she knew from memory. Arthur, meanwhile, pulled several music books from the stack behind her and selected one or two longer works, along with some vocal duets. Putting the latter aside with a frown, she chose a piano transcription of a Bach organ concerto.

As she struck the opening chords, Clarinda thought of her mother, who had transcribed the composition. Jane Franklin Matthias had been a gifted artist and musician, her bohemian nature tolerated for that reason by her staid, affluent family. When she died giving birth to her only child, the Franklins had hoped the little girl would inherit her mother's more desirable qualities. But as Clarinda was painfully aware, all she received from her mother were her green eyes, a talent for music that she ignored, and Jane's free spirit. It seemed to Clarinda she was forever in her mother's shadow, and while it rarely bothered her, there were times, like now, when she wished she could be more like the beautiful young woman whose portrait graced the parlor in the Washington townhouse.

Reaching a difficult passage of music, Clarinda turned her full attention to the score, but as had happened so often before, she lost her place and was unable to find it. Frustrated, she stopped playing in mid-measure and closed the cover with a quick slam.

Bronstein, who was listening with his eyes closed, started at the sudden silence. "Why did you stop, Fräulein? Please continue, the Bach was lovely."

"Yes, Clarinda," Arthur added. "It's been such a long time since I've heard you play it."

She shook her head resolutely, and no amount of persuasion by either man could make her change her mind. While she returned to her seat, the parlor door opened, and Bernice entered, looking for her. With a sigh, Clarinda stood and followed the housekeeper into the hall.

"What do you need, Bernice?"

"I would like to know what you are planning to feed your guests the next two days."

"Now?"

"Clarinda" — Bernice massaged her temples with her fingers — "I have to dismiss the staff for the night. I think Mrs. Royce would appreciate knowing what she is to prepare for breakfast before she retires. After all, she is only filling in while Laura is in Washington."

"Is there fresh bread?"

"I believe I saw two loaves, which need to last until Monday."

"Then have Mrs. Royce make buttermilk biscuits and eggs. That should do."

"Nonsense." Bernice's fingers slid up into her hair. "Never mind, Clarinda. I'll take care of the menu. Just one more thing."

"Yes, Bernice?"

"Is Richard serving, or will there be a repeat of this evening's performance?"

"I want him to serve," Clarinda began, before remembering the vehemence of Bronstein's request. "I'll let you know."

"Try to do so *before* dinner, please." Bernice stared at the girl. "You are old enough now to show a little more concern about what goes on around here. It *is* what is expected of you."

"Good night, Bernice."

Clarinda returned to the parlor. When she entered, Bronstein was standing. "Ah, Fräulein. I hope the problem was not serious."

"Nothing that my housekeeper can't handle, Your Excellency."

"Good. As I was just telling Herr Jamison, I wanted to thank both of you for a pleasant evening before I retired."

"I tried to convince him to wait, Clarinda, but the count insists on going to bed."

"It has been a very long day for me, and I am quite tired. I am sure you understand, Fräulein."

"Of course, Your Excellency. Good night."

"Good night." Taking her hand, Bronstein raised it to his lips and kissed it, then, with a slight bow, made his exit.

After the count left, Arthur came over to Clarinda and slipped an arm around her waist. "I'm glad he's gone. I've wanted to be alone with you all evening."

"Then why did you tell him to stay?"

"Protocol." He chuckled. "Can't have our esteemed visitor feeling neglected. I really am delighted you played for us tonight. Jack says you rarely do nowadays."

"Why should I bother? I'll never be as good as everyone says Mother was, and when I do play, all I hear from Grandmother Franklin is comparison to her."

"Then stop worrying about what the Franklins think. I guarantee you that both the count and myself thought you were wonderful."

"Thank you."

"By the way, what did Bernice want?"

"She wanted me to plan the menus for the weekend, something else I can't do very well."

"Ah, Clarinda, I noticed at dinner that you were, um, watching the help rather closely."

"Was I?" She felt herself start to blush.

"I don't think it was because you thought Richard was going to spill the soup."

"No. He's a very good butler, which is why I don't understand the count's dismissal of him this evening. By the way, Arthur, would you talk to the count about Richard's serving? It is his job, and I don't think —"

"You aren't serious about Richard, are you?" She turned her head away, averting Arthur's eyes, but he caught her chin and forced her to look at him. "You cannot seriously believe Jack would condone any kind of relationship you could have with Richard. And what about his family? If your uncle ever found out, they'd be out on their ears."

"Why wouldn't Uncle Jack understand? Is it wrong to love someone?"

"Of course not, but you have to remember your position."

"It's always protocol, isn't it, Arthur? Protocol or propriety."

"It's only common sense. You and Richard, you come from two entirely different worlds. How can you expect him to fit into your station, or you to fit into his?"

"I think I've heard enough."

"You don't have to fall in love with the first man you meet, Clarinda. You're still so very young, you'll find the proper one for you." He looked down at her, his blue eyes darkening. "You may even be surprised."

"I don't think I'm wrong about this, Arthur."

"We'll see." He released her and kissed her on the cheek. "Good night, dear . . . Clarinda."

"Please talk to the count?"

"Very well. Anything for you."

* * *

Bronstein walked past the garden, dew moistening the edge of his trouser legs. He had spent a restless night, and he thought the early morning air might clear his mind. Nodding to the soldiers milling around the paddock, he made his way down a wooded path behind the stable.

He came by chance upon a crumbling fence. Pushing against a rusted iron gate set into it, the creak of disuse cutting the quiet, the count noticed a side path leading further into the woods. He followed it to a clearing where, to his surprise, a tower-like structure stood. Ivy and moss covered the stone walls, and in a sandstone face above the door was etched the number 1692. A new door, Bronstein realized, with a barely rusted bolt. It slid back with little resistance, and he cautiously entered the building.

The room was nine feet square, a crude fireplace set into one wall, narrow stairs leading to the second story. Bronstein looked around at the incongruous domestic touches in the abandoned building. A faded blue rag rug covered the wood floor, and a broken vase filled with long-dead flowers sat on the sill of the room's sole window, framed by tattered chintz curtains. As he did, an idea came to him, one that would solve his dilemma, and he laughed cruelly. After a second cursory examination, he left.

* * *

After breakfast, Clarinda and Richard cantered down the dirt path that led to the oak stand, instead of taking their usual circuit through the surrounding Maryland countryside. By his silence, she knew the events of the previous evening had disturbed him as they had her, and she had requested the change in route so they could talk about it. Approaching the grove, he managed a smile. A short time later, having removed the horses' tack and releasing them into the adjoining clearing, he sat down beside Clarinda.

"I was very proud of you last night, Richard. You handled things beautifully."

"Then why did you dismiss me? Dinner was only half over."

"Count von Bronstein demanded it. He felt you weren't needed, and Arthur said it wasn't protocol to countermand his request."

"I make the count uncomfortable."

"But he had never met you, and he seems fine around everyone else. What makes you think—"

"Before dinner last night, when I went into the parlor, he kept looking at me as if he'd seen a ghost." Richard laughed a little. "And the way he kept saying my name . . . I think he was trying to remember it."

"Does that mean anything to you?"

Closing his eyes, Richard thought for a few seconds. "I wish it did. I spent most of the night thinking about it." Running his fingers through his hair, Richard continued, "They went out last night, after everyone was in bed."

"How do you know?"

"I heard them leave."

"Do you know why?"

"I'm not a sneak like Iris. I didn't follow them. Besides," his voice dropped, "he taught me what would happen if I left my room at night."

Her throat tightened. "Is that why you're so quiet when you go to the attic?"

He started, the haunted look returning to his eyes. "How—"

83

"I told you when I found you up there. The attic is above my bedroom, and one of the floorboards creaks. Every night, you step on that board."

"I don't mean to disturb you."

"You don't. I look forward to it, and I missed it last night."

"I know I'm supposed to be sleeping, but I have to go somewhere to think."

"Stop apologizing. It's all right. What do you think about?"

"Me, mostly. Trying to remember something."

"Do you?"

"Only what I've told you."

"When you think about yourself, what name do you use?"

He laughed loudly. "Richard, of course."

"No, really. Just Richard? No surname?"

"I've always thought of myself as just Richard. In fact, I do remember them having an awful time making me use Royce. How do you think of yourself?"

"Clarinda Matthias." She sighed, another avenue for discovering his true identity gone for, despite what her uncle thought, she believed what Richard had confided in her to be the truth and not fantasy. Putting her arms around his chest, she felt him wince. "What did Joseph hit you for this time?"

"He didn't," he stammered. "I-I backed into a door latch in the stable."

"You're sure?" she queried, catching the uncertainty in his reply.

"It's only a bruise, Clarinda, honestly. Thank you for caring, anyway." He turned and leaned against the tree trunk.

Settling back into his shoulder, she announced, "I'm telling Uncle Jack about us on Monday."

"Clarinda . . . I'm not sure that's such a good idea."

"Why not? You do love me, don't you?"

"He's got to have more important things to worry about than us."

"What's the real reason you don't want me to talk to him?"

"You know." Richard bit his lip.

"We both know you're just as good as I am."

"Am I? What will Mr. Matthias say about it? I think a lot about that too. I'm a servant, Clarinda, and servants aren't supposed to fall in love with their mistresses. If I could only make something of myself . . . maybe the army's still looking—"

"Richard, why are you thinking that way? What's wrong with being a servant, especially since you're such a good one?"

"Your uncle's got to believe that even a soldier would be better than a servant for you."

She looked into his face. "Are you ashamed of what you are?"

"I didn't think I was. Oh, I knew I was able to do more than what he let me do, but I never minded, not until now."

Taking his hand, she examined it, tracing the long, well-shaped fingers, feeling the calluses. It was a good, strong hand, she decided, despite the dirty cuticles and assorted cuts and scratches, and she laced her fingers between his. "Don't ever be ashamed of what you do."

"But—"

"I would rather be with you than with any number of so-called gentlemen because you truly are a gentle man." He smiled bashfully. "I'm glad you have ambition, but don't feel you have to be something you're not because of me." She squeezed his hand, then kissed him.

"I think we'd better go back," Richard remarked. "I wouldn't want the count to feel you're neglecting him."

"I guess you're right, although I'd rather stay here than listen to"—she deepened her voice—"Fräulein Maa-tee-aas, vood choo . . . ?" They laughed and, rising, prepared to leave.

* * *

On Monday morning, Clarinda paced on the porch, the skirt of her riding habit clinging to her ankles. She was excited and nervous about Jack's return for the weekend had been longer than she had expected. She smiled at Bronstein, who had come out to join her, thankful he had been persuaded to allow Richard to serve in the dining room, although the servant left after each course. She only hoped the king and queen would not be so peculiar.

"Is it always this hot, Fräulein?" the count asked, mopping his brow.

"During the summer, it can get pretty bad, but it's because the air is so heavy. My uncle says Washington is much worse at this time of year."

"Is this why you live out here while your uncle lives in Washington?"

"We've always summered at Landfield. But I expect to be in the city after summer's over." A swirl of dust in the distance caught her attention, and she pointed with great excitement. "Here they come, Your Excellency!"

Soon, a caravan of carriages could be seen moving up the lush, tree-lined avenue toward the house, stopping at the edge of the manicured lawn that stretched out like a green carpet to the woods. Clarinda smiled and waved to her uncle in the first coach, spotting the three other people with him. Jack exited and came up to her while Bronstein went to the vehicle. "Good day, Your Majesties. I trust your trip was pleasant."

"As good as could be expected on country roads in the heat," the king replied.

"Herr Matthias's housekeeper has assured me your rooms are prepared, and I am certain Her Majesty would like to rest," Bronstein proceeded for he could perceive the queen's white face behind her veil.

"Later, perhaps," she answered. "I would first like to meet Herr Matthias's niece."

"Well, you shall not have to wait long, ma'am," Jack said, laughing, and brought the girl over to their visitors. "Clarinda, I have the pleasure of presenting you to Their Majesties, the king and queen of Ahrweiler. Your Majesties, my niece, Clarinda Matthias."

She curtseyed and repeated her uncle's welcome. They moved up onto the porch and, while they continued chatting,

Clarinda—at first awed by the elegant, dignified couple—became more comfortable with them. The king, as tall as Jack, had retained much of the handsomeness of his youth, although there was a great deal of gray in his dark brown beard and fringe of hair that surrounded his large bald spot and a slight thickening of his waist. But it was the queen who held the girl's attention. Her golden-brown hair, barely touched with gray, framed a delicate heart-shaped face dominated by large brown eyes. Clarinda could see that the woman had suffered much during her life, yet when the queen looked at her husband, she could almost feel the love between them. They went into the house shortly after that, and Jack had Bernice set out lemonade in the parlor for his guests. Then he took Clarinda aside and asked her out into the hall.

"Did you miss me, Uncle Jack?"

"What do you think, honey?" He kissed her cheek and, laughing, added, "However did you get along without me?"

"I think I managed." Joining in his laughter, she blushed scarlet.

"You've been out?"

"Not yet. I wanted to wait until you arrived because I have something important I want to talk to you about. Richard has our horses ready."

"Honey, I can't leave the king and queen now. That isn't protocol."

"Protocol." She stamped her foot. "I'm tired of what is and isn't protocol."

"It's also very impolite. They *are* our guests. I'm sure whatever you need to discuss can wait a half hour."

"But, Uncle Jack—"

"I know, it's important. But so is this. We have to make the king and queen feel welcome."

"You're right, and I'm sorry I was so thoughtless."

"As soon as they retire to their rooms, we'll go out. I promise."

\* \* \*

Within the hour, Jack and Clarinda arrived at the oak stand. Riding with her uncle, she wondered how she was going to tell him about Richard for she could see how distracted Jack was by their royal visitors. They dismounted, and while Jack secured the horses, she brushed off the bench and sat down. He joined her, sliding his arm around her waist. "Now what is it you have to talk to me about?"

"Uncle Jack, I . . ." Suddenly, the words refused to come.

"Did something happen while I was away?"

"Yes, no, I mean, I didn't intend for it to happen, but it did."

"What happened, sweetheart?"

"It's Richard and me, Uncle Jack. We're . . . fond of each other."

Shaking his head, he chewed his lip and exhaled. "I was afraid something like this would occur."

"Afraid? Of what?"

"That Richard would become attached to you."

"It's not like that. We're in love with each other."

"Just because you like him and have fun with him, don't confuse that with love."

She started to weep. "I'm not, Uncle Jack. I . . . I've never felt this way about anyone before. I told Richard I would talk to you because he can't yet. We" —she bit her index finger— "Richard and I, someday, want to get married."

As he took her face in his hands, she saw what she could only interpret as discouragement in his mouth and eyes. "Clarinda, sweetheart, you don't know what you are asking."

"Why? Because Richard's a servant and not of my class?"

"That's one reason."

"But when we're together, I feel we're equals, and I don't want more than Richard, whatever his station."

Stroking her jaw, the creases in his face growing deeper, he inquired, "How much have you thought about this, honey? Would you be willing to give up all your advantages, give up Landfield, to go into service with him?"

"Why would I? Richard loves it here, and he wants to make himself better. I know he can. Look at what he's done in a month."

"And what if it is his lot in life to be a servant? I know you far too well to forbid you, but I want you to be absolutely certain about this. The decision you finally make, both you and Richard will have to live with for the rest of your lives. And should you betray him—"

"I know, Uncle Jack. I would never intentionally hurt Richard."

Placing his arms about her shoulders, Jack again thought about the woman she had become, unaware that a tear trickled down his cheek. Clarinda noticed, however, and brushed it away before kissing him. Managing a smile for her, he asked, to change the subject, "What do you think of our guests?"

"The king and queen seem nice, but I don't like Count von Bronstein. She's very quiet, isn't she?"

"The queen?"

"Yes. I suppose it was because of the drive from the city."

"Partly, but she suffers bouts of melancholy."

"I'm so sorry."

"This year has been particularly rough for both of them."

"Is that why they're here?"

He fell silent for several minutes, debating whether or not to tell her, unwilling to involve her in the dangerous game he was playing.

"Uncle Jack?"

He patted her hand. "I'm sorry, honey. I didn't forget your question. At present, it's better you not know why the king is here."

"I won't tell anyone, not even Richard."

"I'm certain you wouldn't, but for your own safety, the less you know . . ." Her eyes widened. "I'm afraid my guest is in a great deal of danger."

"All right. I won't press further. But if you ever need me, I'm ready to help."

"Thank you, Clarinda. Now"—he stood—"we'd better go back to the house. Leaving a king alone for too long—"

"Isn't protocol," she laughed and waited to be put up on her horse.

\* \* \*

Joseph was busy supervising the unloading of the luggage when his employers came from the stable, Spotting them, he stopped what he was doing and walked over, obviously upset by something.

"Yes, Joseph?" Jack said with a sigh.

"I told my boy to help me."

"Richard is busy taking care of the horses. When he finishes in the stable, he can help you."

"Always too busy to help me nowadays."

"That isn't true," Clarinda refuted.

"Then he's too slow." Joseph pointed a bony finger at the girl. "It's her fault, tryin' to make him better," he groused. "Now he's too good to do any *real* work, afraid of gettin' his fancy clothes dirty, too busy to eat his supper with his family. He's too good for nothin' but what she wants him to be."

Jack grabbed the other man's arm, for the royal retainers had stopped their work and begun staring. "That is enough, Joseph. If you did your job even half as well as everything Richard does, you might have a reason to complain. But Richard does more than I ask of him, and without any objections."

Joseph smiled. Immediately, Clarinda felt sick for she knew what he was about to tell her uncle. "Includin' gettin' cozy with your niece."

"*What?*" Jack gasped, first turning deathly pale, then beet red.

"You heard me. My Iris caught them in the stable."

Jack turned to Clarinda, anger growing in his hazel eyes. "Is this true?"

"Yes," she stammered, "but Uncle Jack, it's not like he's making it sound. Nothing happened."

"Apparently, *something* did."

"I told you it were a mistake, trustin' your girl with him," Joseph taunted.

"Enough! Joseph, I want to talk to Iris and Richard immediately. And you, young lady"—Jack gripped Clarinda's arm—"I'll see you in the kitchen."

"Please, let me explain!" she cried.

"You'll get your chance after I've spoken to Iris and Richard." He looked at the girl, and she could feel the disappointment that was so evident in his face. "How could you let things go so far?"

Sobbing bitterly, she buried her head in Jack's coat, and he led her into the kitchen. "Laura," he almost shouted to the surprised cook, "get Miss Clarinda a cup of tea to calm her down." Then he stormed out of the room.

"What on earth happened?"

"Joseph told Uncle Jack." Clarinda fought to regain her composure. "He said Richard and I had . . . and Uncle Jack believes him. Uncle Jack won't even let me explain what really happened."

"Give him a chance, Miss Clarinda. He loves you very much, and he doesn't want anything to happen to you."

The girl laughed. "I had just finished telling him how much Richard and I . . . care for one another, and now Joseph's ruined everything."

"Come on, sweetie. Sit down and have a nice cup of tea. You'll feel better."

"No, thank you, Aunt Laura." But Clarinda sat at the large oak table while Laura busied herself with the tea, and she made no objections when the cook put a steaming earthenware mug in front of her, along with some gingerbread squares.

"Sweet tea and gingerbread, best cure for a sad face, my ma used to say."

Nibbling a piece, Clarinda sighed. "Why won't Uncle Jack listen to me?"

The elderly woman smiled, then hugged the girl. "Don't you worry yourself about that just now. It'll all come right. See if it don't."

* * *

Iris entered Jack's study. She was self-conscious, shifting from one foot to the other as she stood in the center of the room, Jack pacing furiously in front of her. "Papa said you wanted to see me, Mr. Matthias?"

He stopped. "Where's your brother?"

"He's . . . still busy in the stable. Papa'll send him up when he's done."

"Your father informed me that you saw my niece with Richard in the stable."

"She goes there a lot."

"And what does she do when she goes there?"

"Most times, they go out riding together."

"Most times?"

"All the time, every day. 'Cept when the weather's bad." She giggled. "You know that, Mr. Matthias. You're the one who made him groom."

"What do they do when the weather's bad?"

"Like last Thursday?"

"Yes. What did they do last Thursday?"

"Well, Miss Clarinda came running from the house in an awful hurry. I mean, she didn't have no parasol or nothin', and it were raining pretty good."

"Where were you, Iris?"

"In the . . . lacy house in the side garden."

"The gazebo?"

"I guess. Anyway, she ran into the stable. A few minutes later, I walked by there, and I thought I heard something, so I went in."

"What did you see?"

"Richard had his arms around Miss Clarinda tight. She wiggled a little bit, trying to get loose, I think. But she stopped when he kissed her."

"What did Miss Clarinda do after that?"

"I think," Iris whispered, "she kissed him back. She were on tippy-toes, so it were hard for me to see," the girl added, a little louder.

"And?"

"I must've made a noise, 'cause her horse heard me and bumped into her. That's when they saw me."

"I see." Jack started pacing again, the knot in his stomach growing with each step. Finally, he sat behind the desk. "Thank you, Iris. You may go."

"You're done with me?"

"For now. If you see Richard, tell him to come in here and wait for me."

"Yes, Mr. Matthias." Iris bobbed a curtsey and left, while Jack stared at the branches of a maple tree moving listlessly in the humid air.

\* \* \*

"All right, Clarinda. Exactly what *did* happen between you and Richard?"

The edge in Jack's voice cut through Clarinda, and she involuntarily stiffened. Laura pressed the girl's hands and whispered, "Remember, he loves you," then removed herself from the room.

"What did Iris tell you?"

"I want *you* to tell me what happened last Thursday."

"When I received your note, I went to the stable to tell Richard about your change of plans. We started talking about other things, and we . . ." Her tears slid down her cheeks and her voice became thin. "I told him I was in love with him. I will never forget the expression in his eyes . . . and then he kissed me."

"And?"

"Iris interrupted us. It appears she'd been spying."

"Don't you realize what *could* have happened?"

"Yes, but I thought you knew me better than that. I thought you trusted me."

"All Richard did was kiss you?"

"Yes."

"What about when you went riding with him?"

"We were *riding*. How could you think—"

"You heard Joseph. He insinuated—"

"*Joseph*? You believe Joseph and Iris and not me?" Clarinda got out of her chair and paced around the table furiously. "Richard said they'd make it sound like . . . that. But Iris is a liar, Uncle Jack, just like she's a thief. Please, talk to Richard. He'll tell you the truth."

"I will, sweetheart. Now I want you to go upstairs and rest a bit."

"Yes, Uncle Jack." She managed a small grin for him.

"And take this as an example of what can happen." He put his arms around her shoulders. "You are the dearest thing in the world to me, and I do not wish to see you hurt or shamed."

"I know." Returning his hug, Clarinda left the kitchen and went upstairs.

# *Chapter* 6

Richard came out of the stable feeling he was the happiest man in the world. He knew Clarinda had spoken to her uncle, her smile and the look she gave him when she and Jack returned their horses told him there should be few problems. Jack instructed him to cool the mounts, then help with the luggage, but there was nothing in Jack's voice to indicate disapproval of him or his feelings toward Clarinda. And tonight, when he served the king and queen, Richard was certain all Clarinda's confidence in him would be confirmed. Putting his hands in his trouser pockets, he lifted his chest just a little higher.

As he approached the service entrance, however, he realized something had happened for Joseph stood there smiling, his legs spread apart, hands on hips. "Where've you been?"

"In the stable, taking care of the Matthiases' horses."

"And takin' a long time with it."

"They had a hard workout in this heat. It took a while to cool them off."

"Perhaps it's you who needed coolin' off."

Richard's stomach tightened. "What do you mean?"

"I seen the way you been gawkin' at Miss Clarinda, like a moon-sick calf."

"I-I still don't understand."

Joseph came over and, standing toe to toe with Richard, forced the much-taller man to look down at him. "Iris told me what she seen in the stable, and I just told Mr. Matthias. He weren't too pleased—you and his pretty little niece." He started to snicker.

Richard's mouth went dry. "Clar—Miss Clarinda, was she . . . ?"

"Your lady love be there, and her uncle's pretty mad at her. About as mad as he's at you, I suppose."

"Why did you—"

"She has trouble rememberin' your place, just like you. Maybe I figgered she needed remindin' you're only a servant, a clumsy and stupid one at that." Joseph stepped back and shoved Richard toward the door. "Get on upstairs. Mr. Matthias wants to see you in his study." Chuckling, Joseph went back to work.

Slowly, Richard walked up the back stairs to the first floor. *No hope*, his footsteps seemed to repeat, echoed by his pounding heart. How could he have dared to love Clarinda, or to expect her uncle to condone their relationship? He stopped a minute, the pain in his heart unbearable, then opened the landing door.

Iris was wandering the hall as he approached. "Mr. Matthias wants you to wait for him in his study."

"I know," he answered sadly.

"You are *really* in trouble this time, Richard," she gloated.

Wordlessly, he trudged by her and entered the room, while Bronstein watched from the library door. The count rubbed his palms together several times, then motioned Iris over to him.

"Did you want something, Your Excellency?" she said, sketching a curtsey.

"Yes, my dear. I need your help with something."

"What?"

"Some of my jewelry appears to be missing, and I suspect that Richard has taken it."

"He don't steal."

"But if Herr Matthias discovered . . ."

"Oh, I get it. You want me to make it look like he took your things."

"Very bright, Iris. Will you do it?" She nodded. "Good. Be at my suite in ten minutes. Then, when you are done, come back here. I shall have something else to give you."

"All right."

Richard stood at the window, resting his head against the glass, when Bronstein walked into Jack Matthias's sanctum a few moments later. Hearing the door close, Richard turned, surprised to see the count crossing the room. "I-I thought you were Mr. Matthias, Your Excellency."

"No, Richard." Bronstein smiled at him.

"Did you want to see him?"

"I was looking for you. I have a message from Fräulein Matthias. She wishes to meet with you right now."

Hope mixed with skepticism in Richard's eyes. "I was told Mr. Matthias wants to talk to me. I'd better wait—"

"Herr Matthias has left the house, which is why the Fräulein begged me to find you. She does not wish to upset her uncle further, so she must see you in secret."

"Where?" the younger man asked tentatively.

"She said she will meet you in the stable in five minutes, that you would know where." Still sensing Richard's uncertainty, the count added, "She has been hurt also, Richard. She needs to know you still care."

A battle raged between Richard's mind and his heart. He never disobeyed orders, and from the way both Joseph and Iris had told him, it was obvious Jack wanted to see him at once. But the thought of Clarinda doubting his love for her soon overpowered his reason, and he said, "I can see her for a minute, I guess."

"Of course. When he returns, I shall explain to Herr Matthias where you went."

"No!"

"What I mean is I will tell him you needed to leave momentarily. I will not disclose your secret *rendezvous* with the Fräulein. Now go. I would not want you to be late."

Richard bowed quickly and ran out of the study and down the hall.

\* \* \*

"Clarinda?"

After the brightness of the outdoors, the cooler semi-darkness of the stable was like night, and Richard found it difficult to see at first. His eyes adjusted quickly while he headed for Moonbeam's stall, thinking that Clarinda would be waiting for him there. Suddenly, he became aware of a barely audible rustle above him. Looking up, he spotted the yellow-green eyes of the gray tiger tabby maneuvering the crossbeam. Laughing in relief, he asked, "Have you seen Clarinda, Lady?" The straight-up tail as the cat scampered away made him laugh again, and he continued down the row of stalls.

"*Entschuldigen Sie, bitte. Können Sie mir sagen, wieviel Uhr ist es* (Excuse me, please. Can you tell me what time it is)?"

Richard froze. Turning slowly, he saw the blond hair and dark blue braided jacket of the soldier behind him. "I don't understand you."

The other man's lip curled slightly. "*Ja, Sie sind der Mann,*" he said, then he whistled sharply. Within seconds, Richard was surrounded by a half-dozen others.

Glancing around, Richard realized he had been tricked into leaving the house, that Clarinda wasn't here. Another soldier approached them, barking orders. Richard's arms were jerked behind him. As a circlet of rope tightened on his wrists, he rammed into the man directly in front of him. Immediately, he was punched in the abdomen, but years of manual labor and Joseph's beatings had toughened him, so he barely felt it. He made a run for the stable door while two of the soldiers attempted to restrain him, tearing his shirt in the process. Ten feet from the entrance, he heard another whistle, and he was tackled from behind and above by a soldier waiting in the loft. Richard crashed to the floor.

The captain of the guard worked quickly. While his men securely bound Richard's hands and feet, he withdrew a handkerchief and small brown vial from his pocket. Emptying the contents of the bottle on the cloth, the captain handed it to the nearest soldier, who clamped it firmly over Richard's nose and mouth.

He struggled, but it was impossible. As the sweet, pungent vapor invaded his brain, he vaguely recalled the time before . . . *them, the room . . . soft, furry . . . Ma . . .*

The soldier glanced at the captain and nodded. A minute later, Bronstein entered. Seeing the motionless figure at his feet, he smiled and approached his confederate. "Excellent, Bauer. Did you have much trouble?"

"He is very strong, Excellency, but then, these peasant types usually are."

The count laughed nervously. "Yes. You know where to take him?"

"Small building in the woods."

Bronstein tapped the rope around Richard's legs with his walking stick. "When you arrive, take this off."

"He will only try to escape."

"Well, then, it is your and Vogel's responsibility to make sure he doesn't."

"You make it sound so simple, Excellency."

"It is simple, Captain." Bronstein glanced down. "Get him out of here. Herr Matthias will be looking for him shortly." He left, followed moments later by the soldiers.

\* \* \*

Clarinda opened the door to her suite, an occasional tear still rolling down her cheek. She had never been so humiliated in her life, certainly not by any of the servants, and she knew if Iris or Joseph were there at this moment, she would have no trouble in venting her anger on them. *Poor Richard,* she thought, *not only will Uncle Jack bring him to task, even forbid him to be alone with me, but what Joseph will do to him?* That she refused to consider. Going inside, she curtly dismissed a surprised Patsy—for to be with any of the Royces was too much right now—then rushed into her bedroom as a new flood of tears began.

"Oh, my poor little lamb!" Mary exclaimed, taking the girl into her arms. "What's happened?"

"Joseph told-he told Uncle Jack about Richard and me."

"But I thought you were going to tell your uncle this morning."

"I did, and that's what makes this so awful!"

"Mr. Matthias didn't approve?"

"Well, he wasn't happy about it, but he didn't forbid it either, at least not before Joseph spoiled everything. Now I'll be lucky to even see Richard, Uncle Jack is so angry."

"What on earth did the boy's father say?"

"He told Uncle Jack about Thursday, what Iris said she saw."

"I thought nothing happened."

"Nothing did, but Richard and I were kissing, and Iris was spying on us. But Joseph told Uncle Jack that"—a shudder ran through the girl—"that Richard was getting cozy with me. He made it sound like-like . . ." Clarinda cried harder.

"Like Richard was taking advantage of you."

"Richard said Joseph would do it too. How could I have been so stupid not to believe him?"

"Oh, Missy." Mary took Clarinda over to the bed, and they sat down. "You're in love with the boy. Now I want you to lie down and cry it all out. And don't worry about what Mr. Matthias will do. He's a fair man, and he recognizes the truth. He'll do what's best for both you and Richard."

"Thank you, Aunt Mary." The older woman withdrew. Ten minutes later, Clarinda sat up, her tears spent and, after wiping her eyes on the wet linen pillow sham, slipped off the bed and went to her dressing table.

She refused to look at her reflection in the mirror but instead sorted through a neat stack of envelopes. Most of them were invitations: a couple of weddings, two or three parties for the upcoming week, which the royal visit would require her to decline. Sitting at her desk to write the most urgent replies, her eyes once again misted over as she recalled Richard's genuine amusement over what she did every afternoon when they went out. It was inconceivable to him that she spent several hours at four or five houses, just to drink tea and talk about nothing of consequence, and her explanation of the importance of morning calls did little to clear his confusion. "Oh, Richard," she sighed. Breathing a quick prayer Jack would indeed be reasonable, she returned to her correspondence.

The last piece of mail was the thickest. Clarinda had deliberately saved it until the end for she knew the letter inside the ivory envelope with the Philadelphia postmark—her name written on its face in a fine, but firm, script—held nothing but unwelcome news. Opening it, her worst thoughts were confirmed. The five-page missive from Dorothy Franklin, her grandmother, was line after line of reprimand and none-too-subtle advice. What did surprise her was how recent the events recounted were (the episode when she was instructing Richard about the wines for one) and her usual discomfiture was replaced by outrage that someone had felt it necessary to communicate with the old woman. "Now she'll 'have to straighten things out,'" Clarinda complained to the air, "just when I don't need any more problems to worry about." She heard voices in her sitting room. A minute later, Mary opened the door.

"Missy, it's your uncle."

Gathering herself together, Clarinda walked out to meet him. Jack could tell she had been crying, but she smiled at him. "Did you talk to Richard?"

"I-no. Honey, come sit down."

She did so. "You said you would. Why didn't you?"

"I want you to think very carefully. Is there someplace where Richard might go to be alone?"

"The attic."

Jack laughed. "You mean I have been looking all over Landfield for him, and he's in the house?"

"Uncle Jack, he's not up there either."

He stopped. "How do you know?"

"The floorboards in the attic squeak. The whole time I've been here today, I haven't heard one squeak."

Clarinda had never seen her uncle so sad and angry at the same time. "I'm sorry, but I have no other choice but to—"

"Did you look in his room?"

"No, I didn't."

"Please, Uncle Jack. Richard deserves that."

"All right." She stood, taking his hand. "Come on, then," he chuckled.

Hoping beyond hope Clarinda was right, Jack entered Richard's room, the white rectangle lying on the navy blanket catching his eye immediately. He picked up the single sheet of paper and read: *"Dear Mr. Matthias, I apologize for what I have done. I never meant to hurt anyone, especially Miss Clarinda, which is why I have to leave here. I will never forget your kindness. Good-bye."* Jack stared at the wall, the paper like fire in his hand.

"Uncle Jack?"

"I'm so sorry, Clarinda. Richard's left Landfield."

"No, he wouldn't."

"He wrote this, and he isn't anywhere to be found." Jack turned, giving her the note. As he did, he saw the flash of red from the dresser.

Iris had done her task well, for scattered around the austere cubicle were the items Bronstein had given her. Picking up the ruby and diamond cufflink, Jack's shoulders sagged, his faith in Richard's honesty completely destroyed. A sob behind him reminded him that he was not alone, and he took Clarinda in his arms.

"Why, Uncle Jack? Why did he leave? He promised he would never leave me."

"I don't know, honey. But I found this." He showed her the jewel. "How can I believe him now?"

"Because I do. Richard doesn't lie, and he wouldn't steal." She laughed. "He wanted to pay us for his shoes, remember? Why would he steal things like this?"

"Maybe he thought he could support you with them." Caressing her face, he continued, "I wish I knew. You're certain nothing happened on Thursday?"

"Yes. We told each other how we felt, and we kissed. That's all." Her eyes dropped to the cufflink. "I thought you believed me."

"Of course I believe you, and in his own way, I think Richard does love you. But I'm afraid the poor boy is . . ."

"You think he's insane?"

"No, honey, just not completely aware of what he's doing, or perhaps, his fantasy world has become his reality."

"It's *not* a fantasy. It's the truth. It has to be the truth."

Arthur knocked on the open door. "I'm sorry, Jack, but the king insists—"

"Arthur, I've already asked you to tell him I have more pressing matters to deal with."

"More important than my life, Herr Matthias?" The king entered the room. "Fräulein."

"Forgive me, Your Majesty. I did not mean to imply your problem was insignificant. Unfortunately, when it comes to my niece, my heart rules my head."

Nodding, the king replied, "I understand fully for I have five daughters. But we must talk, Herr Matthias."

"Very well. Arthur, take Clarinda back to her room, then go to Oak Store and get Sheriff Tyler. Tell him I've had a theft here."

"Uncle Jack!"

"What else can I do, Clarinda? These items obviously do not belong to Richard, and he is not here to explain how he got them. Besides"—he lifted her hand—"you hold his confession."

"You *could* have believed in him. And as for this . . . I will never believe Richard's done anything wrong." She crumpled the paper into a ball and threw it at Jack's chest, then left the room with Arthur.

"Your niece is very loyal, Herr Matthias."

"She thinks she is in love with him."

"And what is your opinion?"

Jack sighed. "I thought–I believed the boy was honest and reliable. He *was* honest and reliable, until today."

"Perhaps he still is."

Shaking his head, Jack escorted the king out and locked the door. "I shall never be able to completely trust him again."

\* \* \*

An hour later, Arthur returned with the sheriff. The thin, middle-aged man spoke briefly with Jack, then went into Richard's room. After examining the physical evidence, he asked to see Clarinda.

She was in her bedroom, Richard's blanket in her hands, when Jack came for her. Since her return from the servants' quarters, she had been holding the blue square, a talisman against the ugly thoughts she was thinking. She wanted to believe Richard. She *did* believe him, but the memory of Jack's face when he showed her the jewelry made it so hard. Staring at the monogram until the gold thread began to pulse like sunlight, she heard Richard's voice: *Trust me.* Just as he had trusted her with the only thing he considered his own, now it was her turn to have faith in him.

"*Yes.*" She wasn't sure if she answered with her voice or her heart.

"Clarinda, Sheriff Tyler wants to ask you some questions."

"What?" She turned toward Jack, holding the blanket behind her. "I'll be right down."

"That won't be necessary, Miss Matthias." The sheriff ambled into the room, scratching his salt-and-pepper beard. "Your uncle said you know this"—he checked his book—"Richard Royce fairly well. I'm afraid I'm going to have to interrogate you about him."

"Yes, Sheriff." Carefully dropping the blanket on the floor, she followed the two men to her sitting room.

"Now, Miss Matthias," Tyler began after she sat down, "how long did you know Mr. Royce?"

"Just about a month."

"And what did he do here?"

"He works in the stable and on the grounds. He's also our butler."

"So Mr. Royce had access to the entire house."

"Yes, but—"

"When did you first notice items missing?"

"Never."

"You mean your guests or housekeeper never mentioned misplaced belongings or rearranged objects?"

"That's correct."

"I see. Well, has Mr. Royce, to your knowledge, ever taken something that wasn't his?"

She thought immediately of the blanket. Technically, it wasn't really his, and he had taken it from Adele's trunk. Something nobody wanted. The analogy to Richard was too close, and she started to cry.

"So he *has* stolen before."

"No, well, not really."

"Could you explain that?"

"It's just an old blanket he found. No one else wanted it."

"How do you know this?"

"He told me."

The sheriff grinned. "He told you how he 'found' this item."

"He was a little boy when he found it, and he was embarrassed when he told me. I doubt he would lie about the only luxury he owns."

"Perhaps Mr. Royce felt it was time to have more luxuries, or maybe he was embarrassed because he didn't want you to know he was a thief."

"Richard *isn't* a thief! If he were, why would he leave his booty behind when he left?"

"I have to ask you about that also. What made him decide to leave?"

"I don't know."

"When did you see Mr. Royce last?"

"About three hours ago."

"Where?"

"In the stable. We had just returned from riding—"

"You and Mr. Royce?"

"No. My uncle and I. We were bringing our horses in."

"And how did he seem in the stable?"

"Today?"

"Yes, Miss Matthias. Today."

"He was fine, a little nervous, perhaps."

"Oh, he was nervous?"

Clarinda clenched her fists. "This evening, he was going to serve dinner to some very important people. He's never served royalty before. I think he has a right to be nervous."

"Of course." She knew he didn't believe her. "Have you seen him since?"

"No."

Turning to Jack, the sheriff queried, "You said you checked your stable, Mr. Matthias. Were any of your horses missing?"

"None of mine, but I'm stabling more horses than just my own at present."

"Well, I'll check myself later. He may have taken one of the other horses."

"Why can't you believe Richard wouldn't steal anything?" Clarinda screamed.

Jack came over to her. "Sheriff Tyler is only doing his job, honey."

"Then why is he trying to make Richard look guilty?"

"He is attempting to get to the truth."

"According to whom?"

Jack took her over to the bedroom door. "Your defense of Richard is admirable, Clarinda, but you cannot deny we found a number of things in his room that are not his. That *must* not be ignored, no matter how well you think you know him."

The lawman signaled to Jack. "I'm going to need a description of Mr. Royce. If he's on foot, he wouldn't have been able to go very far, and my men will need to be able to identify him."

"I'll be with you in a minute, Harry. I don't think my niece can give you any more information at this time." Then Jack took her into the bedroom, where he spied the blue mound on the floor. "The blanket?"

She nodded. "He asked me to fix it; it was torn."

"When?" he asked quietly.

"The first night he served dinner."

"And he said he found it?" She nodded.

Jack held her face. "*Where* did he find it?"

"In Adele's trunk."

"And you expect us to believe Richard doesn't steal?"

"He said that" — she choked back a sob — "after he found it, and Adele saw him with it, she took it away. How many things did I find in your trunks and desk? He didn't steal the blanket."

"All right, Clarinda." Jack bent down and picked it up, his fingers touching the embroidery. He gave her the blanket, then kissed her. "Keep it safe for him, honey."

"I will."

He gazed at her once more, then rejoined the sheriff.

* * *

Clarinda stood alone in the parlor, waiting for dinner. Staring out the window, she spotted a member of the sheriff's posse searching the woods that joined the garden. Why didn't anyone believe Richard wasn't a thief? Why wouldn't they interrogate that sneak Iris instead of her? And the biggest question of all, where was Richard? The questions repeated in her mind like a litany until she thought she would scream. A sudden brightness in the shadowed room caused her to turn around, and she watched Adele lighting the lamps.

"Oh, Miss Clarinda . . . have you heard anything more?" the woman asked when she finished.

"The posse hasn't found him. Sheriff Tyler doesn't think he's been able to go very far." A tear rolled down the girl's cheek, and she brushed it away.

"My Richard's a good boy, Miss Clarinda. This . . . trouble is not of his doing because I know him, and I see how much he loves you."

"They think he's a thief; that he's been stealing from the guest suites. Uncle Jack found some jewelry in his room earlier."

"A thief?" Adele shook her head. "No, not Richard. Joseph wouldn't have it." Taking Clarinda's hands, she added, "Don't lose faith in him, please. When he is found, *all* the truth will be told."

"Yes. And Richard will be proved innocent." Clarinda smiled wanly, then as she looked at Adele's thin, sad face, continued, "I'm glad you trust him too."

The older woman excused herself and left the parlor. Clarinda made her way to the piano; lifting the cover, she let her fingers meander over the keys for several minutes before once again attempting to play the Bach organ concerto. She became lost in the music floating more in her mind than from her hands; no longer the composition of a deceased composer reworked by an equally dead mother, but something new — her song, wild and unique. For the first time, she truly was the music and not just the musician, and she began to understand a little better the freedom her mother had.

She continued playing, oblivious to everything, until the parlor door crashed back against the wall. Looking up with a start, Clarinda stared at the stout, white-haired woman, her mouth in its perpetual frown, entering with Jack.

"I'm sorry, Clarinda," Jack began. "I tried to explain—"

"Nonsense," the woman interrupted. "Clarinda knew I was coming, didn't you, girl?"

"Yes," Clarinda managed to utter as she rose from the piano stool and began to cross the room. "I knew she'd come, Uncle Jack." Reaching the two of them, the girl curtseyed, then kissed the woman's finely wrinkled cheek. "Good evening, Grandmother."

# Chapter 7

Quickly regaining her composure, Clarinda smiled at her grandmother. "Forgive my surprise, but I only received your letter today. Did Grandfather come with you?"

Dorothy Franklin sniffed. "What a ridiculous question, Clarinda. He is outside with Gerald and his wife. I assume there will be no problem with the four of us staying for dinner."

At the mention of dinner, the girl blanched. "Oh no! I forgot to tell Bernice—"

"It's all right, Clarinda," Jack assured her. "I took care of informing Bernice about what happened today."

"No, it is not all right," Dorothy argued. "It is Clarinda's responsibility to maintain communications with her housekeeper concerning the running of her household, not yours, Jack."

"Grandmother, please, not now."

"When, then? After you're married and don't have your uncle or the old family retainers to smooth over your lapses? By then, it will be too late."

"Dorothy," Jack said, his voice tinged with irritation, "leave it alone for tonight. Today has been hard enough on Clarinda without having you rail at her."

"I am not railing at the girl, just offering some advice. I *am* permitted to do that, or is that a Matthias privilege?"

"Only when it's bad advice, Aunt Dorothy," Gerald Franklin commented as he entered the room. "How are you tonight, Jack?" he added, extending his hand.

"Could be better; it's too humid too early for me."

"And, Cousin Clarinda, you seem quieter than usual. Are you feeling ill?"

"No, I'm fine, Cousin Gerald," Clarinda replied with a little sigh.

"Well, let me have a look at you, just to be sure." Gerald led the girl closer to the window and began a cursory examination.

"Gerald, I'm a bit tired this evening. It's nothing you need to be concerned about."

The doctor smiled at her. "I know Aunt Dorothy can be overbearing, but she does care a great deal about you. However, I don't think that's all that's bothering you, is it?" He took her chin in his right hand and checked her eyes. "Hm. Just as I suspected, a definite redness. You've either been crying or drinking in excess, neither of which is particularly healthful."

Clarinda laughed at his diagnosis. "If it were drink, Bernice would have called for you before tonight. I suspect she has the open bottles marked. I guess I have been crying a lot today."

"I noticed the sheriff leaving when we arrived. Does that have anything to do with it?"

"Some." She felt the color creeping up her neck.

"Aha. Another symptom: patient flushes easily." Gerald chuckled, then his gray-green eyes became serious. "Unfortunately, this humble country doctor has no cure for heartache."

"Humble indeed, darling." Gerald's wife, Arliss, joined them. "Pay him no mind, Clarinda. I think Gerald was born conceited." She cast a loving glance toward her husband. "By the way, did you receive the invitation to dinner next week?"

"Yes, but I'm not sure I'll be able to come. Uncle Jack has house guests."

"If you can, you are welcome to bring an escort if you desire."

"Thank you, Arliss, but—"

"If not, I'll find someone to fill out the sitting."

"Are you planning on monopolizing my granddaughter's time all night, young Gerald?" a warm bass voice rumbled.

For the first time since that morning, Clarinda genuinely smiled. "Grandfather! I'm so happy to see you!"

Charles Franklin's neatly trimmed white moustache twitched as he laughed. "More than Grandmother, I suppose."

"Well . . ."

They both laughed. The younger Franklins made their excuses, returning to where Jack and Dorothy, now joined by the royal couple, stood while Charles took Clarinda's hands and kissed her.

"How is my little girl?"

"I'm fine, Grandfather."

"No, you're not. I could always tell when something was bothering your mother, and you're too much like her for me not to notice. What is it?"

Clarinda laid her head on the elderly gentleman's chest. "Grandfather, I have never been so miserable in my whole life. Just when I thought everything would be wonderful, today . . ." The tears once again began running down her face.

"And our visit doesn't help."

"It's not that I don't love you and Grandmother, but she wants me to be like Mother. I wish I could be as pretty and as talented as she was, but I'm not."

"And what happened today?"

Clarinda's body shook uncontrollably. "It's all a lie, everything they're saying about him, but nobody will believe me. Even Uncle Jack's believing the lies, and he knows Richard."

"Who's Richard, Clarinda?"

"He's . . ." She started moaning.

Charles signaled to Jack, who rushed over to them. "Shall I get Gerald, honey?" Jack asked.

"No, Uncle Jack," she answered in a shaky voice. "I'll be fine in a minute."

"You're certain? You don't have to stay for dinner if you're not up to it."

"Grandmother will expect me at dinner." She wiped her eyes with the handkerchief offered by Jack, then wandered over to the window.

"Believe me, Jack, I tried to convince Dorothy not to come down here, but she said it was her duty."

"Unfortunately, your arrival came at the worst possible moment. I'm dealing with a very delicate matter of state, plus I'm short-staffed."

"Those things shouldn't affect the girl this way."

"On the surface, no, they shouldn't, but . . . she's become very fond of the servant who left this afternoon."

"This Richard she mentioned?"

"Yes. She's taken his departure very hard."

"Maybe we should take her back to Philadelphia with us for a few weeks. Dorothy was going to suggest a long visit."

"Charles, I know you and Dorothy mean well, but the only thing that's going to help Clarinda now is time, not your wife's attempts to try and make her what she isn't."

"I'll take that from where it comes, Jack."

As the clock struck seven, Bernice entered the parlor. "Mr. Matthias, dinner is ready."

"Thank you, Bernice. Do you have additional places set for the Franklins?"

The housekeeper stiffened. "Of course."

"We'll be right in."

Bernice nodded and left the room. Jack turned to Clarinda and asked, "You're sure you'll be all right?"

"I have to be." Straightening her shoulders, she walked over to the king and, giving him her best smile, offered him her arm.

* * *

Entering the dining room, Clarinda was amazed by the transformation of the meal. The simple but elegant dinner for six she and Bernice had planned the day before had been replaced by the first course of a banquet for ten, complete with an ornate floral arrangement in the center of the table and place cards at each sitting. Bernice stood by the sideboard, her face an unreadable mask, while in Richard's usual corner, Lily Royce — her wheat-colored hair caught up in a tight bun and wearing a dress two sizes too big — tried not to show her excitement at being asked to help serve. Jack seated the queen on his right, then, after everyone else found their places, Bernice and Lily began to circulate with the julienne soup and salmon à la *Genévése*.

It was Dorothy who first mentioned the absence of male domestics. "I thought you had a butler, Jack."

"I do, Dorothy. He's . . . indisposed at the present time."

"The something Clarinda forgot to tell Bernice, I presume."

"Does it matter who informed Bernice so long as she *was* told? What is really bothering you, Dorothy?"

"Who says anything is upsetting me? From what I have heard, it is Clarinda who is acting irrationally."

"Perhaps your granddaughter is involved in an *affaire du coeur*," the queen commented.

Dorothy laughed. "Whom could she possibly meet in this backwater? If she were living in Washington, perhaps, but not here."

Bronstein turned to the woman at his right. "Frau Franklin, I share your views about your granddaughter marrying the right sort of person. Unfortunately" — his hooded gray eyes shifted toward the queen — "we cannot always predict where one will find love and, more often than not, are bound to be disappointed."

Dorothy nodded in agreement, then turned her attention back to the slice of fish in front of her.

At the other end of the table, both of Clarinda's dinner companions noticed her lack of appetite. "You have to eat something, sweetheart," Charles Franklin commented as the girl laid her spoon down after three mouthfuls of the vegetable soup.

"I don't feel much like eating, Grandfather. Even thinking about food upsets my stomach tonight."

"At least try to finish the soup."

"I can't." Clarinda sighed deeply, then, once more, picked up the spoon.

The king's kind russet eyes focused on his hostess. "I know it is hard, especially in the beginning, but, if you are lucky, the pain will ease in time."

"Uncle Jack told me earlier about your wife, Your Majesty, that she suffers from melancholy."

"Yes."

"Is that why you're here?" Clarinda caught her breath, putting her hand to her mouth. "I'm sorry, Your Majesty. I promised Uncle Jack I wouldn't pry."

The monarch smiled. "It is quite all right, Fräulein, but I hope you will not think me rude if I don't answer."

"Of course not." She sipped the Riesling, grimacing slightly at the taste of the wine.

"You do not appreciate fine wines, Fräulein?"

"I've never acquired a palate for them, Your Majesty. I prefer sherry."

Charles laughed. "Especially at eleven in the morning."

"Grandfather, it wasn't like that. I wasn't drinking the sherry."

"Even though Bernice caught you with a glass of it?"

"A *full* glass. Or did whoever wrote to Grandmother fail to mention that?"

"The fact remains that you were in the dining room, surrounded by Jack's liquor supply, when you should have been speaking with Bernice."

"Even though Uncle Jack asked me to show Richard the liquor cabinet?"

"Your butler did not know which wine to serve?" the king asked.

"His training was limited, Your Majesty." Clarinda caught Bernice's raised eyebrows. Nodding, she signaled Lily to remove the first course.

Waiting until after the veal cutlets and *ragoût* of duck had been served, Jack asked Bernice to remove the lavish centerpiece, saying it impeded conversation among the diners. For Clarinda, however, the large spray of roses and lilies was a barrier from the scrutinizing eyes of her grandmother. With it gone, she became increasingly nervous and ill at ease, something that did not go unnoticed by the rest of the party.

"Clarinda?"

"What is it, Arthur?"

"I just asked you if you would pass the cauliflower."

"Oh, certainly." She picked up the dish in front of her.

Charles placed his hand on her arm. "Mr. Jamison asked for cauliflower, dear, not potatoes."

"Forgive me." Setting the serving bowl down, she found the vegetable platter and passed it to Arthur, nearly upsetting her wine glass in the process.

"Clarinda," Dorothy commented from the other end of the table, "what has gotten into you? You never used to be so clumsy."

Charles shot a look at his wife, then turned to his granddaughter. "Don't worry about it, sweetheart. We understand you've been under a great strain."

"That is no excuse for ineptitude, Charles," Dorothy countered. "A real lady never allows her emotions to interfere with her duties."

"Then maybe I'm not a real lady, Grandmother," Clarinda sobbed, "because I can't . . ." Her voice trailed off, and she dabbed her eyes with her serviette.

The queen, her eyes misting, looked at the elderly woman opposite. "I think Fräulein Matthias is handling herself quite well, Madame, considering the circumstances. I know I would not have been hosting a dinner party after the kind of afternoon your granddaughter has just had."

"You misunderstood me, Your Majesty," Dorothy simpered. "I did not mean to imply —"

"But you did, Aunt Dorothy," Gerald broke in. "You have a blind spot where Clarinda is concerned."

"Are you saying that I am not permitted to voice my opinions?"

Jack stared at the woman to his left. "Not when you insinuate Clarinda is any less a lady because she reacts like any normal seventeen-year-old to something that has upset her very much."

"I see. And what will be the accepted reason for her lack of interest, for what anyone with her background should be interested in, when this episode is long forgotten?"

Charles left his seat and approached his wife. "I think you've said enough, Dorothy. Forgive her, Jack."

"I'm not the one who is owed the apology." Glancing down the table to where a white-faced, teary Clarinda sat, Jack smiled reassuringly at her. "You know, Dorothy, that young lady is at this table tonight only because she knows you expect it of her."

The woman cleared her throat and, waving off her husband, resumed eating her dinner. Shrugging, Charles returned to his chair.

"She'll never change, will she, Grandfather?" Clarinda whispered as he sat down.

"Hardly. She's as stubborn as they come, but then, dear, so are you."

She laughed a little, recognizing the truth of his statement. "I thought my being stubborn was something I got from my father."

"Your grandmother would like to believe that."

Clarinda said nothing in reply, but focusing her attention on her food, the corner of her mouth began to twitch.

The sweet course revived, to some degree, Clarinda's appetite for she dearly loved sweets, and the array of tarts, puddings, and creams was out of the ordinary for a Monday night at home. She helped herself to surprisingly large portions of strawberry cream and iced pudding, along with two gooseberry tarts, after Bernice and Lily had removed the fowl course, of which she had taken nothing, sighing with pleasure as she tasted each one in turn.

"Perhaps we should have had the third course first," Charles commented. "Then I wouldn't have been so worried about your appetite."

"But this isn't real food, Grandfather. I'm not hungry for real food."

He laughed heartily. "Just like a child, isn't she, Your Majesty? They'll always choose the bad over the good."

"I believe that is a feminine trait, Herr Franklin. I know my wife prefers desserts over more substantial fare when she is upset."

"All I know," Clarinda said, a dollop of strawberry cream on her lip, "is it tastes delicious."

With that, both men laughed, while to the king's right, Arliss Franklin nodded her agreement.

Finally, Bernice put out the dessert dishes, and the dinner party helped itself to the fresh fruit and chocolates, while Lily circulated with the lemon-water ice. Once more, Clarinda's penchant for sweets came to the fore, and with a spoonful of ice melting in her mouth, she felt happier than she had since the morning, so much so that she was astounded to find her grandmother staring at her, a deeper frown than usual on her face.

She stared back, confused. Eventually, Arliss leaned over and whispered something to the king, who nodded in understanding.

"Fräulein Matthias, I think your grandmother is waiting for you to take the ladies into the drawing room for tea," the monarch said *sotto voce*.

"Oh, of course." The girl stood, and the other ladies followed suit. Then she led them into the parlor.

* * *

After Bernice had set up the tea tray and Clarinda had passed the cups, Dorothy remarked, "I cannot understand why your uncle spent so much money trying to educate you. You obviously haven't learned anything about the way a proper lady behaves."

"I forgot, Grandmother, about the ladies. I apologize."

"Something that should be second nature to you—really, Clarinda."

The girl's face began to redden. "I-I don't usually leave the dining room after dessert."

"What! How do you expect the gentlemen to discuss whatever they talk about with a young, and I emphasize the word *young*, lady in their midst?"

"It seems silly to me, Grandmother, that I should have to sit in here by myself, and Uncle Jack wait a decent time in the dining room alone or with one or two other men, just for the sake of convention. Uncle Jack doesn't seem to mind having me there."

"Then he's more of a gentleman than I thought."

"Aunt Dorothy," Arliss interrupted, "why are you causing such a tempest in a teapot? Clarinda simply needs to be exposed to more social situations. Then she'll learn what to do."

"And how will she do that here? She needs to be—"

"In Philadelphia, where 'she can meet the right sort of people.' I happen to like it here, Grandmother, and I don't like Philadelphia, or your friends."

"Clarinda!"

Arliss came over to her young cousin and grasped her shoulders. "I don't think this is the time for this."

The girl turned toward the woman behind her. "Then when *is* the time, Arliss? Every time Grandmother and I see each other, it's the same thing over and over. I can't help being who I am, and I do try to please her, but it's never enough."

The sound of light strains of music from the piano caught Clarinda's attention. "I didn't know you played, Your Majesty."

The queen smiled at Clarinda. "I don't, not really. But music helps me cope sometimes."

"Perhaps you could honor us with a little something, ma'am," Dorothy gushed.

"No, I don't think so." The queen returned to her seat and addressed the elderly woman to her left. "Herr Matthias told us your daughter was an accomplished musician."

"Yes, ma'am, she was," Dorothy gloated. "It was such a pity that she died so young. There were many of my set in Philadelphia who said she would have had quite a career had she lived."

"But you have your granddaughter. That must be some comfort. I know my daughters have been so to me."

"But it is not the same, ma'am, especially when I so rarely see Clarinda. Not the girl's fault, you know. We would have been very happy to have her with us. Her father's family disapproved of letting us raise Clarinda after he died."

"Aunt Dorothy." Arliss shook her head. "How many children do you have, Your Majesty?"

"Five daughters and . . . my oldest daughter has a son, so we are both grandmothers, Madame Franklin."

"Grandchildren are so rewarding, aren't they, ma'am?"

As Dorothy Franklin rhapsodized on the joys of being a grandmother, Clarinda watched the other woman's expression change from polite deference to sorrow. Poor woman, the girl thought, how she must suffer, her own hurt returning with full force.

The men rejoined the ladies shortly after, and as everyone sat around, almost afraid to speak, Jack came over to Clarinda.

"Arthur mentioned to us that you played for him and the count the other night. Would you play for us tonight?"

"Uncle Jack, not while Grandmother is here."

"Well, it is your decision, but" — he looked into her eyes — "I think it will help you far more than it will entertain us."

"All right, but only for you." She walked to the instrument.

Once more, the early summer air was filled with the strains of Mozart, Beethoven, and Chopin. As she had before dinner, Clarinda found herself becoming lost in the music, a beloved friend instead of the terror she had made it so often in the past. Even her thoughts of Richard seemed far away. All that mattered were the sounds emanating from the grand piano, and the feeling of peace it gave her.

The round of applause at the end of her performance astounded her for it was not the polite acclaim she was used to, but rather acknowledgment of her talent. Clarinda glanced at Jack, her delight evident on her face. Then she saw Dorothy's frown, and her expression changed.

Jack immediately came over to the girl. "You were wonderful, honey. In fact, I cannot ever remember hearing you play so well."

"Then why isn't Grandmother pleased? Just look at her. She looks as if I've done everything wrong."

"I'm afraid I can't answer that one for you, Clarinda, but I do know everyone else seems to share my opinion." Jack hugged her. "You have a wonderful gift, and it worried me that you chose to ignore it. Neither your mother nor your father would have wanted you to do that." They smiled at each other, then Jack brought Clarinda back to her seat.

The queen was the first to thank the girl. "Your music, it was superb. You are an exceptional pianist."

"Clarinda is nothing beside her mother, ma'am," Dorothy Franklin butted in. "My Jane—words cannot describe what she could do at the piano. She lived for her art."

"Perhaps Clarinda would also, if you allowed her to, Dorothy," Charles commented.

The old woman looked at her husband. "I suppose you would want another musician in the family, Charles."

"If it makes Clarinda happy, yes."

"As if pleasure was all that mattered." Dorothy's violet eyes became hard. "What did Jane's life amount to, happy or not? She was dead before her twenty-third birthday. Her daughter has—"

Clarinda heard no more for she ran from the parlor, tears streaming down her face.

Jack came out to find her. "I'm sorry, Clarinda."

"Why do I bother? All she ever does is compare me to Mother."

Taking the sobbing girl in his arms, Jack tried to reassure her. "It's her pride, honey."

"Then why can't she be proud of me? You are, aren't you?"

"Do you really have to ask? But I, at least, have had the joy of watching you grow up. Your grandmother sees you so infrequently. Perhaps she doesn't realize how much you've matured."

"Sometimes, I don't feel grown up."

"Like now?"

She nodded, then asked Jack for his handkerchief.

Giving it to her, he laughed. "Do you ever have one of your own?"

"Usually," she replied, a discreet blow following her answer.

"All right." Seeing that she seemed to be feeling a little better, he walked her over to the staircase. "Why don't you retire for the night? I'll make your excuses to the rest of the party."

"Grandmother—"

"Your grandmother be hanged. You've been through too much today, and you should never have stayed for dinner. They should never have come. And I apologize for asking you to play tonight when you weren't up to it."

"No, Uncle Jack, you were right. The music did help me a great deal. It's just that Grandmother always makes Mother sound so perfect."

"I know. We all do you an injustice by comparing you to your mother, but unfortunately, the comparisons are so easy to make."

She smiled at him through her tears. "I'll try harder to be what she expects me to be, Uncle Jack."

"Just be yourself. That's all anyone can ask. Good night, honey."

"Good night." Kissing his cheek, she went upstairs.

* * *

Mary was waiting when Clarinda came into the bedroom. "Did you have a nice dinner with your family, Missy?"

The girl stared at the older woman. "How did you know they were here?"

"Everyone downstairs knew. We've been busy for hours preparing for their visit—making. dinner, getting extra rooms ready, which, may I add, wasn't easy with your uncle's visitors— the usual fuss and bother."

"Why didn't you tell me, Aunt Mary?"

"You got her letter. You must have known she'd be here. Besides, with all the trouble from the morning, I didn't want to upset you further." Mary began undoing Clarinda's hair. "Was that you playing earlier?"

"Uncle Jack asked me to."

"It was so nice to hear. Even Bernice commented on how fine it was." The servant looked in the mirror at her mistress's face. "What did old Mrs. Franklin think?"

"She wasn't pleased."

"I am sorry to hear that. Someday, I'll have to tell her not to be so demanding of you."

Clarinda turned and stared at Mary. "Do you often communicate with my grandmother?"

"No more than the rest of them, I suppose."

"Rest of whom?"

"The old servants, Miss Clarinda. We thought you knew."

"No. I didn't know."

Clarinda dismissed Mary shortly after that, astounded by what she had learned. No wonder her grandmother seemed to be aware of everything that was happening. But she never would have suspected those she trusted the most to betray her.

"They're no better than Iris and Joseph," she cried, "and I believed they loved me." She picked up the blanket, which lay on the chair where she had put it earlier. "Oh, Richard," she sighed, "why did you have to disappear now?"

# *Chapter* 8

---

Richard sat in a corner, his wrists raw from rubbing against the rope. He was surprised he had slept, for the heat and stench in the tiny, windowless room were unbearable, and the sharp pangs in his stomach reminded him it had been a long time since he had eaten. Footsteps on the stone stairs roused him from his half-sleep. Focusing his eyes, he stared questioningly at Bronstein.

"Well," the count began, coughing, "I see you have come around."

"I don't understand, Your Excellency. Why am I here?" Richard tried to stand; Bronstein caught his ankle with his foot. Landing with a thud, he found the blade of a bayonet pointed at his chest.

"Don't be a fool. My men have orders to shoot you should you try to escape."

"Your men?" Richard recognized the soldier with Bronstein. "You were in the stable, with the others."

"*Ja wohl, mein Herr.*" Bronstein glared at Captain Bauer.

"But what have I done to you or the king, Your Excellency, that I'm being kept against my will by your soldiers?"

The count laughed. "Do not play games with me. You know very well what you have done." Even in the semidarkness, the older man could see the denial in the younger's eyes. "It is no use. Everyone at Landfield knows exactly what you are."

"I demand to see Mr. Matthias. I have a right to—"

"*You* demand? *You* have a right?" Bronstein laughed. "You have nothing, you *Kind des Teufels* (child of the devil)." After saying something else in German to his confederate, Bronstein again addressed Richard. "Captain Bauer will bring you water and something to eat. We will talk again later." The two men left, and a minute later, Richard heard the door bolt slide shut.

Once outside, the count confronted the soldier. "You fool!" he hissed. "How dare you treat him with respect!"

"Forgive me, Excellency, I forgot myself. It will not happen again."

"It better not. I cannot afford any more complications."

Bauer stared at Bronstein. "You are going to allow this one man threaten everything we have struggled for all these years? Let me kill him now and be done with him."

"No, Bauer. He is far more important to me alive. But when I have the throne . . ."

\* \* \*

Clarinda glanced at the assortment on the sideboard. The chafing dishes of eggs *a la maitre d'hôtel*, broiled rashers of bacon, oatmeal, and blueberry muffins beckoned, the aroma of freshly-brewed coffee and chocolate hung on the morning breeze, but neither food nor drink enticed her. Finally, selecting a muffin and two strips of bacon, she sat at the empty table.

Walking into the dining room, Arthur smiled at Clarinda. She looked absolutely charming in a *broderie Anglaise* morning gown, her chestnut curls caught up with a white ribbon, and he exhaled slowly.

He filled a plate, then sat beside her. "Good morning, beautiful."

"Oh, good morning, Arthur," she replied.

"You're not eating very much again this morning."

"I'm not hungry." But she broke off a piece of bacon.

"What's troubling you?" he asked for he could detect the faint circles under her eyes. "You look like you didn't sleep well."

"I didn't." Putting the bacon back on her plate, she sighed, "Where could Richard have gone, Arthur?"

"Is that all?" He laughed as she nodded. "You've probably seen the last of that one. You and Jack are well rid of him."

"He hasn't done anything wrong."

"You have to face facts, Clarinda."

"What facts?"

"A small fortune of jewels in his room, for one."

"Lying out in the open so anyone could see them. Richard's smarter than that."

"Perhaps he wanted to get caught."

"Then why did he leave?"

He had no answer for her and turned his attention to his breakfast.

"Maybe he did not have the time to hide them, Fräulein Matthias," Bronstein said as he joined them in the dining room. "I have found servants in general to be extremely shifty and secretive, and your stableboy was shrewder than most."

"You don't know him at all, Your Excellency," Clarinda countered. "How dare you make such an accusation!"

"May I remind you, Fräulein, it was my jewelry he stole?"

She opened her mouth to reply, but Arthur stuck a piece of muffin in it. Choking on a crumb, she glared at the attaché, but he laughed, his blue eyes twinkling. "That's one way to get some food into you."

"I don't think that was very polite, Arthur," she complained.

"I didn't want you to say something you'd end up regretting."

Swallowing, she muttered, "Because I'm defending Richard? And don't tell me it's not protocol to believe an innocent man."

The gentlemen stood as Jack and the king entered the room. Clarinda also made as if to stand, but the monarch waved her down with a smile. "We are not in my court, Fräulein Matthias, but in yours." He whispered something to Jack, who laughed. The two men approached the sideboard.

"Is the queen coming down for breakfast?" Clarinda asked after they sat down to eat.

"I am afraid not, Fräulein," the king answered. "My wife breakfasts in her room." Stroking his beard, he continued, "The morning hours are not her best."

"I guess she's like my grandmother. I've never seen her at a breakfast table." The men laughed.

"You were out early, Your Majesty," Bronstein commented, taking notice of the king's riding clothes.

"Herr Matthias was kind enough to give me a tour of his estate. He recommended I see it before the heat settled."

The count cleared his throat, then smiled. "I, too, have been exploring, Your Majesty. Herr Matthias's property is mostly woods, nothing of importance or interest."

"I am surprised I didn't see you, Your Excellency," Charles Franklin said as he joined the group. "It has always been my habit to take an early morning constitutional." He sat down across from his granddaughter. "How are you today, Clarinda?"

She smiled weakly at him. "I guess I'll be all right, Grandfather. I'm just a little tired."

"I spoke to your grandmother last night. We both seem to feel a change of scenery would be the best thing for you at present."

"Grandfather . . . I can't leave now. Uncle Jack has guests."

Charles gazed benignly at her. "Of course, we would not want you to neglect your responsibilities, but, my dear, if your health is going to decline because of it . . . you have to think of yourself first."

"Then I'd rather stay here. I'd be miserable if I didn't know what was going on."

"Clarinda, honey," Jack gently countered, "what can you possibly hope to learn? Unfortunately, the boy is gone and, for all I know, not coming back. You have to forget about whatever you thought you had with him and get on with your life."

"But—"

"Believe me, Fräulein," the king added, "if you do not do what your uncle says, you will only become more miserable."

Nodding his head, Jack added, "Listen to the king, honey. I would hate for you to suffer the way the queen has."

"Yes, Uncle Jack." Clarinda picked at her muffin, tears filling her eyes.

The monarch turned to his host. "Your niece appears to be quite strong, Herr Matthias. It is just that the *Herzweh* is so new. All she needs is some time."

"My niece has never had a loss like this before, sir. It is new to both of us."

"But the loss of her parents—"

"She never knew her mother, and she was so young when my brother died, she actually grieved very little. Of course, her family and the staff helped her at that time."

"Perhaps we sheltered her too much, Jack," Charles commented.

"No, Grandfather, you didn't," Clarinda answered quietly. "And I think the king is right. I'll be fine soon."

Bernice knocked and entered with the sheriff. Since the previous afternoon, when Jack informed her about Richard's disappearance, she had been increasingly bitter toward both the young man and her employer, especially as she had had to assume Richard's duties in the dining room. And then this bumpkin sheriff and his men asking the entire staff questions and searching the grounds . . . it was too much, and she could feel another migraine beginning. "Sheriff Tyler would like to speak to Clarinda, Mr. Matthias."

"Thank you, Bernice. Would you make sure the queen and Mrs. Franklin have trays?" he added as she started to leave.

"Of course, Mr. Matthias." She seethed inwardly.

"Miss Matthias," Sheriff Tyler commenced, "did Mr. Royce ever mention where he would like to go someday?"

"He wanted to stay here," Clarinda almost shouted. "Richard hated moving from place to place."

"He told you that?"

"How else would I know, Mr. Tyler?"

"Harry," Jack interrupted, "I don't think this is the best time to question my niece."

"On the contrary, Mr. Matthias, the suspect has had almost a full day to make his escape. He could be anywhere by now."

"That's true. Clarinda, did Richard say anything to you about going somewhere?"

Reducing the remainder of her muffin to crumbs, she mumbled, "He thought about joining the army."

"What did you say?"

She looked up. "He said he thought he might join the army. He tried once, years ago, but Joseph stopped him."

"There haven't been recruiters in Oak Store in months," the sheriff offered.

"Then he might have gone to Washington to enlist," Jack said. "I'll make sure the recruitment stations there are on the lookout for him."

"No, Uncle Jack! You can't!"

"At this point, only Richard can prove his guilt or innocence, and he can't do that unless we find him."

"But you think he's guilty. Even if you do find him, why should he come back?"

"Clarinda," Jack began, then stood and came over to her. "I think we need to talk privately."

They went into the parlor. Jack looked at Clarinda as he walked around the room, trying to understand her. She had always been so reasonable, so rational, why was she different now? Then, almost without realizing it, he had his answer. She was in love.

"Richard doesn't want to be a soldier, Uncle Jack. He only said he was considering the army because he believed that you'd think a soldier was better than a servant for me. As if it really matters."

He touched her hair. "You sound like your father, when he told his mother about a certain young lady from Philadelphia he planned to marry. 'Not the doctor's cousin!' she said, if I recall correctly."

"Mother?"

"Your grandmother thought no girl was good enough for her Ralph, certainly not 'one of those stuck-up Franklins.' Of course, Dorothy felt the same way about your father."

"Then you do understand how I feel about Richard."

"Yes, sweetheart, but what if Richard *is* a thief?" She dropped her head. "I know, you believe he isn't. But your unwillingness to cooperate isn't helping matters any. All we want — all anyone wants — is to get to the bottom of this. And despite what it sounds like, I do trust your judgment because I don't think Richard would consciously do anything wrong."

"Meaning he's unbalanced."

"Meaning, we won't know until we find him."

"Or he comes back."

He put her arms around her. "Why don't you go upstairs? I don't think you'll be wanting any more breakfast."

"All right, Uncle Jack." Hugging her, he led her into the hall.

* * *

Mary was surprised to see Clarinda back so soon. "You're done early, Miss Clarinda. I haven't had time to lay out your riding clothes."

"I wasn't very hungry."

"And not very sleepy last night either. I noticed the bed sheets were more rumpled than usual."

"You notice a lot, don't you, Mary?" Clarinda asked pointedly.

"Not any more than others. All servants see things about their employers if they're good servants. It helps us to know what you need."

"Or what I'm doing wrong?"

"I don't understand, Miss Clarinda. Who said you were doing anything wrong?"

"Isn't that why Grandmother is here? Because I'm not acting like someone in my position should act?"

"Perhaps she wanted to get away from the city, or to see Dr. Gerald. Before your mother and father were married, Mr. and Mrs. Franklin would come to Oak Store all the time."

"I just wish I'd known she was coming a little sooner. Then I'd be prepared for her." Clarinda sat at her dressing table, and Mary began to comb out the tangle of curls.

A couple minutes later, Clarinda asked, "How often do you write Grandmother, Aunt Mary?"

"Once or twice a year, Miss Clarinda, mostly to tell her how well you were doing in school. Mr. Matthias used to share your letters with us, and I knew you wouldn't be writing Mrs. Franklin that much, so I did it for you."

The girl turned and stared at the maid. "I wrote her every other week! Even when I was at home, I'd write her. Uncle Jack said I had to because he didn't want Grandmother and Grandfather to feel I was deliberately neglecting them."

"She-she didn't believe what you wrote, that you were coloring the truth so they'd think everything was all right. Mrs. Franklin asked us to write her, every once in a while, to let her know what was really happening."

Covering her face with her hands, Clarinda slumped in the chair, her head finally resting on the table before her. "I never lied to her," she wept. "Everything I told Uncle Jack I told her. Why can't she trust me?"

"I wish I could answer that, Miss Clarinda. All I know is that she insisted on us writing her about what you were doing."

"Who else wrote Grandmother?"

"Laura did a couple of times, but she wasn't comfortable doing it, so she stopped. And Bernice, of course."

"Mattie and Jacob?"

"They were Matthias servants, they didn't come from your grandmother's house with your mother when she married. Besides, they couldn't read or write very well, just sign their names."

"Did Uncle Jack know about your arrangement with Grandmother?"

"If he did, he didn't say. It was private between Mrs. Franklin and us."

"How long has this arrangement been going on, Aunt Mary?" the girl whispered.

"Only the last few years, Miss Clarinda. Since you've been at school."

"And before then?"

"I don't know."

"I think I do." *There was no need for her to check up on me,* Clarinda thought. *Before I went to school, the way I acted could be attributed to my being a child. After, I was grown up and expected to act so.*

"Will you be dressing to go out, Miss Clarinda?"

"Not right away. I want to talk to my grandmother first."

Clarinda knocked lightly on the closed door. Receiving no response, she opened it. Her grandmother was seated at the small dressing table, while Bernice, a rare smile on her face, was busy arranging the elderly woman's coronet of white braids. This astounded the girl for she had never seen the domestic in any other role but housekeeper, and she watched for several minutes before interrupting.

"I didn't realize you enjoyed playing the abigail, Bernice."

The two women turned sharply. "Clarinda," Dorothy sputtered, "you should have knocked."

"I did, Grandmother, but I guess you didn't hear me. May I speak with you for a few minutes?"

"Certainly, dear."

Dorothy started to wave Bernice out of the room, but Clarinda stopped her. "I want Bernice to hear what I have to say, Grandmother."

"If it is private enough that you must address me in my bedroom—"

"I would like to know why you insisted you be informed about every little thing I do. I'm not a child anymore. Or weren't my letters to you good enough?"

"Clarinda, dear, you're overreacting," Dorothy purred. "What is the harm in a couple of letters a year from some former retainers who just happen to be in my granddaughter's service? If you were mentioned at all, it was in the kindest light. Mary and Laura love you deeply."

"And Bernice?" The girl stared at the thin housekeeper. "Does she share Mary and Laura's opinion of me?"

"Of course I do, Clarinda," Bernice answered. "Perhaps it is just that I can see things a little more clearly."

"So you felt it your duty to catalog everything I do."

The servant's eyes shifted down to Dorothy Franklin, then she rubbed her forehead. "You really are making too much of this, Clarinda. If you will excuse me, Mrs. Franklin, I need to lie down for a spell."

Dorothy dismissed Bernice. When she was out of the room, the woman turned to her granddaughter, fury darkening her face. "Thank you very much, Clarinda. Now that Bernice has one of her headaches, who is going to finish my hair?"

"I'll send Mrs. Royce up to help you dress, Grandmother." Clarinda started to leave but stopped. "It has always amazed me how you never seem to travel with staff of your own."

"There has never been any need for me to bring Nellie, at least not here. Mr. Matthias and Gerald, when I visit him and Arliss, have always been generous about providing enough help. It is something you should have learned from them."

"There would have been plenty of help for you if you had timed your visit a little better. Unfortunately, Uncle Jack's guests take precedence over family."

"Even though they brought more than enough retainers with them to augment your own staff?"

"Maybe it is you who should take the lesson, Grandmother."

"How dare you speak to me like that, girl! I had never expected to hear impudence from my own daughter's child."

"Stop saying that!" Clarinda screamed. "I'll never be what you remember her to be." Quickly wiping her eyes on her sleeve, she added, a little more calmly, "I'll send Mrs. Royce up to you shortly." Then, with none of her questions answered, Clarinda left the room.

\* \* \*

Arthur and Clarinda entered the stable, after one of the king's retinue had taken their horses to cool. While Jack and his guest continued to discuss his problems and the sheriff's posse prowled the woods surrounding the house, Arthur took the girl away for a few hours to help her cope with things a little better. Unfortunately, all Clarinda cared about was the situation with Richard, which, for Arthur, resulted in a tiresome outing. Stripping off his gloves, he leaned against the corner of a stall. "This feels terrific, after that ride."

"We didn't have to go out, Arthur."

"I think we did."

Clarinda removed her jacket, the white cotton blouse clinging to her figure. Arthur inhaled sharply, then added, "You need to forget what happened yesterday."

She tossed back her head and laughed. "That's funny. Everyone else wants me to remember every possible detail of the last four weeks. 'Where did the suspect go? How did he spend his time?' If they really want to know, why don't they question Iris? She followed Richard and me everywhere."

"Iris is a child."

"Iris is a sneak and a liar."

"Then why should Sheriff Tyler believe her? Clarinda, you're not making any sense."

Her eyes narrowed. "Iris stood right there and told Richard Joseph would put him back in his place. And Joseph doesn't just talk."

"If he was doing something wrong, Richard should have been punished."

"He wasn't doing anything wrong. He kissed me, and I kissed him."

"And what about the jewelry in his room?"

Pounding the door of Moonbeam's stall, she screamed, "He's *not* a thief! They should question Iris about *that* too!"

Arthur grabbed her. "Calm down, Clarinda." She wrapped her arms around his neck and, laying her head on his shoulder, cried as though her heart would break.

Her crying slowed. She lifted her head and wiped her eyes. "I'm sorry, Arthur. I didn't mean to do that."

"It's all right. I know you've been quite upset."

She smiled slightly. "I'm beginning to sound like Richard. I think his favorite words are I'm sorry." Suddenly, the note flashed in her mind: *I apologize for what I* . . .

"What is it?"

"The note in Richard's room. He didn't write it."

Shaking his head, Arthur tried to reason with her. "You can't seriously believe that."

"You don't understand. Richard would never have—"

A rustling behind them in the stall caught their attention. Arthur opened the door, and the gray cat ran out, dragging something in her mouth. They watched the feline play her hunting games with the scrap of cloth, pounce and fight, until Clarinda noticed the red and blue tattersall pattern. Snatching the fabric from the indignant Lady, who hissed and scratched at the girl, she exhibited it to Arthur.

"This came from Richard's shirt, the one he was wearing yesterday."

"So he was in the stable and tore it."

"Or someone else did." She clasped her hands, a smile spreading across her face. "Someone forced him to leave."

Arthur's forehead creased slightly. Who?"

"Joseph. He hates Richard, and he wanted to humiliate him."

"All Joseph needed to do was send Richard to your uncle. He disgraced the both of you pretty well in the courtyard."

"So he made Richard look guiltier by making him leave, then had Iris put those things in his room." Clarinda ran to the door. "I have to tell Uncle Jack right away!"

\* \* \*

"Uncle Jack!"

The study door flew open, and the two men looked up from the architect's plans they were examining. "Yes, Clarinda, what is it?" Jack asked while the king discreetly signaled his bodyguard to lower his weapon.

"It's Richard —"

"He's back?"

"No, but I don't think he ran away."

Jack scratched the back of his head. "What makes you think that?"

"The note we found in his room." She took a deep breath. "When did Richard ever apologize?"

"Clarinda," he laughed a little, "you know as well as I that Richard was always apologizing."

"No, he wasn't. He was always saying he was sorry. Uncle Jack, Richard's not that sophisticated. He wouldn't write words he didn't use. He would have written, 'I'm sorry.'"

"Hm." Drumming his fingers on the desk, Jack pondered what she had said, and while it made sense, he wasn't completely convinced it was true. "Is that all, honey?"

"No." She laid the scrap of cloth on the desk. "Arthur and I found Lady playing with this just now."

He examined the piece of faded plaid cotton. *Nothing unusual about it*, he thought, and he started to return it to her when he spotted the neat mend. "Where did you get this?"

"In the stable."

"This is from Richard's shirt?"

"Yes, the one he was wearing yesterday." Her eyes glistened. "He was forced to leave Landfield and, whoever did, tore his shirt doing so."

"Who, Clarinda?"

"Joseph. It had to be Joseph."

Jack shook his head. "No, honey. He had nothing to do with Richard's disappearance."

"Uncle Jack—"

"Joseph told me, and I have no reason to doubt him at this point, he sent Richard here. Iris even said she saw him come in here."

"They've both said things before that weren't true."

"It doesn't fit, Clarinda. Why would Joseph, who watches every move his son makes, all of a sudden just send him away?" Her face fell. "I'm sorry, honey. Until someone gives me more than this, or Richard returns, I have no choice but to believe that he left on his own. Now if you will excuse us, I have some serious matters to discuss with the king."

"All right, Uncle Jack."

"We'll see you at dinner."

Clarinda curtseyed to the monarch, then kissed her uncle before leaving the study.

"Your niece could be right," the other man offered.

"But what would be the rationale behind it?"

"I'm afraid I can't answer that." The king turned his attention back to the drawings. "You are certain I will be safe in the study?"

"Yes. When the house was built, there were still some Indian raids occurring, and my great-grandfather, whose mother's first husband was killed by Indians, wanted to make sure he would lose none of his family that way. So he had a secret passage built behind this part of the house where, in case of attack, they would be able to hide."

"And did it work, Herr Matthias?"

"Fortunately for us, we never had to use it." Jack laughed. "Remember, sir, when the count does make his move, you must appear defenseless."

"In other words, no guards."

"It would be best." Jack looked at the sober uniformed man behind the door. "You expect him to act soon?"

"My guess would be Friday."

"You seem certain of that."

The king rose and dismissed the guard, then stood by the window. "If I were to die then, my wife would be completely incapable of handling it." He rubbed the top of his head. "That would be Bronstein's style."

"I don't understand, Your Majesty."

He sighed. "Bronstein and my wife . . . the count was her father's rival long before he was mine. As I told you last week, the count had a privileged position in my early reign, and I think he expected too much. He has a younger sister and tried very hard to arrange a match between her and me. Unfortunately for Ferdinand, I fell in love with Marta, and after I married her, I would turn to my father-in-law for advice instead of him, which angered my prime minister. Then, when the baby came . . ."

"What happened?"

"Nothing I can prove, and without proof, I cannot accuse a *Reichsgraf*, a count of the Empire, of anything. Unless, of course, I wish to be at war with my neighbors."

"But you *are* at war with Bronstein, and he intends to win."

"That, my friend, he shall never do."

\* \* \*

Bauer kicked the soles of Richard's shoes. "*Der Graf möchte Ihnen sehen* (The count wants to see you)."

"What?" Richard said sleepily.

"*Was, was–die ganze Zeit, 'Was*? (What, what–all the time, 'What?')" He pulled Richard to his feet and pushed him down the steep stairs.

Blinking rapidly from the blaze of light from the window, Richard was forced down to his knees by the soldier beside him. He heard the door open and someone walk in.

"I trust you are feeling better, Richard," the count said, "now that you have eaten."

"I wasn't very hungry," Richard replied, refusing to admit the warm water and rancid stew had made him sick.

"I see. Well, then, perhaps your memory has improved, and you can recall what you have done."

"Done? I haven't—"

Bronstein thrust the end of his walking stick under the young man's chin. "Do not pretend to be innocent with me. No one believes you are."

"Miss Clarinda. She knows what happened."

"Fräulein Matthias doesn't care about you anymore."

Anger exploded in Richard's eyes. "I don't believe you."

The count's beard twitched slightly as he smiled. "Think what you like, but the Fräulein spent the better part of the day with Arthur Jamison. *Ach*, such a charming couple." His gaze narrowed slightly. "The Fräulein took him riding to all her favorite places, I understand. And this morning, Herr Jamison actually fed the Fräulein her breakfast. She was so touched she had no words to adequately express her feelings. Why would she care about a liar and a thief like you?" Raising one eyebrow, he added, "Herr Matthias seems agreeable to the arrangement, and of course, the grandmother. Her sense of propriety would not allow her precious granddaughter to involve herself with anyone of the lower classes. When Fräulein Clarinda decides on Herr Jamison, Frau Franklin will be quite pleased with the girl's choice, I can assure you."

"Mr. Jamison's Miss Clarinda's friend." But Bronstein's barbs had found their mark, and a shadow crossed Richard's face.

The count became uneasy. "Your devotion is touching," he said sarcastically, then signaled to the captain to take Richard back upstairs.

When the soldier returned, Bronstein ordered, "He is to be fed what the rest of the guard eats, Bauer."

"Excellency?"

"He must not look ill-treated. Oh, yes, Captain," Bronstein continued, seeing the surprise on the other man's face. "He will be found. And when I am finished . . ." He snickered as they left the building.

# *Chapter* 9

Clarinda paused in the doorway to the dining room. The third day of waiting, she thought, hoping that Richard would return to clear himself. At least the sheriff and his posse weren't around asking their interminable questions. Having found no trace of Richard, they had left the day before.

A motion by the window caught her eye. There was something familiar about the man standing there, but when he turned, she was surprised. "Your Majesty," she sputtered, dropping a curtsey.

"Forgive me, Fräulein. I was waiting for your uncle. He said he would meet me here."

"It's just . . . I was so sure it was—"

"Your stableboy?"

She nodded, her eyes filling with tears.

"It is the not knowing. You begin to hear things, see things, believing that . . . But kings do not become stable hands, just as shadows do not become little boys," he sighed, then he gazed at Clarinda. "You remind me of my wife, Fräulein. She still expects our son to . . . come back to us."

"Your son? I didn't know you have a son."

"I don't . . . not any more."

"He died? I'm sorry, Your Majesty."

"No need to be, my dear."

"Oh, here you are, Clarinda," Arthur remarked, entering the room. "Good morning, Your Majesty."

"Has Herr Matthias come down, Herr Jamison? We were to go riding, but with the weather, I am not sure."

Clarinda glanced out the window at the storm clouds gathering in the west. "You should be able to go out, Your Majesty. The storm won't arrive until this afternoon."

The monarch laughed. "How do you know?"

"The way the clouds look. Jacob—he was our caretaker before the Royces—he taught me how to read the sky patterns, among other things."

"And how did Jacob know?" Arthur probed.

"He learned from his mother, who learned from her mother."

Jack chuckled as he joined the little group. "I thought I educated you, Clarinda Matthias. Now I find you believe more in Jacob's voodoo than what you learned in boarding school."

She giggled in reply. "And how many times did Mattie scold you for coming home drenched because you ignored the signs?"

"More times than I'd care to remember, young lady. By the way, it's good to hear you laughing again." Jack kissed her on the forehead and escorted her to her seat as Laura and Lily brought in the griddle cakes and sausage patties.

They had already begun eating when the count entered with Charles Franklin. Since Tuesday, Charles had been Bronstein's companion on his morning walks, and as a result, the count had been unable to visit the abandoned structure as often as he would have liked. Bowing to the king, Bronstein smiled and said, "Good morning, Your Majesty."

The king nodded in reply. "You were out early again."

"I was speaking to Captain Bauer, Your Majesty. He informs me the garrison has not maintained discipline in the past few weeks."

"I doubt our American hosts would have appreciated foreign troops marching up and down their streets."

"Perhaps if they bivouacked in the woods, rather than the stable, they would be better able to remain sharp."

The king shifted his eyes slightly toward Jack. "Tell Captain Bauer to do whatever he deems necessary, Bronstein."

"Of course, Your Majesty."

The ruler looked fully at Jack now. "Herr Matthias, my wife spends June 22 in seclusion. Do you have a chapel on your property where she may go?"

"I'm afraid not, Your Majesty. The closest thing to a chapel is the family crypt. I doubt she would want to go there."

Smiling slightly, the monarch answered, "Oddly enough, she might."

Clarinda tugged on her uncle's sleeve. "What about the old house?"

"It's in disrepair, honey."

"It was, but Jacob fixed it up for me, remember? Of course, I haven't been there in a few years."

"All right, Clarinda. Why don't you see that it's made ready for the queen this afternoon?"

"It's going to rain this afternoon."

Jack laughed. "Then go this morning."

Putting down his fork, Arthur asked, "Where is it, Jack? I've never seen it."

"In the woods behind the stable, if I recall correctly."

Clarinda nodded, and Arthur smiled at her. "Now I'm curious. What's it like?"

Laughing, she replied, "It's very small, just two rooms. When I was younger, I'd use it as a playhouse, and sometimes, my governess would give me my lessons there. In fact, I used to pretend I was Rapunzel in her tower because that's what the old house is like."

She went on describing the building, Bronstein becoming more and more distressed. "Your Majesty," he interrupted, "perhaps this year, the queen could forego her silly rituals."

The king's russet eyes burned with rage. "How dare you! My wife has never stopped mourning for our son."

"Maybe it is time for her to face reality."

"What do you mean?"

"What good has all her grieving done? Has it brought the prince back? No. Meanwhile, she has a grandson she barely acknowledges because she refuses to admit her son is dead."

"You know very well that the queen loves Ferdinand, but he will never be my son. And until *she* is ready to accept that the child is never returning, I shall indulge my wife her beliefs, however misguided they might be."

It wasn't until after the king began eating again that Arthur realized Clarinda had left the dining room. Excusing himself, he went to find her.

She was on the portico, half-hidden by a marble column, the rising wind ruffling the skirt of her pale blue gauze dress. Arthur crossed to where she stood and, placing his hands on her shoulders, glanced at her tear-stained face. "What is it?" he murmured.

"Is that what I'm doing? Believing in an impossibility?"

"They weren't talking about you."

"Oh, I know, but earlier, the king said I reminded him of his wife, and he seems to feel—"

Arthur's finger stroked her neck. "Their son has been gone for twenty years. Richard is missing only a few days."

"What happened, Arthur? I mean, with their son?"

"He was kidnapped and killed." A distant rumbling intruded. "It looks like your forecast was wrong."

"No, the storm is still a few hours away."

"Why don't we go and look over the old house now so we won't get caught in the storm?"

"I need a half hour to change." Holding out the sheer overskirt, she laughed, "I'm not exactly dressed for cleaning."

"Thirty minutes, then." He escorted her back into the house.

\* \* \*

The two guards stopped them at the entrance to the building. "What are you doing here?" one of them asked.

"I should be asking you that question," Clarinda countered. "But since you asked us first . . . I need to check the house."

"*Nein . . . verboten!*" the other guard shouted.

"Forbidden? By whose orders?" The two men stared at each other. "I'm going inside despite your orders."

She had taken one step toward the door as Arthur tried to hold her back, when it opened and a third soldier came out, pistol drawn. "Ah, Fräulein Matthias, Herr Jamison."

Clarinda stared at the steel barrel of the weapon while Arthur demanded, "What is the meaning of this?"

The guard lowered the gun. "Maneuvers, the captain approved them."

"I'm sure your captain would not expect you to hold unarmed civilians, ah—"

"Sergeant Vogel."

"Vogel. Yes. Now if you will allow Miss Matthias and me to pass, Sergeant, you may continue with your maneuvers."

"No one allowed inside. Captain's orders."

"Well, you were inside," Clarinda observed.

"I . . . lookout." The man smiled at his cleverness.

"Come on, Clarinda, let's go," Arthur urged. "If we can't get in, we can't get in."

She shook her head. "I want to know what's going on."

"If you want to get yourself in trouble, go right ahead." Arthur turned to leave.

"The king gave his permission for this barely a half hour ago," she continued to argue. "These men have an established camp here. You can't do that in fifteen minutes. Sergeant Vogel," she asked the soldier, "how long are you here?"

He held up three fingers. "*Drei Tagen.*"

"Three days?"

"*Ja.*"

"You've been *here* three days, Sergeant Vogel?"

"*Nein.* We take turns. All of us, three days."

Arthur laughed. "He doesn't understand what you're asking him, Clarinda. He thought you wanted to know how long they've been at Landfield."

She angrily waved six fingers in Arthur's face. "Then he would have said *sechs Tagen*. They came with the count. The soldiers have been *here*, in the woods, for three days." Her hand flew to her mouth. "Sergeant, have you seen my stablehand? Tall, dark brown hair and eyes?"

He screwed up his face in thought. "*Nein*," he finally responded.

The three soldiers snapped to attention, and the sergeant said, "Good morning, Excellency."

"Gentlemen. And Fräulein Matthias, it is a pleasure to see you again." Bronstein sketched a kiss on her hand.

"Your Excellency, would you please tell the sergeant to let Arthur and me into the house?" As she spoke, large drops of rain began falling, and she laughed. "I was wrong, after all."

Bronstein took Vogel aside and quickly issued orders, then allowed Clarinda and Arthur entry before he and the sergeant followed them in, the count silently cursing the rain.

Clarinda twirled in a corner of the room. "Isn't it wonderful?"

"It's rather small," Arthur commented.

"But that's what makes it special, just big enough for one."

"Or two?"

The count carefully made his way upstairs while the girl continued to reminisce, knowing he would not be missed by either of them. He nodded to his subordinate, who sat on Richard's legs, holding his pistol against the gagged man's forehead.

Three days in the squalid upper room had taken their toll on the man at Bronstein's feet. More and more, Richard found himself retreating into the soft, fuzzy area of his mind where he knew he'd always be safe—the place he thought of as home. It was there his mama and papa were, joined now by Clarinda, her chestnut hair tumbling from under her white bonnet, down the green riding habit to her waist. They loved him, or said they did, until someone in a blue uniform with bright gold buttons took him away. Now they existed only in a place he couldn't reach, no matter how hard he kept trying to.

It was the dark thoughts, the memories, crashing in on him like the ocean waves he had seen once or twice on the passage to America, which kept him away, hitting him harder than the switch. He recalled vividly each blow he had received over the years as he remained in the twilight world between reality and madness, the searing pain in his soul torturing him until, as a final, desperate act, he screamed with every part of his being. Or had he, for no one had come, not even his captors.

Raising his eyes, he saw Bronstein. *"What do you want now?"* they asked the count.

"It is something you want, Richard. Fräulein Clarinda is downstairs." Disbelief replaced disinterest, but Richard listened and, hearing her voice, smiled briefly over the gag.

"She and Arthur Jamison were walking when the rain started. Apparently, this was the nearest shelter." Bronstein chuckled softly as Richard fought against the bindings on his wrists. "They have been inseparable since your disappearance. Young Arthur is quite in love with the Fräulein, and she is learning very quickly to love him."

*"But . . . she loves me,"* Richard's eyes said as clearly as if he had spoken the words.

"Listen to her. She is laughing, with Arthur." Almost on cue, their laughter floated up the staircase. "That should tell you how she feels about him . . . and you."

Richard's eyes shifted away, his desolation making him ill. Watching, Bronstein smiled. "Do not worry, Richard. It will all be over soon." Turning to Vogel, he commanded, "If he attempts to alert the Fräulein to his presence here, shoot him." Then he went downstairs and, despite the rain, left the building.

\* \* \*

"It's really coming down," Clarinda noted, peering out the window.

"You're sure we'll be safe here? I mean, the roof's not going to leak, is it?" Arthur asked facetiously.

"Why don't we go upstairs and check?" She laughed as she approached the stairs.

He caught her around the waist and drew her to him. "That's not necessary." His heart throbbed while he stroked her back; snatching her hair in his hands, he raised it to his face. "So sweet," he moaned, inhaling the faint scent of lilac in it. She pulled back, but he refused to release her.

"Arthur, I don't think Uncle Jack would—"

"I spoke to Jack last night. He's given me his blessing."

"About what?"

"About us, of course." He kissed her cheeks. "Clarinda, you had to have known how I feel about you."

"Arthur, I-I didn't—" His mouth was on hers, his hands taking liberties which she had no intention of giving. "Please, stop!" she managed finally to mumble.

To his surprise, and her relief, he did. "I'm sorry, dearest. I didn't mean to." Removing his hands from her back and putting them on her shoulders, he added, "I love you, Clarinda, more than anything else in the world. At least give me a reason to hope."

She went partway up the stairs. "Perhaps if you had come sooner, but I can't promise what I don't feel."

"Because of Richard? Face it, Clarinda. He's gone, and there is someone here who loves you very much."

"I wish you wouldn't, Arthur."

"You say you can't help whom you're in love with. Well, neither can I. I just hope you come to your senses before it's too late."

"I'd rather be an old maid than give up Richard just because it's the proper thing to do."

"If he really cared about you, he wouldn't have turned tail and run as soon as Jack found out about your little escapade in the stable."

"Richard didn't run away! Why won't anyone believe that? Something's happened to him. I just know it."

"It's been three days, and while I know that you want to believe the best of him, I think the facts speak for themselves."

"Richard doesn't have a dishonest bone in his body."

"Maybe his bones aren't dishonest, but I wouldn't be so sure about the rest of him," Arthur quipped.

She leaned against the wall, focusing on an imperfection in the stone opposite. "I wish I could tell you how I feel whenever I see him or hear his voice. It's as if my heart begins singing. And when he touches me . . ." Her eyes closed, and she sighed.

Arthur studied her, recalling the way she had watched Richard a week earlier. She had never looked at him that way and, in a voice filled with envy, said, "You actually believe it's real, Clarinda, don't you."

"Yes, and I will until the day I die."

"What if you're wrong?"

Turning to him, the pain as visible in her eyes as the love earlier, she whispered, "Maybe then, Arthur, I'll be able to love you."

Once more, he took her in his arms and led her to the window. "The rain's stopped."

"Look, there's a rainbow."

"I think we'd better be going back."

She nodded, and Arthur kissed her wet cheeks. Smiling at each other, they left the house.

Richard barely heard the door close. Three days of turmoil over—Clarinda loved him, not Arthur. No matter what the count told him about them now, he knew the truth. Finally, he had something to fight for, and although he couldn't see it, Richard knew there was a rainbow. It shone in his heart.

\* \* \*

Jack paced in the study. He greatly disliked waiting for something to happen, and as Friday approached, he found himself becoming more and more tense, the king's almost cavalier attitude toward the threat to his life disturbing him more than he wanted to admit. Watching the slowly-breaking clouds, the muffled thunder announcing the passing of the storm, Jack hoped his storms would also soon be at an end.

The knock on the door startled him. "Come in."

"Uncle Jack," Clarinda began, "I have to talk to you."

"Yes?" Seeing the serious expression on her face, he smiled then sat behind the desk. "What's wrong?"

"It's Grandmother. She keeps complaining about everything that I've done this week, and I've even caught her 'fixing things,' as she puts it."

"Such as?"

"Last night's dinner. She insisted on having roast lamb and curried lobster, even though we'd already had lamb three times this week, and getting the lobster meant Laura had to make a special trip into town."

"What had you planned?"

"A roast beef and stewed chicken. But it's not so much what she does but how she does it. She keeps going behind my back to talk to Laura and Adele, then upbraids me because I'm not managing my household. I would if she'd let me. And since I found out about the letters—"

"What letters?"

"The letters Bernice and Mary send her. I worry that they're telling her everything I'm doing. I'm surprised she hasn't reprimanded me for what's happened between Richard and me."

"Maybe she doesn't know."

"Uncle Jack, everybody here knows how I feel about him. I haven't exactly been quiet about it."

"No," he chuckled, "that you haven't." Jack looked at Clarinda and smiled. "Do you want me to talk to your grandfather about this?"

She was silent for a long moment. "I thought I did, Uncle Jack, but now, I'm not so sure."

"What changed your mind?"

"What you told me about Joseph and Richard—that he'd never gain confidence if I fought his battles for him. I guess this is one battle I'm going to have to fight myself."

The door creaked open, and almost apologetically, Joseph entered. "I hate to disturb you, Mr. Matthias, but . . . Adele and me been talkin', and Count von Bronstein . . . the king is in danger."

Holding up his hand to silence the other man, Jack turned to Clarinda. "Honey, I want you to leave."

"Now?" She glanced at his face. "I guess I could ask Adele for cleaning supplies."

"Thank you."

Jack waited until the girl was out of the hall to address Joseph. "How do you know this?"

"We . . . hear his people. Mr. Matthias, I want to help you protect the king."

Looking skeptically at the servant, Jack asked, "Why, Joseph?"

The man hesitated. *"Tell Mr. Matthias everything,"* Adele had implored him before he came upstairs. But now, he was afraid.

"I need to know I can trust you, Joseph."

Looking Jack straight in the eye, Joseph said, "I made an oath, long ago, in my home country, and I broke that oath. It's time for me to make it right. I ain't gonna betray you, Mr. Matthias."

The study door opened again, and the count's secretary entered. "Pardon me, Herr Matthias, but I have run out of ink. Would you have some I could use?"

"I believe so." Rummaging through his desk drawers, Jack asked, "Didn't you just buy some in Washington last week?"

"Yes, but Count von Bronstein is a prolific letter-writer. I use much ink on his correspondence."

"You write his letters?"

"The count rarely writes his own."

"Well, I can imagine a man as busy as he—"

"It has nothing to do with his schedule. Count von Bronstein is left-handed. When he writes, the ink smears, so for legibility, I write for him. All he does is sign."

"I see." Jack handed the squat bottle to the secretary.

"Thank you, Herr Matthias." He bowed crisply and left.

Joseph also started to leave, but Jack stopped him. "Joseph, is Richard right-handed or left-handed?"

The other man thought for about ten seconds. "Right-handed. Why?"

"Oh, just curious. And Joseph?" The servant stopped once more. "Thank you."

"You're . . . welcome, Mr. Matthias."

After Joseph left, Jack opened the locked compartment in his desk and withdrew the scrap of cotton and the crumpled note. Flattening out the paper, he noticed the streaks of black haloing the letters, particularly the lower loops. Even a note written hurriedly by a *right-handed* person would not be smudged from left to right, he realized, but to be sure, he attempted several times to duplicate the smudges himself without success. "How could I have been so blind?" he asked, knowing it was his outrage over what Joseph had implied that morning which had prevented him from believing Clarinda completely or trusting Richard's honesty. Jack rubbed his forehead while he stared at the items before him. Replacing them in the cubbyhole, he went back to studying the papers on his desk.

* * *

Walking into the kitchen, Clarinda was not surprised to see her grandmother deep in conversation with Laura. "I think a saddle of mutton will do nicely tonight, Laura, in addition to the boiled ham. You have been able to get one of those nice Virginia hams, haven't you?"

"No, Mrs. Franklin."

"Why not? Jane always had them when we'd come to visit."

"I think Miss Clarinda wants the ham on Sunday."

"You can save the beef for Sunday. We'll have the ham today."

"No, Grandmother, we won't. Laura, I would like the meals as we discussed yesterday."

"Yes, Miss Clarinda," the cook said, smiling, then she quickly withdrew.

"I don't appreciate your interference with my orders, Grandmother," Clarinda continued. "You keep telling me what a poor job I'm doing around here, but you don't let me try to do a better one."

"Well," Dorothy sniffed, "you've been reliant on Bernice for so long, perhaps I didn't think you were capable of—"

"Maybe Bernice's migraine was a good thing after all."

"Have you been to see her?"

"Several times. She can't abide being disturbed right now. In fact, I've even had Gerald out to examine her."

"When? I don't remember seeing him here."

"Yesterday morning, while you were upstairs having breakfast."

"I am surprised. I thought you didn't care about the rest of your staff as much as you do your uncle's butler."

Clarinda blanched. "How . . . who told you?"

"I wish it had been you. Instead, I have to find out through servants' gossip that my daughter's only child is foolishly enamored of a *stableboy*. How Jack Matthias could allow such a thing is beyond me. What must the neighbors think?"

"He didn't allow it, Grandmother, it just happened. And nobody outside of the family knows, so you needn't worry about your ruined reputation. Besides, once you meet Richard, I know you'll—no, you won't because you can't see beyond your own ideas of what's right and wrong. Just because Richard's a servant doesn't mean he isn't a gentleman."

"And oil and water don't mix. While I've often felt you were irresponsible, Clarinda, I never thought you were stupid."

Adele came into the kitchen then, carrying a pail and a stack of rags. "Here are the cleaning supplies you asked for, Miss Clarinda. The broom and dust pan are just off the kitchen. Will you want one of the girls to come with you?"

"No, thank you, Adele. This is something I want to do myself."

"What about water?"

"I'm sure the soldiers at the old house have some I can use."

"Very well." Adele looked at Clarinda. "You're sure you won't need help?"

Dorothy remarked, "Of course not, Mrs. Royce. My granddaughter's going to have to get used to this kind of work if she expects to have any kind of a future with your son." Turning back to Clarinda, who, at that moment, resembled Jack at his angriest, she added, "Think about it, girl, before you do something rash."

"Believe me, Grandmother, I have." Clarinda stormed out of the kitchen.

* * *

Sitting in one of the ladderback rockers on the porch, Bronstein saw Clarinda make her way around the corner of the house and head for the path into the woods. "Fräulein Matthias," he called out, "may I speak with you one moment?"

She stopped and waited as he lumbered down the stairs and joined her. "How can I help you, Your Excellency?"

"I see you are preparing to return to the building in the woods. If you will permit me, I would like to arrange an escort for you."

"That isn't necessary, Your Excellency," she giggled. "I'll be perfectly fine."

"An old man's folly, then. Beautiful young ladies should never be allowed to walk in the woods alone. You never know when you may meet a hungry wolf."

"I'm not carrying a basket of good things for my grandmother, but if you insist . . ."

"I do." The count led her toward the stable.

Captain Bauer was surprised by their presence there. "Fräulein Matthias, may I help you?"

"Actually, Bauer, you can help me," Bronstein said. "I have promised the Fräulein an escort to your camp. Do you have someone available?"

"Certainly, Excellency." Signaling to one of his subordinates, the captain relayed the count's request. The skeptical private nodded, then took Clarinda's equipment.

"You know what to do, don't you, Private?" Bronstein asked.

"Of course." With a slight nod and bow, he left the stable with Clarinda.

Bauer turned to Bronstein. "Excellency, has something happened?"

Glowering at him, the count replied, "Yes, Bauer, something has happened. The queen intends to use the little house in the woods tomorrow for her day of fasting and prayer."

"But, Excellency, everything will be accomplished tomorrow morning. Our forces are ready to strike at dawn."

"And the queen does not sleep, especially on *this* night. At first light, she will be out."

"Then she will have a surprise waiting for her when she arrives. I'll take care of the stableboy tonight."

"You fool!" Bronstein spat. "Not before the king is dead; the blame must fall completely on the boy."

"So what are we to do, Excellency? The inactivity has made the squad restless."

"As you have already mentioned. Come. Walk with me." The two men headed out of the stable and down the broad lane, away from the house.

\* \* \*

Returning from her second visit to the old house that day, Clarinda deposited her broom and dust pan in the mud room off the kitchen before looking for the queen, finding her in the conservatory, sorting strands of embroidery silk. The older woman smiled as the girl, her face streaked with dust, curtseyed. "Your Majesty, the old house should be ready for you tomorrow. I didn't realize it was so dirty."

"I am grateful, Fräulein Matthias, but you didn't have to clean it all yourself."

"I wanted to. It kept my mind off . . . other things."

"Frau Royce's son?" The queen laughed a little at the surprised look on Clarinda's face. "It is so obvious, my dear, how much you care for him."

Noticing the pile of white fabric in the other woman's lap, Clarinda asked, "What are you making?"

"It is for my grandson. I, too, need something to occupy my thoughts." She laid out the dress. "Do you like it?"

"It's lovely." A glint of gold caught Clarinda's eye. Wiping her hands on her apron, she asked, "May I hold it? I'll try not to soil it."

"Certainly. And do not worry about the dirt. It will be laundered before I give it to him."

Taking the offered garment, Clarinda ran her fingers lightly over the nearly completed design that adorned the bodice. The silver-dollar sized medallions of embroidery felt so familiar she gasped, but when she examined one of them, she realized she had been mistaken. "Oh. It's an 'F.'"

"My grandson's name is Ferdinand. The design is his cipher."

"He's just a baby, isn't he?"

"About eighteen months old. But all princes of the house of Ahrweiler receive a cipher at birth, just in case."

"In case of what?"

"If the ruling monarch dies, it legitimizes their right to the throne."

"Only your family has ciphers?"

"Any member of the nobility may have a coat of arms, but only the king and his heir are entitled to display the crown." She pointed to the design on the dress. "See? Here."

Clarinda glanced again at the small circle, seeing the tiny crown topping the letters. "Your Majesty, forgive me for prying, but who was your husband's heir before your grandson?"

The older woman sighed. "My son. Before we left Ahrweiler, my husband named Ferdinand his successor, even though I pleaded with him not to press the matter."

"Why?"

"Oh, I understand why it needed to be done, and in my head, I accept it, but here . . ." She put her hand on her breast and, looking past Clarinda, focused on a Boston fern swaying on a wall bracket. "So hard we tried, my father and I, to keep my little son alive."

"Isn't he dead?"

"It is believed so, because, shortly after my little boy's disappearance, a gutted cottage was discovered about an hour from the castle. Inside . . . the soldiers found objects indicating he had been there, but not his body. My father rejected the official ruling that the baby died in the fire and refused to support a change in the succession, even after my oldest daughter married Bronstein's son and Ferdinand was born. Now my father is dead, and Bronstein has had his way regarding the succession."

"But if everyone else thought—"

"In my country, Fräulein, my husband's heir can be named only by a unanimous vote of the Grand Council. My father's steadfastness in not agreeing to a change . . . The only thing keeping my baby alive to our subjects, and now, even that is gone."

Clarinda had never seen such profound anguish as she did in the queen's dark brown eyes. Quietly, she left the conservatory and ran to her room.

Taking out the blanket, she reexamined the embroidery. The queen had called it a cipher, the mark of a prince. She traced it over and over, her fingers stopping on the crown. "She said only the king and his heir have the crown," Clarinda whispered. "The king's son." Suddenly, a surge of heat shot up her spine, stopping at the base of her skull, and her eyes widened. She knew beyond a doubt that this blanket, the one Richard had found in Adele Royce's trunk, had once belonged to the missing prince of Ahrweiler, for it bore his cipher.

# *Chapter* 10

As soon as she could begin to think clearly, Clarinda looked over the fabric. There had to be a rational explanation for how Adele happened to have an item which came from Ahrweiler, when she and Joseph were from a place nowhere near it, and why she had kept it hidden until Richard found it. "Perhaps they bought it somewhere after the prince's death," she wondered aloud, for the blanket showed no sign of scorching or burns, but the queen's denial of her child's demise made that option seem unlikely. "She would never have disposed of his things because she expected . . . expects him to return. Then, how—?"

Walking over to the window, Clarinda spotted Bronstein heading into the woods behind the stable. "He never goes out in the afternoon," she muttered. "It's too hot." Shaking her head, she turned back, but the sight of the count jogged her memory, and she remembered the covert glances between him and Adele the week before. Suddenly, the girl realized that Adele did know Bronstein, and more than just casually. "So you're not from Austria or Switzerland, Adele, and the village you and Joseph lived in was in Ahrweiler. But where did you get this?" Clarinda shook the blanket at an invisible opponent.

A moment later, she had an answer. Adele and Joseph had discovered the cottage where the prince was and taken the blanket for their own child. But why just the blanket, and why wasn't it damaged by the fire?

*Richard's a foundling. Mama and Papa got him twenty years ago.* Patsy's words cut through the questions swirling in Clarinda's mind.

*They got Richard the same time the queen's son disappeared, she reasoned. That means they were possibly the last people to see the prince alive and left him to die in that place, or —*

"Clarinda?"

She turned abruptly. "Grandfather? What is it?"

"Your grandmother and I have been speaking about your behavior as of late."

"I shouldn't have argued with her earlier, but she keeps interfering, and it makes me look incapable."

"It wasn't about dinner, sweetheart, and to tell the truth. I'm glad you finally put her in her place about that. It's been a long time coming . . . Clarinda, what did I say to upset you?" for she had begun to weep.

"It's . . . nothing, Grandfather. I'll be all right in a minute."

"We've been discussing your obsession with this servant. It isn't healthy, and that you refused to tell us of it disturbs me a great deal."

"Maybe I thought you and Grandmother wouldn't understand. No, that's not fair. I haven't been able to tell you. After all" — she laughed a little — "it's something one just doesn't blurt out over tea: 'Grandmother and Grandfather, I'm planning on marrying Uncle Jack's butler.'"

Charles Franklin smiled. Then his sides began to shake. "How do you think your mother told us about your father? Of course, with her, it was a *fait accompli*. She and Ralph had already come to an understanding, and if I recall correctly, your grandmother spilled three cups of tea that afternoon. But that's not what I wanted to talk to you about. We think it would be a good idea if you came back to Philadelphia with us tomorrow."

"Tomorrow? I-I can't."

"Clarinda, you aren't going to get over this by staying here."

"But Uncle Jack--"

"I've spoken to him already. He thinks some time away from Landfield right now would be good for you."

"How long?"

"For the summer."

"The whole summer in Philadelphia?"

"No, just a few weeks here and there. For the rest, we could go to the mountains, or perhaps you would prefer the seashore. We have friends at either place."

"Friends with proper sons or grandsons to take my thoughts away from Richard. After all, with everything *they* would have to offer me, how could I continue to seriously consider a servant suitable? Or have you arranged with Arthur to 'conveniently' meet us?"

"What has Mr. Jamison to do with this?"

"Apparently, he's spoken to Uncle Jack about him and me."

"You are doing your grandmother and myself an injustice, Clarinda. You accused your grandmother earlier of narrow-mindedness. Isn't that what you're doing? Coloring every suggestion we make for your welfare with what you believe are our secret motives? We love you, dear. All we want is what is best for you."

"And you think Richard's unsuitable."

"I've never met him, so it would be difficult to judge."

"Then trust me."

"But you are very young and, don't take this in the wrong way, susceptible to being misled by your feelings. You may be absolutely correct in your relationship with this young man. All I'm asking is that you allow yourself the time to know."

She looked at him, tears shimmering in her eyes. "Do I have to go?"

"You and your grandmother need to restore your relationship. She has been terribly hurt by what she considers your rebellious and antagonistic attitude toward her, and

I know you feel that she doesn't care about you, which, by the way, couldn't be further from the truth." Charles took the girl in his arms and kissed her. "Think about what I've said, sweetheart. You never know when it will be too late to mend fences."

She turned her face up to his. "If I promise to come to Philadelphia, could I please stay here until after Uncle Jack's visitors leave? After all, it wouldn't do to neglect my duties as hostess."

Charles let out a loud guffaw. "I think your grandmother can be persuaded to agree to that."

"Thank you." Joining in his laughter, she led him to the bedroom door.

\* \* \*

Waiting in the downstairs room of the tiny building, Bronstein noticed the thoroughness of the job Clarinda had done in preparing it for the queen. "It is too bad the Fräulein's efforts are for naught," he said. "When this night is over . . ."

Footsteps echoing on the stones behind him brought an end to his contemplations. "Leave us," he said to Sergeant Vogel, before turning his attention to Richard, who stood near the window, rubbing his wrists.

"The heat's broken," the boy said quietly.

"It will make things much easier." Bronstein chuckled, seeing the confusion on Richard's face. "Surely, you didn't think I kept you here just so I could release you."

"I didn't know what was going to happen to me."

"Well, you need not wonder any longer. Tonight, I will make it appear that you have murdered the king of Ahrweiler."

"Murder the *king*? Me?"

"That shall be what the local authorities and the Grand Council of Ahrweiler will conclude."

"But . . . what reason would I have for killing him? I've never met him."

"You've done many irrational things lately." Again, Bronstein saw the denial in the other man's eyes. "I see. You believe seducing your employer's niece is normal. Stealing my jewelry is normal. Disappearing for three days is normal."

"I . . . didn't."

"But everyone thinks you did." Bronstein laughed again. "Herr Matthias even had the local constable here for two days looking for you. It will not stretch their imaginations to surmise you are a murderer as well since you will not be around to tell anyone differently."

"I'm going to be killed too?"

"After you shot the king, they will determine you returned to your senses, and unable to face what you did, you hanged yourself. Simple, no?"

Richard stared out the window. "Why me? I've done nothing to you."

"This is true. And you do deserve an explanation." The count snickered. "Unfortunately, you will not be getting one." Heading for the door, he looked one last time at the tall, dark-haired man in the stained clothes. "*Auf wiedersehen, mein Herr. Requiescat in pace* (Rest in peace)." He bowed and left the building.

\* \* \*

Clarinda sat at the piano, reviewing some vocal pieces which had been left on the music holder, while a breeze ruffled the sheer curtains at the open windows. There was a feeling of congeniality which had been missing since Monday, as if the rain earlier had done more than just clear the outside air. She smiled at Arthur, who crossed the room with a glass of sherry.

"I see you found the duets, Clarinda."

"It was hard not to." Accepting the glass from him, she added, "I hope there are no resentments about this morning."

"I'd be lying if I said there weren't, but at least you've been honest with me." He stood behind her, laying his hands on her shoulders. "I hear you're going to Philadelphia soon."

"In two weeks. How did you know?"

"Old lady Franklin's been boring everyone this evening with the announcement." Spotting the slight reproach in Clarinda's eyes, he whispered, "I know she's your grandmother, but she certainly is tedious."

"Arthur, I'm trying to be on good terms with her."

"Will you play the duets later?"

"Only if you'll help me sing them."

The look in his eyes betrayed his elation. "I was hoping you'd ask. And you'll write me when you're away?"

"If you wish."

"I do, my dear. Very much."

She began feeling uneasy, and rose. "I-I don't think Uncle Jack would want me to ignore the count, Arthur, so if you will excuse me . . ." Slipping out of his grasp, she made her way over to Bronstein.

A few minutes before seven, Jack entered with the royal couple. The queen drew stares from everyone, for her clothes and hair were of an earlier fashion and she wore a magnificent diamond tiara. *She almost looks happy,* Clarinda thought, as the older woman stood next to the black marble fireplace, her husband and Jack beside her. The count, however, was not so generous.

"Was this necessary, Your Majesty?"

The queen glared at him. "Tomorrow is my son's birthday, and I shall celebrate it the way I always have."

"Not always," Jack heard the king murmur.

"You silly woman," Bronstein jeered. "You think that by dressing up in your ancient gowns and saying your prayers, you will bring back the dead?"

"Bronstein!" the king growled. "I thought I made my position clear this morning." Embracing the queen, who had started to tremble, he whispered, "You look lovely, Marta," and began stroking her cheek.

She clung to him. "Am I being foolish, Johann? I just want my baby to know me."

"Oh, darling." The queen's body shuddered against her husband's. "Of course he will know you. You're his mama. And if it makes you happy to wear your old clothes"—the king glowered at Bronstein—"then I want you to wear them."

But the queen could not be comforted. She ran from the parlor in tears despite the king's pleading to stay and returned to her room. Reentering the parlor, the incensed monarch addressed his prime minister. "I do not appreciate you humiliating my wife in front of our hosts or, for that matter, in front of *anyone*. She is your queen and is due your respect, whatever you may think of her personally."

"And, Your Majesty, do you think I am the only one who questions the queen's sanity?"

"She is grief-stricken, not insane."

"A year or two, yes. But twenty?"

"So you ridicule her attempts to cope with our son's abduction and murder."

Bronstein laughed harshly. "The queen does not cope. She lives in the past, pretending that her little darling is going to toddle in one day, ignoring facts everyone else in Ahrweiler, yourself included, Your Majesty, have accepted for years now. The queen and her father, nothing more than deluded fools."

"That will be enough, Bronstein!"

"Even if by some miracle the prince did escape the fire and had somehow managed to survive, he would be a man, not a child. A twenty-two-year-old man who wouldn't recognize her now if he saw her, no matter what she wore."

"*She* would know!"

They continued arguing in rapid German while Clarinda struggled to get out of her chair. Pieces of conversations were arranging themselves in her mind like letters in a game of Anagrams, revealing an answer so astonishing it had to be true. Running toward the hall, she was stopped by Dorothy. "Where on earth are you going, Clarinda? Dinner's about ready to be served."

"Not now, Grandmother. There's something important—"

"Surely, it can wait until after dinner. This impulsiveness of yours—"

"That woman has been told for twenty years she's believing a lie, when all the time it was the truth, and I think I can prove it."

"What woman? What kind of lunacy is this?" Dorothy frantically waved to Jack.

"It isn't lunacy, Grandmother, it's a miracle."

"As if they happen nowadays." Turning to Jack, who had just joined them, Dorothy commanded, "Talk some sense into your niece, Jack Matthias," then flounced over to her husband.

"What was that all about? I thought you were going to try a little harder to understand her."

"I am, Uncle Jack, but she doesn't know . . . I have to see the queen right away."

"She's very upset at present, honey. It would be inadvisable to disturb her further."

"I know, but I think I can help her."

Jack smiled, knowing he could not stop her, and let her pass.

\* \* \*

Clarinda stood outside the queen's room, the blanket securely under her arm. Ever since that afternoon, when she realized who the blanket's original owner was, something had been niggling at her which—until the argument between the king and Bronstein— she had thought impossible. Now it was the *only* logical solution. Throwing back her shoulders, she knocked on the door.

The door was opened by a woman in a dark blue gown covered with a starched white apron. Looking beyond her, Clarinda could see the queen sitting by the window, clutching a small leather diptych, while tears ran down her face. The maid went to her mistress and said a few words. Surprised, the queen glanced up. "Fräulein Matthias, I did not expect—"

"Your Majesty, may I come in? I have to talk to you."

"I don't think—"

"It's important," the girl insisted.

"Very well."

Clarinda closed the door. After the queen dismissed the domestic, she asked, "What is it, Fräulein?"

Cautiously, the girl asked, "What happened the day your son disappeared?"

The older woman stood by the window and watched the gray clouds drift across the darkening sky. "It was one of the happiest days of my life. I had discovered I was expecting another child, and my husband and I wanted to tell my parents privately before the official announcement was made. So . . . I tucked my little boy into bed and kissed him good night. Two hours later, he was gone." She clutched the draperies. "A week after, two weeks, I don't remember, the soldiers came and told us of the cottage they had found and showed us" — a shudder ran through her — "a little shoe, his rattle . . . a piece of scorched material, from his nightdress. 'Where is my baby?' I screamed. 'I'm sorry, ma'am,' the soldier said. 'We didn't find a body.'"

"Your Majesty, you don't have to continue."

"We had to sit through the inquest, Johann and I. The fire, in the cottage, it had been deliberately set, they said, and the baby — my baby — apparently drugged and left to die there. 'What is your proof,' my father asked, 'since there is no body?' They even questioned me about the articles that were found. 'You do not deny, Your Majesty, that they belonged to your son.' How could I? They were his things.

"It took the Grand Council twenty minutes to declare my son dead.

"A period of mourning was declared, and we all went to the church for a memorial service." The queen hiccoughed. "In the church is a little tomb, an empty tomb, with angels on the top and my son's name carved in the side. But I know he has to be alive somewhere. The people who took him, they couldn't have — not to my baby." She staggered back to the chair and sank into it. "I'm sorry, Fräulein. You had something to say to me?"

Clarinda, who had been listening in shocked silence, came over and knelt down. "Are you going to be all right, Your Majesty? I can call your maid if you need her."

"No, Fräulein. She will just give me something to make me sleep. They all believe I am deranged, even, sometimes, my own husband. All I want is some proof that my little boy is dead, and until I see that, or die myself, I will believe he lives." Taking the woman's hand, Clarinda exhorted, "Please, Your Majesty, don't give up hope. Your son needs you to be strong for him."

Slowly, the queen turned her head, as if seeing Clarinda for the first time. "You sound so certain, Fräulein, almost as if you know what happened."

"Maybe I do," Clarinda said quietly.

Suddenly, the other woman smiled and picked up the diptych from the table beside her. "This is my son. It was painted just before—"

With shaking hands, Clarinda opened it. On one side was a replica of the cipher, surrounded by a singed piece of material: the nightdress, she realized. The other side was an oil portrait of a toddler with curly, dark-brown hair and nearly black eyes, underneath, written in copperplate by a strong feminine hand, the single word *RICHARD*. Tears filled Clarinda's eyes as she saw in the portrait the expression of happiness that she knew so well and was so rarely shown and, without realizing it, exclaimed, "Yes! Yes! Oh, yes!"

"Fräulein?"

"I think—no, I'm certain—that the man I know as Richard Royce is your son."

"Frau Royce's son is *mine*? It is impossible. They are Swiss."

"And before they said they were Swiss, they said they were Austrian. Besides, I'm sure Mrs. Royce knew Count von Bronstein before he came here last week."

"She knew Bronstein? That still doesn't mean she took my baby."

"Perhaps this does." Standing, Clarinda crossed the room and picked up the bundle she had dropped on the chaise longue. "Richard found it in Mrs. Royce's trunk."

The queen stared at the embroidery, then screamed. At once, the door to the bedroom opened and the maid rushed in.

"No, Tilde, I'm all right," the queen said, her voice shaking. "I will not need your services at present."

The maid curtseyed and removed herself.

Clarinda looked at the queen. "I'm sorry, Your Majesty. I didn't mean to—"

"No, Fräulein Matthias, I really am all right," the woman replied tearfully. "It is just a shock, after so many years, to know . . ."

"This is your son's blanket, isn't it?"

"Yes, this is his cipher. You are certain? My little boy is Frau Royce's son?"

"As soon as I saw this"—Clarinda held up the portrait—"I was sure. Of course, he's not a little boy anymore."

"A man. And he is well? He was a good baby, always laughing and smiling. Did he grow up so?"

"I think Mrs. Royce should be the one to tell you about that," Clarinda replied for she was loath to reveal to the queen exactly how her son had grown up.

"Yes. She is the one I must talk to. Fräulein?"

"What, Your Majesty?"

"You love my son, and he must have told you—"

"Told me what?"

"His mama and papa. Did he miss them?"

"Oh, Your Majesty." Clarinda began to weep. "More than you could begin to imagine."

"No, Fräulein. I can."

A knock on the door interrupted their conversation. "Excuse me, ladies," Jack said, entering the room, "but we are waiting for you so we may begin eating."

"I'll be right there, Uncle Jack."

"And you, Your Majesty?"

"May I have a tray sent up, Herr Matthias? I would not be able to face the count again this evening."

"If you wish, ma'am. I'll tell Laura—"

"Ask Frau Royce to bring it." The queen smiled at Clarinda. "We have a great deal to talk about."

The girl returned the smile, then joined her uncle.

\* \* \*

Entering the dining room, Clarinda immediately sensed the earlier tranquility had been replaced by a tension thicker than ever. Everyone, it seemed, was looking at her as she sat at the foot of the long table and waiting. For what, she did not know. Jack signaled to the Ahrweiler footman, who had been pressed into service due to Bernice's continued illness, and as the pea soup was being circulated, the king leaned over to the girl beside him.

"Fräulein Matthias, my wife, she will be all right? Your uncle informed me you had gone to see her."

"I believe she will be now, Your Majesty. She just needs a little time."

"I had hoped the time away from Ahrweiler would be beneficial for her, but it seems her madness . . . especially at this time of year. She can never forget."

"Your Majesty." Clarinda paused briefly, debating whether to tell him what she had told the queen, deciding this was not the place. "I think your wife's melancholy is a thing of the past."

Hearing the conversation, Bronstein looked at the girl. "So she has come to accept the truth at last."

"Yes, Your Excellency, she has."

Bronstein smiled cryptically, then returned to his soup.

"I have always maintained, Your Majesty," Dorothy declared, "that removing oneself from a particularly troublesome *milieu* does wonders. Which, of course, is the reason why my husband and I are taking Clarinda for the summer. She needs to forget about this ridiculous liaison of hers, and she can't do that here."

"Thank you, Dorothy," Jack remarked for he watched Clarinda's face turn scarlet, and the corners of her mouth begin to twitch.

Charles looked over at the girl as well and was shocked by what he saw. Far from being upset, she actually seemed to be laughing silently, a wicked twinkle in her eyes. "You find what Grandmother is saying funny, dear?"

"No, not especially, Grandfather." She took a spoonful of soup.

"What is it, then?"

"Just that" — she suppressed a chuckle — "when Grandmother finds out, I think she'll be changing her song about . . . a lot of things."

Suddenly, the service door opened, and a haggard Bernice entered, holding a screaming Iris by the ear.

"What is the meaning of this, Bernice?" Jack asked.

"I just found this scalawag going through my closet!" She twisted Iris's ear a little tighter.

"Is this the truth, Iris?" demanded Jack.

"I-I weren't stealin' or nothing. Everybody knows Richard's the thief. I were just looking to see if he hid more of his stuff in Miss Lycoming's closet. After all, that would be the obvious place to look."

"That's absurd!" Bernice asserted. "The boy was never in my bedroom."

"Oh, I heard you, Miss Lycoming," Iris went on. "Every night, Richard'd have his supper with you, and you'd be talking real sweet and nice to him. Of course, he's too stupid to know what you was trying to do. He thought you was just being friendly, like Miss Clarinda."

"Mr. Matthias! You cannot believe what this child is implying!"

Jack stood. "Bernice, this is not the place to discuss this. Wait in the kitchen."

"Very well, Mr. Matthias. Come along, Iris." Pulling the girl, they left.

"Ha!" Dorothy exclaimed. "I knew it! This paragon of virtue of yours, Clarinda, is nothing more than a Lothario. You weren't the first of his conquests, and I doubt you would have been the last."

Jack waited at the service door. "Clarinda, shall I handle this, or will you?"

"You, please, Uncle Jack."

"Very well. If you will excuse me, I shouldn't be long."

After Jack left, Clarinda signaled the footman to remove the soup, then addressed her grandmother. "How dare you make judgments when you don't know the facts. Richard would *never* have done the things that Iris accused him of. He couldn't even tell me that he loved me at first."

"Then he is shrewd, Fräulein," Bronstein offered, "just as I have always suspected."

Clarinda stared at him, a sly smile growing. "Your Excellency, I happen to know Richard has loved only two women in his entire life—myself and his mama."

The count blanched and took a swallow of wine, choking slightly. "If you insist, Fräulein, but I fear you are still too young to be any real judge of character."

The arrival of the fish stopped the war of words, but for Clarinda, the evening that had started off so magically had been ruined, and even the sweet courses did nothing to improve her mood.

* * *

As Clarinda and Dorothy were leaving for the parlor, Jack took the girl aside and told her briefly what had taken place in the kitchen, then allowed the ladies to withdraw. Clarinda knew her grandmother's curiosity had been piqued by the exchange, but rather than discuss it at once, she decided to wait for the old woman to broach the subject.

It happened after Lily had brought in the tea. "Your uncle appears to have taken care of his domestic problem."

"Yes, Grandmother, he has."

"And, of course, your stableboy has been exonerated."

"Of course."

"You realize that Bernice should have come to you about her little problem, not your uncle."

"I don't think it was a little problem. She was accusing Iris of stealing or trying to steal. Uncle Jack should have handled it."

Dorothy settled back in her chair, an imperious smile on her face. From experience, the girl knew this meant she was preparing to launch into her favorite topic for discussion, but what the old woman said stunned her.

"What did your uncle do?"

"This evening?"

"Of course this evening."

"He told Joseph to lock Iris in her room without supper, and he sent Bernice back to bed and told her to take a sleeping draught."

"Which, naturally, you were incapable of doing."

"It could have been more serious. We may have had to send for the sheriff again."

"Clarinda, when are you ever going to grow up? You continually neglect your responsibilities to your home and to your set, then wave them off without a thought here or there. And if I were to rely on your correspondence, I would think you hadn't a worry in the world."

"Why should I burden you with my problems? I thought you wanted to hear the good things that were happening to me, not the bad. Which, by the way, are the same things I wrote Uncle Jack."

"So I found out."

"Grandmother, about the letters you got from Bernice and Mary. Who wrote the last one?"

"I find it highly improper of you to be asking such a question. In fact, it borders on bad taste. Whom I receive correspondence from is no business of yours."

"Even though it concerns me?"

"Absolutely. I see no need — "

"But you came here because of it. I read your letter, Grandmother. 'How could you do such and such?' 'You should know better than to?' Five pages of that! Most of the things you criticized me for were taken completely out of context."

"Such as your indulgence in sherry at an inappropriate hour."

"I wasn't *drinking* it. Uncle Jack wanted me to instruct Richard about the wine service since he had never been taught, and as part of that instruction, I asked him for a glass of sherry. All I did was take one sip. Bernice walked in after that and drew the wrong conclusion. I suppose she failed to mention that in her letter."

"I haven't had a letter from Bernice in months."

"Then who?"

"Oh, you're going to find out sooner or later. Laura wrote me two weeks ago, right before they were planning to go to Washington."

"Laura?" The blood began pounding in Clarinda's ears. "She never writes you."

"Which is why I took it so seriously." Dorothy came over to the girl. "If it had been Bernice or Mary, I would have simply written them in return and, possibly, your uncle. But Laura—I had to respond in person. Even your grandfather saw the urgency of it."

"What-what did she say?"

"Mainly that you were spending too much time with the new help, and it was causing you to act capriciously. She didn't think it proper that a male servant, especially a young and handsome one, should be your sole companion. Of course, she was right."

"Laura?" Clarinda still couldn't believe her ears.

"When you were born, your grandfather and I had such high hopes for you. We don't want to see you waste your life with someone who can give you nothing."

Clarinda began to cry. "So you came down here to take me to Philadelphia and teach me how to be a lady like Mother."

"Like your *mother*? Your mother was never a lady."

"But I thought—"

"Apparently, Bernice and I aren't the only ones drawing the wrong conclusions."

"I don't understand. I thought you wanted me to be just like her."

"Why do you think I disapprove when you play and criticize the way you act socially?" Tears began filling the old woman's eyes. "Your mother was the same—carefree, impulsive, totally unconventional. To lose her so young . . . And then, we see the same pattern developing all over again with you. Make you like your mother? Hardly."

"But you loved her."

"Of course we did, girl, and we love you too. It would be better all around if you weren't so much like her, that's all." Regaining her composure, Dorothy kissed Clarinda's cheek, returning to her seat as the men joined them.

Arthur came over at once to Clarinda. Taking her hands, he declared, "I think it's time for some music. After all, you did promise."

She stood and pulled them away. "Not tonight, Arthur. I'm not up to it now."

"What is it, dear?" His arms found their way around her waist.

"Please! Leave me alone—all of you!" Breaking free from his grasp, Clarinda bolted out of the parlor.

* * *

The girl heard a noise coming from the small alcove next to the pantry, the room Mary and Laura called "our parlor," and pushed against the swinging door. Turning, Laura saw her. "Oh! Miss Clarinda, I had no idea you were there."

"Laura," she began, then sat in a chair at the damask-covered table. "Why did you feel it necessary to write my grandmother?"

"She told you. I guessed it was only a matter of time before you found out it was me, the way you've been questioning Mary and Bernice. I thought she should know about—"

"Richard and me."

"Well, yes and no. I mean, everybody below stairs saw what was happening: you spending so much time with him and all, and him always so much happier after he'd be with you. In a way, I was glad Richard was going to Washington. It would give you both a chance to think."

"But he didn't go."

"And that's when I started worrying. You and him alone in this house, without anyone to properly chaperon—"

"Bernice and Mary were here, and so was Adele. Besides, Joseph came back before the rest of you."

"But I didn't know before we left that he would be returning so soon. Then I wouldn't have worried because that boy sure do mind his father."

"So you wrote Grandmother Franklin."

"I thought somebody should know, Miss Clarinda, and Mrs. Franklin said we were to keep an eye on you."

"Why not tell Uncle Jack?"

"I don't rightly know. Maybe I thought he saw it too. But Monday, when you told me what happened—all my worst fears coming to pass and Mr. Matthias not knowing—I was glad I had written Mrs. Franklin, and that she would be here to take care of it."

"How did you know, Laura?"

"In the letter, I told her we'd be in Washington. She sent me a telegram there. So when Joseph came back last week, I gave him a letter for Bernice." Laura looked down at Clarinda, whose face had begun to flush. "I did it because I love you, and I didn't want to see you hurt or make a mistake. I guess I was wrong."

"No, Aunt Laura," Clarinda whispered. "It's just I've felt so betrayed by the people I love the best, that I could never talk freely to them ever again. I didn't know about the letters to Grandmother until Aunt Mary told me." The girl gazed up at the cook. "Was Richard trying to . . . like Iris said he was?"

"With Bernice?" Laura began laughing. "Even if he were, which, by the way he looked at you, I highly doubt, *she* wouldn't even have noticed. Bernice's had her eye on a bigger prize for years."

"You don't mean—" Clarinda joined in the laughter. "She's after Uncle Jack?"

"Well . . . him being a bachelor, but while Mr. Matthias admires Bernice, I don't think he's ever had a single romantic notion about her. In fact, if it weren't for her feelings for him, I'm pretty sure Bernice would have returned to your grandfather's house years ago."

"Poor Bernice," the girl giggled. "No wonder she has migraines."

"No, them she's always had, Miss Clarinda."

Clarinda stood and wrapped her arms around the plump cook. "I'm glad we talked."

"I am too, sweetie."

Smiling, Clarinda quietly withdrew from the alcove.

# *Chapter* 11

---

Downing the remainder of his brandy, Bronstein sat in the front bedroom he occupied, eyeing the dueling pistol lying on the occasional table and listening as the clock in the hall below chimed the hour. "Ten o'clock," he grumbled, "and still the king stays downstairs." At last, the count heard voices echoing in the hall, and he smiled as they moved away from the stairwell. "Just a few moments longer," he breathed, then lifted the candle beside the gun from the table and approached the window.

It was dark, the moon was not rising for several hours, but the count knew Bauer would be waiting by the stable. He raised the taper high and lowered it, repeating the motion a second time, then moved it twice from right to left. Turning away, he returned the candle from where he had taken it, breathing a curse that there wasn't more brandy. "A sober man does not commit murder, only drunkards and madmen," he muttered, before sitting down once more. "You must show patience," he added, for he knew that surprise was essential to the success of his plan. Finally, all was quiet. Bronstein picked up the pistol and stalked down the hall.

\* \* \*

Captain Bauer nodded to the cluster of soldiers around the fire and continued on into the house. As he entered, they began to secure a noose around the branch of a maple, setting a small log below it.

When the door opened, Bauer found Vogel in the lone chair, his rifle trained on Richard, who stood at the window watching the three men preparing the execution site. "It's time?" the sergeant whispered.

"Yes." Bauer glanced at the young man across the tiny room, seeing in the lantern light something disturbing. "You left him untied?"

"Where is he going to go?" Vogel laughed. "Besides, Bronstein wanted him untied."

"We can remove the rope after we've finished." The captain again looked at Richard, who listened uncomprehendingly. "Take care of him. I want to get this over with."

Nodding, the sergeant propped the rifle against the door jamb and picked up the length of rope. *"Mein Herr?"* Richard stiffened and turned toward Vogel.

Fifteen years of soldiering had not prepared Vogel for the look in the other man's eyes. He had seen many men before their deaths, most of them resembling cornered rabbits, others resigned to their fate, but this man . . . There was a determination that astounded the sergeant, and he knew the unsophisticated stableboy was not about to die without a fight. But when Richard almost meekly put his hands out in front of him, Vogel was taken by surprise.

Beginning to coil the rope around Richard's wrists, he was stopped by Bauer. *"Hinter, nicht vor* (Behind, not in front)," the captain barked from the door. As the sergeant started to comply with the order, Richard jerked his arms upward, catching the other man hard under the chin. Vogel staggered, dazed, and Richard slammed him into Bauer, who had started crossing the room. The two men fell back into the door. Richard stripped off the rope and, covering his face with his arms, hurled himself through the window.

He lay amid the broken shards of glass for a second, knowing that he had to move quickly. As he pulled himself to his feet, he saw one of the soldiers looking toward him, and he could hear movement from inside. He ran toward the clearing.

The door flew open, and the two men rushed out, weapons drawn. Bauer, seeing the rapidly moving figure, shouted, "*Achtung! Achtung!*" and discharged his pistol. The night immediately erupted with gunfire, bullets flying in all directions as Richard wove, trying to avoid being hit. He fell but staggered to his feet and began running again, only to fall a second time. The captain gave the order to stop shooting, until, incredibly, Richard stood up. Another round was unleashed into the darkness; a loud shriek from the woods ended the barrage. Bauer waited a minute. When no further movement occurred, he regrouped the squad, and the five men began searching the underbrush with torches fashioned out of broken tree limbs and the remains of the chintz curtains smeared with grease.

* * *

Reaching the king's door, Bronstein heard a noise behind him. "Excellency! Wait!"

Spinning around, he saw his valet rushing toward him, arms waving frantically. "Be quiet!" the count whispered angrily. "Do you want the king to know—"

"Shots, Excellency," the man gasped, "from the woods."

Bronstein flushed, then blanched. "Are you certain?"

"Yes."

"Damn." Gunfire could only mean that the boy had resisted or, worse, escaped. "When?"

"Just now, Excellency."

"Single shots?"

"No, Excellency. Rifle and pistol."

"Escape." Bronstein was barely aware he had spoken.

Doors opened, and the hall filled with people. Dorothy Franklin, her white hair in disarray, pounced on Jack. "It's Indians! I know it! They're going to kill us all!"

"Will you calm down, Dotty?" her husband argued. "There haven't been Indian raids here since . . ." He looked at Jack, who shrugged his shoulders.

"Calm *down*? There are rampaging, murderous *savages* out there, with *rifles*!"

"Nonsense," Bronstein answered, saying anything to try and shut the old lady up. "The king's soldiers are in the woods. If your savages *were* rampaging, I am sure they would be able to take care of them."

"Then what were the soldiers firing at?" Jack posed.

The king appeared at his door. "What on earth is going on, Bronstein?" he demanded. "When I authorized maneuvers, I did not expect my sleep to be disturbed by them."

"Captain Bauer has not informed me of plans for any night action, Your Majesty."

"Find out what the trouble is and put an end to it." The monarch motioned to Jack. "When you have things back in order out here, I would like to see you."

"Of course, sir." The door slammed shut.

Jack addressed Charles Franklin. "Take Dorothy back to her room, Charles, and if I may so advise, give her some laudanum."

The older man nodded, then slipped his arm around his wife's shoulders. "Come back to bed, dear. I'll pour you a cordial, and you'll soon forget about this."

"Oh, very well, Charles," she huffed. "But I still maintain it's Indians."

After they left, Jack turned his attention to Clarinda, who had been standing at the end of the hall. "I think you should return to bed also, honey."

"Uncle Jack?"

"What?"

"Does this have anything to do with . . . you know, why the king is here?"

Jack glanced at Bronstein, who was storming back toward the stairs. "I don't know."

"If you need me to help—"

"I just want you to be safe. Go back to bed."

"You're sure?"

"If I need you, I'll come get you, all right?" She nodded. "Good." Jack kissed her cheek and took her to her room.

A few minutes later, Jack entered the king's bedroom. The monarch stood by the window, peering out through the drapery. "Can you see anything, sir?" Jack asked.

The other man turned toward his host. "No, but the shooting's stopped." The king sat down and rubbed his beard. "Whatever it was, it may have just saved my life."

"Your Majesty?"

"Bronstein has a pistol."

Jack joined his guest. "Get your wife and meet me at the end of the hall in ten minutes."

"Of course."

* * *

Sitting on the bed, Jack took Clarinda's hand. "Honey, you said you wanted to help me."

"Yes, Uncle Jack. What is it?"

"I need you to go to the servants' quarters and tell Joseph to wait for me on the back stairs. I'll be there shortly."

"Joseph? Uncle Jack, he's a kidnapper and . . . and other things. You can't—"

"Honey." He grasped her shoulders. "I don't have the time now to explain. Just do what I've asked."

"All right." Throwing back the coverlet, she reached for the candlestick on the stand beside the bed.

Jack seized her wrist. "I'm sorry. No lights."

"But—"

"Clarinda, it is imperative that no one knows you are downstairs."

"Uncle Jack? Why not?"

"Sweetheart . . ." He hesitated a moment. "For your own sake . . . please, just do what I've asked."

"Can I take the back stairs?"

Once more, he hesitated, but time was of the essence. "All right, honey, but just going to the Royces' bedroom. When you return here—and do so as soon as you've spoken to Joseph—you *must* take the hall stairs. And keep your door shut. Whatever happens, stay in your room."

"I will."

"Good girl." Tying the sash on her blue wrapper, he added reassuringly, "Everything will be fine."

She nodded, then Jack walked her to the stairs.

The door opened almost before Clarinda knocked. "Miss Clarinda," Adele said, "what—"

"My uncle wants Joseph to meet him on the back stairs." In the dim light in the bedroom, the girl could see Joseph pulling on his shoes.

"We heard the gunfire. Joseph figured he'd better be ready."

He came over. "Where on the stairs, Miss Clarinda?"

"Uncle Jack said the back stairs. I don't know exactly where." The girl saw the curve of a pistol butt protruding above his belt.

Joseph patted it. "It's been a long time since I used her. I hope I remember how."

Adele smiled, but Clarinda noticed the slight glistening of her eyes. "Of course you'll remember. A good soldier never forgets, and you were one of the best."

"I gotta get goin'." Caressing Adele's cheeks, he whispered, "*Ich liebe dich*," and made his way to the stairwell.

"God protect you, my Joseph," Adele murmured, then turned to reenter the bedroom.

"Mrs. Royce?"

"What is it, Miss Clarinda?"

"It is true about Richard, isn't it?"

"Yes." The woman sighed a little. "The queen told me you were the one who found us out. How did you guess our secret?"

"It wasn't too hard to see he wasn't your child, but that he was the queen's son . . . I only figured that out this evening."

"'*Sie sind nicht meine Mutter.*' He was five years old when he told me that—the last thing he ever said in German, at least consciously. I was so sure Richard would forget his home, that Joseph and I, well, I would become his parent. He was such a little boy, and he had such a huge hate, right from the very first day."

"Richard? Hateful?"

"He don't show it like others, Miss Clarinda, but it's there, buried deep inside him like the tears he never cries. '*Sie sind nicht meine Mutter.*' When he said that, that's when I saw the hate, and I knew it was hopeless."

"But you kept him. Why?"

"I couldn't send him back, not to what was waiting for him."

"A loving mother and father who thought he was dead? They would have—"

"If Joseph and I had sent him back, and you do not know how many times Richard begged us to do so, he would be dead. Count von Bronstein would not have allowed him to live."

"The count? What has he got to do—"

"Everything, Miss Clarinda. Why do you think Richard's missing?"

"I thought Joseph made him leave, putting him in his place for—"

"My husband would never have sent him away, and Richard wouldn't have dared leave on his own." Adele paused, wiping her eyes with the thin challis shawl draped about her shoulders. "This evening, when Laura told me the queen wished to see me, I was so afraid she would be angry when she found out the truth, but she just sighed and questioned me about what he is like. Twenty years in an hour. I hope I did Richard justice. Of course, I couldn't tell her everything, how Joseph . . ." She paused again to dab away tears. "That's for Richard to tell her, if he chooses. I only hope that . . ." She turned from Clarinda, completely overcome by her emotions.

Clarinda stared at Adele, trying to comprehend everything the woman had just told her. Events of the past week flashed in sharp relief through her mind, and she saw for the first time the danger Jack had only alluded to. Recalling Jack's admonition a few moments earlier, she tugged on Adele's sleeve. "Mrs. Royce, my uncle wants me back upstairs. Would you take me to the kitchen? I didn't bring a candle."

"I'm sorry, Miss Clarinda. What did you want?"

"I'd like to go back to my room."

"There's a door from the stairs—"

"I can't use them. I have to go through the house."

"Of course, Miss Clarinda." They headed down the dark, narrow hall.

* * *

Richard lay in the thick underbrush, catching his breath. He was barely aware of the pain in his right ankle, or of the caked mud and blood that covered his arms. All he knew was that, for the moment, he was safe.

Suddenly, he heard them—voices, first to the left of him, then the right, but he recognized only Bronstein's. Crouching lower, he forced himself to breathe more slowly, afraid a gasp would be detected. A moment more; the voices began moving toward the clearing, away from him. He raised his head and looked for the torches his captors were using, but all was dark. Then he exhaled and, filling his lungs with clean, rain-damp air, began searching for something he recognized.

An owl hooted, and Richard heard the flutter of wings as it moved to another tree. In his weakened condition, he had no idea how long he had been crawling silently through the woods—minutes, hours—but his mission remained as clear to him as ever. Since the late afternoon, when the count had told him of his fate, Richard determined that if he was to die this night, it would not be the coward's death, but the hero's, attempting to save the king of Ahrweiler from certain assassination. All Richard had to do was figure out where he was.

There was a different sound in the mist, the nickers and whinnies of horses at rest, and he smiled. Spotting the cupola atop the stable, he continued on toward the side of the white wooden building, praying he wasn't too late.

He reached the paddock, only to discover a new obstacle. A soldier was patrolling the porch, scanning the drive, and although he couldn't be sure, Richard guessed there were others. The voices started getting closer again and it was only a matter of time before someone would find him. He had to get into the house, but with the soldiers . . .

The impatient stamps and neighs of one of the horses caught Richard's attention, giving him an idea. He limped over to the gate and unlatched it, then picked up a small stone and threw it at the chestnut gelding's withers. The animal reared and charged out, followed by three more. Immediately, the man on the porch spotted them galloping free and shouted, *"Die Pferde!"* as he ran after them. When no one else joined him, Richard assumed the other soldiers had not heard the shouts, that they were in the rear of the building. Moving as fast as he could on his swollen ankle, he crossed the yard and, entering the garden, crept around to the side of the gazebo.

He pushed against an old oak door, the hinges, rusty from years of disuse, groaning on their bolts. Quickly slipping into the darkness behind it, Richard waited, listening for the expected footsteps. When, after a minute, there was nothing but the sound of crickets, he let out his breath, then began groping his way down the slimy brick walls.

During those first weeks at Landfield, before Clarinda's return gave him a reason for staying, Richard had often thought of the old service tunnel as his means of escape from Joseph's tyranny. It was *his* secret, discovered one afternoon when Mr. Matthias was in Washington and Joseph was getting supplies in Oak Store. He had almost missed the entrance at first—thick ivy and brambles had grown up around the doorway, the garden reterraced after the old kitchen's demolition. But the tunnel remained and was, as best as Richard could determine, still sound.

He reached a right angle, but in the total darkness, he failed to see it and walked into the wall. Reeling from the impact, he felt his knees buckle, the food he had eaten earlier turning his stomach. It would be so easy, he thought, just to give in to the nausea and the lightheadedness, to wait for one of Bronstein's soldiers to find him. "No," he whispered, "I can't do it." He slowly raised himself up off the earthen floor and once more moved forward.

From the turn, it was only another thirty feet to a second door. Pulling off the layer of cobwebs blanketing it, Richard took the knob with shaking hands, praying that it wasn't locked or boarded over. When a shaft of light pierced through the crack in the door, Richard almost wept with relief. Bending slightly, he stepped into the alcove by the pantry.

Arthur was sitting at the table, a half-empty bottle of whiskey at his elbow. "Well, well. The stableboy," he mumbled, observing Richard through bleary eyes. "Coming back to steal some food?"

"Mr. Jamison, do you know where the king is? I have to—"

"She loves you, you know. Don't know why, but she does." Staggering to his feet, the attaché took hold of the other man's arm. "If you know what's best for her, you'll disappear for good." He giggled. "Maybe you're not here after all."

"Never mind," Richard said contemptuously, pushing him back into his chair. "I'll find the king on my own." He backed out through the swinging door and, quiet as a cat, made his way up the kitchen stairs.

\* \* \*

The flickering lights guided the group of men to the clearing. Surrounded by loyalists, Bronstein tried to think of a way to divert them so he could return to the house. Captain Bauer, shocked to see the count, approached him.

"Captain, the king demands this disturbance be stopped at once," Bronstein bellowed.

"The *king*?"

"Yes, Captain, the king. He wants to know, as do I, what happened here this evening."

Bauer's mouth dropped open. There was no story other than the truth, and to divulge that to the king's soldiers was out of the question.

"Well? I am waiting."

"Excellency, Sergeant Vogel's squad and I were discussing our upcoming maneuvers when we heard a noise in the woods. We investigated and, although we couldn't see clearly, it appeared to be Herr Matthias's stableboy. I fired into the air to stop him, but he shot back. Then the squad opened fire."

"Is he dead?"

"I don't know, Excellency. He disappeared into the woods."

"I see." Suddenly, Bronstein had an inspiration. "The stableboy was armed?"

"Yes," Bauer replied hesitantly.

"That can mean only one thing—he means to murder the king. Which direction did you say he went?"

Bauer caught the count's train of thought. "He entered the woods there," he answered, pointing to a spot near the house. "After that, he could have gone anywhere. We have been able to search only the area surrounding the building."

"Well, then, I think the best strategy would be to have the soldiers spread out and search the woods. That man must not get near the house."

Bauer called Vogel over. "Sergeant, take charge of the detail."

"*Ja wohl, Herr Rittmeister.*" Saluting, Vogel began to dispatch the king's guards, making sure they were sent in the opposite direction from where Richard had actually entered the forest.

Bronstein pulled Bauer aside. "What *really* happened?"

"He escaped."

"*How?*"

"Vogel was preparing him for execution. He struck the sergeant, then crashed through the window."

"*You* should have been making sure my orders were carried out!"

"And I trust my men, Excellency, particularly Vogel." They walked away from the house. "He ran in here. He may have been shot; we heard a scream."

"So he could be dead."

"Or wounded."

Bronstein smiled. "Then leave him to the soldiers. We have more important matters to attend to. You positioned men near the house?"

"Just as you commanded, Excellency."

"One more thing; give me your revolver."

"Excellency?"

Bronstein held up the dueling pistol. "The king saw me with this earlier, and he will be expecting me to return. Surprise is no longer possible. Therefore, I must make sure he is dead."

"Personally, I would trust the weapon you have over mine."

"And if I need more than one shot?" The captain handed over his gun, then signaled Vogel to muster his squad.

Returning to the path, Bronstein declared, "I have waited long enough."

# *Chapter* 12

Clarinda entered the dining room, still absorbed in Laura's gossip. "Bernice and Uncle Jack?" she said out loud, and a smile spread across her face. A beam of light from the butler's pantry reflected off the polished silver plate in the center of the table, making it simple for her to maneuver around the room. *The rest of the way should be easy,* she thought; out the door, turn left, then up the stairs.

She stood there, increasingly aware of the eerie silence of the house, and her mood suddenly changed. She felt for the wall, the well-known hall unfamiliar in the darkness, and she wished anew she had brought a candle.

Soon, however, she was able to make out shapes—the table with its vase of roses, the tall clock between the library and parlor. Groping her way around furniture, she spied the banister. She ran toward it, but the sound of the front door opening behind her stopped her in her tracks. She thought it was the wind at first, then smiled when a man crossed the portal. "Uncle Jack," she began, "I didn't think you'd go outside, not when you told me—"

A deep rumbling laugh froze the rest of the words in her throat. "And just what did your uncle tell you, Fräulein?" Bronstein asked. "Where he is hiding the king, perhaps?"

"No-no, Your Excellency. He told me to go back to bed."

Seizing her arm, the count laughed again. "Of course he did, my dear. Surely, you don't believe I am *that* naive."

"I'm not a liar, Your—"

"Then what are you doing down here, in the dark?"

"I'm checking the house. Our housekeeper is indisposed, if you recall. Which is why I was surprised my uncle would be outside since he wanted me to lock the doors."

Bronstein reflected a moment. It was plausible the girl was only carrying out her domestic obligations, that she was indeed unaware of his conspiracy. But her remarks at dinner belied her innocence. She knew who the boy was and had most certainly told the queen. It did not strain his imagination to presume she had informed others as well, which made her a dangerous liability. But he had always been one to turn his disadvantages to his favor. "My dear, you can't expect me to believe that feeble excuse."

"It's not an—"

He grabbed her by the hair and pulled, snapping her head back. "Do not play me for a fool. You know everything, don't you, Fräulein?"

The terrified girl shook her head, but he wasn't satisfied. "What has your uncle told you?"

"He hasn't . . ."

The count tightened his hold. "He trusts you. Of course he has told you what he and the king were doing in secret all those hours. Answer my question!"

"He wouldn't tell me. He said it was better I didn't know."

"Then why are you wandering around in the dark, if it isn't to help your uncle protect the king?"

"I already told you," Clarinda cried. "Uncle Jack asked me—"

The dull *thud* of a door closing in the rear of the house captured the count's attention. He pressed the muzzle of the revolver against Clarinda's ribs and, covering her mouth with his other hand, whispered harshly, "One sound, Fräulein Matthias, and it will be your last. *Verstehen Sie?*" Feeling the girl nod, he pulled her back into the shadow behind the stairs and waited.

\* \* \*

Jack slipped into the study from the musty chamber behind the bookcases. The king immediately began to follow, but Jack waved him back. Moving to the window, Jack pulled back the heavy drape as far as he dared and, raising the dark lantern in his other hand, stared out into the night, exhaling deeply when he saw nothing out of the ordinary, only the flickering torches in the woods. He quickly released the thick gold corded tieback. After the panel fell straight, he repeated the process with the remaining draperies until the study was completely black. Only then did he open the door on the lantern and allow the king and queen into the room.

"What now, Herr Matthias?" the queen asked, sitting on the horsehair sofa.

"We have to wait, ma'am, for my man. Without firearms, we're completely vulnerable, and I can't barricade the study until he arrives with them."

The solitary rap sent Jack to the door. He rapped back once, and a succession of rapid taps from outside followed — three, one, one, two. Jack opened the door, and Joseph entered with a cache of weapons, which he laid on the desk. "Did you have any trouble finding them?" Jack asked.

"No, Mr. Matthias. They were right where you said." Joseph smiled. "I'da never thought that linen closet was a secret magazine."

Jack turned to the king. "How much experience do you have with a rifle, sir?"

"Mostly recreational, Herr Matthias, but I am a fairly accurate shot."

"Good. Joseph? How about you?"

"Twenty years ago, I was the best marksman in my unit. I ain't been able to keep up my skills, but I'm sure I could still take care of a few traitors." He withdrew his antiquated pistol from his belt and checked the sight.

Satisfied, Jack approached the queen. "Your Majesty, I need you to make sure the guns are always ready to be fired because we will not be able to do it if an assault begins. Can you handle it?"

The woman looked up at her host with eyes that, for the first time in many years, were resolute and unclouded by grief. "Herr Matthias, my father fought Bronstein and his quest for power until the day he died. Now it is my turn to save the crown for my son." Then she went to the desk and, with Joseph's help, loaded the assortment of rifles and pistols with cartridges, while her husband and Jack began stacking chairs against the door.

* * *

Footsteps clicked on the polished oak floors. Bronstein laughed softly, his grasp on Clarinda's mouth relaxing. "It will all be over soon, Fräulein," he whispered. "My men have entered the house."

"How do you know it isn't the king's soldiers?" the girl challenged.

"Because, my dear, they are busy searching the woods for your stableboy. And when they find him . . ."

Clarinda's mind reeled, the fleeting joy of knowing Richard was at Landfield replaced by an overwhelming sense of doom. "They wouldn't. He's their king's son."

"All they know, Fräulein, is that he is attempting to murder the king, and being the loyal soldiers they are, they will eliminate any threat to the crown. As for the other, the prince died twenty years ago. *That* is what everyone accepts as fact." The count laughed again, a little louder. "The ultimate victory over von Kegel. *My* grandson on the throne, not his."

"You're going to kill the king? That's treason!"

"On the contrary, when I return to Ahrweiler, I shall be proclaimed a hero for having executed the king's assassin, and in gratitude for my service to the state, the Grand Council will name me regent. Then Ahrweiler will know what a *real* king is."

Suddenly, Clarinda comprehended the madness that possessed the count, and the diabolic perfection of his scheme. "You can't believe you're going to get away with this," she declared.

Bronstein's eyes glittered. "But I have, Fräulein. Twenty years ago, when that hovel was found . . . And now—"

Captain Bauer approached them from the front hall. "Excellency, we have secured the premises. The king cannot escape."

"You are certain?"

"I have men at each door; the rest are awaiting your orders."

"*Sehr gut.* Now, Fräulein Matthias," he growled, pulling her face closer to his, "where has your uncle hidden the king?"

"I tell you, I don't know."

Bronstein's lips tightened, and he cocked the hammer of his pistol. "I do not have all night, Fräulein. Where is the secret room?"

"This-this is an old house, Your Excellency. It has many secrets."

Only the heightened excitement in his eyes indicated Bronstein's delight. Finally, he was getting the answer he wanted, the baited question about the hiding place breaking the girl's facade. "And where is this one?" he asked, his voice deadly quiet.

"There's a passage—the priest's hole—from Uncle Jack's room. Jacob said that's what my grandfather called it, but he couldn't tell me why."

"And where does it lead?"

"Somewhere downstairs. Jacob said it was too dangerous for me to play in."

The count kissed her forehead. "Thank you, my dear." He turned to Bauer. "Did you notice anything unusual when you approached the house?"

"The windows in the right rear corner of the house; the drapes were covering them."

CARYL C. BLOCK

Clarinda laughed. "All the downstairs windows have drapes on them, Captain Bauer."

"How many of them are tied back, Fräulein?" the captain demanded.

"All of them."

Bauer addressed the count. "Then the king and Matthias are in that rear room. The drapes are over the windows, not drawn back."

"The study," Bronstein declared in triumph. "Of course. Herr Matthias's sanctum, where he and the king spent all of their time plotting. Come, Bauer!"

"And the girl?"

"For the moment, she remains with us." The count slid an arm around Clarinda's waist. "She may still be of use to me."

* * *

Jack stood by the window. Since the original barrage in the woods, there had been nothing, and he was beginning to wonder if the king was mistaken about the whole thing. *Well, better to be safe than sorry*, he thought, and he stretched back against the wall.

Suddenly, Joseph signaled from the study door. "What is it?" Jack demanded.

"Footsteps in the hall, comin' right toward this room!"

"How on earth? Never mind. Your Majesties, into the passage. This room is no longer safe."

The queen retreated at once, but her husband picked up one of the rifles on the desk and joined Jack. "Herr Matthias, this is not your fight. It is mine. I will not cower in a corner while good men such as yourself and Herr Royce risk your lives."

"Sir, as soon as you made the decision to come here and seek my help, you made your protection my responsibility. But if you insist upon defending yourself, I am in no position to stop you."

"I only wished to force Bronstein's hand, to end this rebellion once and for all. This has been accomplished. What the outcome

194

will be, that, I'm afraid, rests with God." The king positioned himself at the other window.

The first assault came from inside the house. The three men trained their rifles on the locked door, which shook with each blow from the rebels in the hall. Then came the inevitable sound of a pistol discharge followed by splintering wood. "They've shot open the lock, Mr. Matthias," Joseph shouted. "We need to reinforce the barricade."

"We'll have to move the desk; it's the heaviest piece in here."

"Will that stop them, Herr Matthias?"

"It's our only option, Your Majesty. Everything else will give under pressure."

Setting down their weapons, the men began pushing the massive mahogany desk toward the door, the scrape of wood against wood drowning out the sounds from the hall.

A thundering sound from the garden halted their progress. "Crossfire!" Joseph shouted, and the men fell to the floor as a five-pound cannonball crashed through the far window, shattering a large vase before imbedding itself in the wall opposite.

The king stared at the hole in the drape. "I should have guessed they would use artillery."

Joseph nodded. "Small cannon."

"What do you suggest?" Jack asked.

The servant quickly surveyed the situation. "Our only advantage is that we're above the action from outside. Got to take out that piece, then we could concentrate on the door."

"Good." Jack went to the window by the desk and broke the glass, then aimed. His shot was answered by a volley of rifle fire, and he fell back, blood seeping from his shoulder and scalp.

At the sight of his blood, he lost consciousness. Realizing that they were defenseless, Joseph bowed, then addressed the king. "*Mein Herr*, you have to hide. We can no longer prevent Bronstein and his troops from taking the room."

The monarch concurred and, while Joseph dragged Jack behind the bookcases, the king picked up their arsenal and the lantern before closing the entrance.

* * *

The king's bodyguard made his way back to the fire, having found no evidence that anyone had been in those woods beyond the little house. He whistled to Vogel, who was busy in his sector. The other man acknowledged the signal and joined him.

"Vogel, are you sure that he ran in that direction?" he asked.

The sergeant cleared his throat. "I did not see anyone, Dietrich, it was Captain Bauer. He was certain the stableboy went that way."

"Then why are you looking over here?"

"Does it matter where I look?"

"If he means to kill the king, as the count insists, why would he be heading *away* from the house instead of *toward* it?"

"The stableboy works here. If there is another way to the house, he will know it." Dietrich nodded and started back to his men.

A shout from the woods stopped him in his tracks. Drawing his pistol, he turned around while his squad ran from their positions. They joined Vogel, who was heading into a break in the brush.

"What is it?" Dietrich questioned.

"We may have found something." They moved deeper into the woods.

It was a dry brook, four feet deep and three feet wide, which one of the king's soldiers had discovered. Carefully, the two sergeants lowered themselves between the banks. While Vogel questioned the private, Dietrich investigated. In the sputtering light from the torch, he saw a depression in the mud as if someone had slipped and, under a tangle of twisted undergrowth, a flash of white. Retrieving it, he examined the scrap of cloth, quickly recognizing it as the same material Clarinda had found in the stable.

"The Royce boy was here and recently." Dietrich held up the cloth. "The mud's not even dry."

"What do you have, Dietrich?" Vogel inquired.

"Part of his shirt. Fräulein Matthias found a scrap like this in the stable on Tuesday."

Vogel crossed the brook and, along the bank closer to the main house, found the corresponding tracks into the overgrowth. "There. He is heading in that direction, back to the house. It's just as Count von Bronstein said."

"Is it?"

"You're suspicious all of a sudden," Vogel growled.

"It's my job to be suspicious," Dietrich countered.

Another of Dietrich's men came running toward the bank. "Sergeant Dietrich!"

"Be careful, Littauer, there's a gully."

He stopped just short of the edge. Dietrich climbed out of the brook bed and faced his subordinate. "What is it?"

"There appears to be a noose in one of those trees."

"A noose?" Dietrich repeated.

"Made with new rope."

"*Now* do you believe His Excellency, Dietrich?"

"Why the noose?"

A shaken Vogel replied, "The boy is deranged. Why else would he decide to kill himself?"

"What?"

"I meant, kill the king."

Turning back to Littauer, Dietrich ordered, "Show me this noose."

The three men circled the building, coming upon the remains of the broken window. Dietrich started to question the other sergeant about it.

"It's an old building," Vogel said. "Who knows how long that glass has been lying there?"

"Sergeant Dietrich," a soldier who had just joined them said, "there is fresh blood on some of the glass."

"Fresh blood?" Vogel replied. "How ridiculous."

"No, sir, it isn't. See? It hasn't dried in spots."

"Private, I was inside the building all evening. Don't you think I would have some recollection of someone trying to break in?"

"But, Sergeant, wouldn't the glass then be on the inside?"

Dietrich's gaze narrowed, and his blue eyes turned steely. "Yes, Vogel," he snapped, shoving him against the wall. "Perhaps you are lying about everything that occurred tonight. I know where *your* loyalties lie."

Vogel's eyes flickered. "It's a ruse!" Dietrich shouted. "Private, arrest this man. The rest of you, quickly! Back to the house!"

* * *

Catching his breath, Richard paused at the top of the stairs. He had been lucky. He should have encountered some of the soldiers by now, but everything downstairs had been normal. *Too normal*, his mind whispered. "Then I still have a chance," he murmured and, stepping into the hall, started toward the west wing.

A shot of pain from his ankle focused his concentration. The king and queen had been given one of the two three-room suites in the west wing, but he didn't recall which side of the hallway it was on. He stared a long time at the twin sets of doors, one on the right, the other on the left, then, limping across the corridor, entered one of the apartments, relieved to find it occupied.

But Dorothy Franklin lay on the chaise longue, a damp cloth on her forehead. She became increasingly aware of an odor in the room and muttered, "How many times do I have to tell that girl not to put us near the necessary in the summer?" Sitting up, she turned toward the door.

Gawking at the disheveled, white-haired woman, Richard quickly remembered himself and bowed. "Your Majesty," he began, only to have the woman scream, "Charles! *Charles*! There's one of those filthy savages right *here*! In my room! *Charles*!"

Richard didn't wait for the unknown Charles to appear. He ran out of the suite and into the one directly opposite. Waiting until his eyes adjusted to the dim light, he crossed to the connecting door, the one he knew led to the king's bedroom and, shaking slightly, knocked.

When there was no response, Richard said, loud enough to be heard through the oak portal, "Your Majesty, it's Mr. Matthias's butler. I need to speak to you."

But he heard nothing. Summoning up his courage, he turned the knob and passed through to the next chamber, only to discover it vacant. "Was I wrong?" he wondered, until he spotted the neatly laid out silk dressing gown on the foot of the canopied bed and the half-full glass of water on the nightstand. *So,* he thought, *someone has already warned the king.*

He turned back toward the connecting door, only to find the way blocked by a small, plump woman wearing a white apron over her immaculate navy blue dress. The ceramic ewer she was holding crashed to the floor as her hands flew to her mouth and she exclaimed, "*Der Kind!*"

Fear paralyzed Richard, and he recalled what Bronstein had gloatingly told him: "*Everyone at Landfield knows exactly what you are.*"

"No, you're wrong!" he shouted back at the maid. "I didn't do anything! He's been spreading lies. *He's* the one going to kill the king, not me! Please, tell me, where is the king?"

But the bewildered Tilde could do nothing but repeat her tearful litany of thanksgiving, which Richard had no way of understanding. Finally, she dared to approach him and, touching his arm, said softly, "*Mein Herr, bleiben Sie hier. Ich muss Berthold finden* (stay here. I must find Berthold)."

"No!" Throwing off the woman's hand, Richard stumbled to the door and, managing to open it, ran down the hall to the back stairs.

He cowered in a corner of the landing, trembling. What had made him think he could be a hero—clumsy, stupid Richard? But then he heard Clarinda saying, *You're neither clumsy nor stupid. You're clever and resourceful, and I'm quite impressed with your abilities,* and her words broke through his doubt. He reminded himself, "Mr. Brown always said there's more than one way to skin a cat. I guess there's more than one way to be a hero too." He started down the stairs, step after agonizing step.

He thought about using the service entrance to return outside, but the sight of the soldier at the door changed his plans. He drew back into the mud room, then limped through the passageway into the kitchen and returned to the pantry alcove where Arthur snored heavily, the sight of the aristocratic attaché resembling the hard-drinking stablehands Richard knew in Baltimore bringing a grim smile to his lips.

He looked for the catch that would open the tunnel door. It swung back on its rusty hinges and taking the candle from the center of the table, Richard disappeared into the darkness.

The journey from the house was more difficult than his earlier trek, even with the illumination. Richard found himself fighting off fatigue and pain with increasing frequency, and when he reached the outer entrance, he ran out into the garden and collapsed on the fieldstone path circling the gazebo. Lying still, he knew his only choice was to reach the stable, where the soldiers had been quartered. "They can't *all* be traitors," he concluded and, one more time, forced his battered body to do the impossible.

He hugged the walls of the summerhouse, partly for protection, but mostly for support, each footfall demanding more of him than the one before it. Finally, the stairs leading to the raised floor came into view. Steeling himself against the pain stretching up his right leg from the ankle, Richard began to run toward the garden gate.

He had taken a dozen steps when the still night erupted with a deafening explosion, followed by an exchange of rifle fire from the far corner of the house. "Have to go back," he mumbled, wondering which way was the quickest, and chose the front door.

He was stumbling through the rose garden, thorns gouging his palms as he tried to steady himself, when a figure emerged from behind the boxwood hedge and he saw the blade of a bayonet pointed at his chest. "Halt!" shouted a young private in German. "Halt or I'll shoot!"

# Chapter 13

The private was quickly joined by the rest of his company, and once more Richard found himself surrounded by men in blue uniforms. This time, however, there was no fight left in him, and raising his arms above his head, he surrendered.

They shoved him through the gate to where Dietrich stood waiting, a sterner than usual expression on his face. "What is the meaning of this?" he demanded. "We do not have time—"

"Sergeant," one of the soldiers declared, "we have captured Matthias's stableboy. He was coming from the house." Richard was pushed forward, further abusing his ankle, and he fell, his face landing on the sergeant's boot.

Two of the men hoisted Richard to his knees, and a third jerked back his head. The sergeant, meanwhile, torch in hand, paced impatiently. Finally, he stopped and, thrusting the flickering light toward his prisoner, snarled, "Herr Royce, did you leave the king alive or dead?"

The expression in Richard's eyes changed from resignation to confusion. Startled, Dietrich approached the boy for closer scrutiny. He knew of only one other person whose eyes reflected emotion so completely as this servant's and, if what he was thinking was true, then it was nothing short of miraculous.

Within a minute, Dietrich knew he was not mistaken. During the past two years, he had spent many hours listening to the queen's rambling memories of her son, her irrational conviction that he still lived. Furthermore, he had often seen her most cherished portraits—the king at the time of his marriage, the little boy. Unless he was now as unbalanced as she, the man before him had to be that child.

Drawing himself erect, Dietrich addressed his men. "This man has done nothing. Take him to a place where he will be safe."

The soldier who had first encountered Richard snickered, "I did not think you could be so lenient on the man who would murder our beloved king, Sergeant Dietrich."

"And you believe what that traitor Bronstein tells you?"

"Why else would he be coming from the house?"

Another one added, "And what if the king is dead? Will *you* swear allegiance to a regime headed by Bronstein?"

Dietrich's face relaxed. "Not while there is another who has a stronger claim to the throne." Handing the torch to the man on his right, he ordered the privates who still flanked Richard to help the young man to his feet.

The bewildered soldiers did as they were bidden. When Richard was finally standing, Dietrich withdrew his long sword and, kneeling before him on the stone drive, recited the Ahrweiler oath of loyalty.

When he finished, Dietrich's men started laughing. "Are you as mad as the queen, Sergeant?" one of them scoffed. "You have just proclaimed this peasant *Stahlknecht* king of Ahrweiler. That's treason, should the Grand Council discover—"

The set of Dietrich's jaw stopped the laughter. "Six months ago, all of us would have done it, Private, by decree of the Grand Council, and we would have considered ourselves fools for doing so." His gaze traveled around the circle of men. "Do you stand with King Johann and his rightful heir, Prince Richard, or the usurper Bronstein?" he asked, adding, a little less forcefully, "We finally have the upper hand in this rebellion, gentlemen. Do we simply discard it because of the improbability of it?"

As one man, the squad responded in the same manner as their leader while an astounded Richard watched. Within minutes, the revitalized loyalists launched their counteroffensive against Bronstein's troops with their battle cry, "By the Grace of God, for Ahrweiler and for Richard!"

\* \* \*

The sentry Bauer had positioned at the front door approached Bronstein, his rifle still trained on his post.

"What is it?" the count snapped.

"Dietrich and his men are returning from the woods, Excellency."

Bronstein smiled and looked down at Clarinda. "You see, my dear? Your precious Richard is no longer a threat to my plans."

"He could have avoided them," she argued, tears beginning to fill her eyes.

"One uneducated man, most likely wounded, eluding a squad of highly trained militia?" Bronstein's laughter declared his opinion of Richard's chances, then he signaled Bauer. "Have the artillery cease fire. I don't want our men accidentally killed when we take the study."

The captain saluted and, dispatching the soldier with him outside, returned to the cluster of soldiers laboring to open the study door.

With each blow, Bronstein's jaw clenched tighter and tighter. "They should have broken through by now," he grumbled. "What is that door made of, anyway? Iron?"

"Something just as good, Your Excellency — Landfield oak," a proud Clarinda retorted.

"Bah! What is the problem, Bauer? I expected a quick end to this."

"They've jammed the doorknob," one of the soldiers replied. "Even with the lock gone, the door won't yield."

"Then shoot it open," the edgy count ordered, knowing every second of delay reduced his chances of total success.

"No, please don't," Clarinda implored, her plea cut short by the rifle blast ripping through the door.

* * *

"What happened?" a dazed Jack muttered, groaning slightly.

"You've been shot, Herr Matthias," the queen replied, who was tending to his shoulder. "Fortunately, your wounds are not serious."

"Hurts like . . . the devil, though." In the dim lantern light, Jack saw the king and Joseph on either side of the entrance, pistols pointed toward it. "Anything new?"

"It's hard to tell, Mr. Matthias," Joseph replied, "bein' difficult to hear through the wall, but I don't think they're in the study yet."

With the queen's assistance, Jack sat up. "There's a peephole just to the left of the door—you can keep watch on the room from it—and a second in the wall to the outside."

"Your ancestor thought of everything," the king said as he and Joseph positioned themselves at the lookouts.

"Well, sir, he needed to know when he could leave." Jack laughed weakly.

Peering through the short, narrow slit in the gray brick facade, which to the casual observer outside appeared to be mortar, the monarch watched the rebel forces, certain of victory, prepare to join their compatriots in the house, only to be stopped by a volley of rifle fire from behind the boxwood hedge. "Thank God," he whispered, "Dietrich has returned."

The queen joined her husband. "Johann?"

"It may not be hopeless after all, my darling. It is now a fair fight between . . ." As the words of his supporters rose from the garden, the king leaned against the back wall, sighing heavily. "They do not forget him either, Marta, our poor little boy."

"No, darling, listen! They are fighting *for* Richard, not in his memory. He lives, Johann! Our son lives!" She turned to Joseph. "Please, Herr Royce, tell my husband. He will not believe me."

Joseph rubbed his nose with his finger. "The queen is right, Your Majesty. My wife and I, we were the ones who took him away from the castle after Bronstein gave him to us."

"*You* took my son?" The king's voice shook with rage. "*Why?*"

"Because of my wife. She was a chambermaid in Bronstein's household, and more, I guess, but she never told me. He said I could have her if we helped him with a problem he had. I wasn't one of the count's spit-lickers, and if I'd have known what he wanted us to do, I'd never have agreed."

The queen said softly, "I knew the people who had my little boy couldn't kill him."

"That was Adele's doing. Otherwise, he'd have been found in that cottage, just like Bronstein planned it." Joseph's face hardened. "Every time I looked at him, I was reminded of my broken vows, first to you, Your Majesty, then to Bronstein."

The sound of splintering wood stopped conversation. Immediately, Joseph resumed watching the study. As he did, they could hear the furniture with which they had barricaded the door being pushed away from it. "They're in," Joseph whispered.

The king started toward the rickety iron ladder on the wall behind him. "Your room, Herr Matthias?"

"Not yet, sir. We haven't been discovered. We're still safe here."

Joseph signaled them that someone had entered the room and, carefully cocking his pistol, leveled it at the catch on the trap door.

It was Bauer. He scanned the study, surprised to find it empty. Clearing the remaining furniture from the doorway, he reported back outside, "*Nicht hier.*" A few seconds later, following a garbled reply, Joseph heard him shout, "*Nein, niemand. Sehen Sie selbst* (No, no one. See for yourself)." With that, Bronstein pushed by the captain, his arm still securely around Clarinda's waist.

Joseph saw no more. Leaving the peephole, he headed for the ladder, only to be restrained by Jack. "Are you indeed a turncoat, Joseph? You swore to me—"

"I'm not going to betray you or the king, Mr. Matthias. I just gotta stop that boy of mine before he does something stupid." Shaking Jack's hand off his leg, Joseph returned upstairs.

"*His* boy?" the king murmured, adding sadly, "Of course, he would feel that way. After all, he did raise him."

"No, sir," Jack reassured his guest. "I would be willing to wager this is the first time Joseph has called Richard his boy and meant it."

\* \* \*

Righting one of the chairs, Bronstein shoved Clarinda into it. "Now, Fräulein Matthias, where is the king?"

"I don't know," she stammered, staring beyond him at the gaping hole in the door.

"We both know your uncle and the king were in here. These chairs did not pile themselves by the door. What did they do? Jump?"

"Maybe."

"Then they are quite dead, I assure you." The count looked over to his men positioned at the windows and, from the shaking of their heads, knew the king had not used them as a means of escape. "Perhaps, Fräulein, they are still in your priest's hole instead." He leaned down to the girl and breathed, "It is only a matter of time before I find their hiding place, my dear. Your silence will not save them."

"But I don't know where it is!" she cried.

Leaving her for a moment, Bronstein confronted Bauer. "Well?"

"There is no way out of here, except through the door or the windows, and we would have known—"

"Then their sanctuary must be somewhere in here. Search for anything that could hide a man."

Clarinda watched in stunned outrage as Bauer and several of his squad began ripping portraits off the walls and punching holes in hundred-year-old plaster, until one of the soldiers cheered from the bookcases, "*Herr Rittmeister*! Over here!"

While the soldiers analyzed the difference in sound between the plaster and wood walls, Bronstein gloated, "So, Fräulein, we have finally found your priest's hole. How very clever of your uncle to conceal it with bookcases." He dragged Clarinda out of the chair. "Now, my dear, *you* will show us how to enter it."

"But I don't—"

Bronstein slapped her hard across the face. "I am tired of your refusal to cooperate. Do what I've told you!"

Clarinda held her hands on her throbbing mouth and cheeks, trying to control her trembling, then stared at the oak stacks, completely ignorant of what she should be looking for. All she had ever been told was, if there was danger, to wait in her uncle's room.

"Let me help you," Bronstein snarled. Walking down the row of bookcases, he swept books off their shelves with his forearm, then grabbing her hand, plunged it into one of the empty spaces. "Now look!"

She began running her fingers over the smooth surfaces of the cabinetwork, finding nothing. The same was true of the next two shelves she examined, but in the fourth, she located the concealed latch. Touching the recessed piece of wood, she hesitated, then continued feeling around the back and sides before moving on to the next shelf.

The sound of gunfire from below drew Bronstein's attention away from the girl. "I thought you told the artillery to cease fire, Bauer!"

Observing the action from the window, the captain replied, "It's the king's men. They're attacking the front of the house!"

"*Quickly*," Bronstein shouted back. "We must declare for Ferdinand."

"But you don't know that the king is dead," Clarinda argued. "Besides, Richard—"

The count slapped her a second time. "Even if, by some miracle, he is still alive, my grandson is the only claimant to the throne the Grand Council will recognize, and to say otherwise is treason."

"Then why is it so important to you that Richard be killed? He doesn't know who he is."

"And if he should find out, Fräulein? What would stop him from challenging me then?"

"I swear. I'll never tell him. Just let him live."

Bronstein gripped her neck and drew her face close to his. "You have already told too many people, Fräulein." Then, the revolver once more pressed into the girl's side, he withdrew with Bauer to the rear of the house, after ordering the rest of the soldiers with him into the skirmish outside.

* * *

A cheer rose from the loyalist forces as they took out the artillery in the garden. Two or three men staggered back to their feet, only to be cut down by a second round of rifle fire. Flushed with victory, the sharpshooters reconnoitered with Dietrich at the front of the house.

The sergeant and the rest of the squad stood around Richard, who knelt on the ground and, in the torchlight, was drawing a large rectangle in the dirt. "*Das Haus, mein Herr?*" Dietrich asked.

"House," Richard repeated, nodding.

"*Wo sind uns* (Where are we)?" Dietrich pointed around to his men.

Quickly, Richard sketched a series of short lines in front of him and, to the right, a circle with an "R" in the middle.

The soldiers laughed as Dietrich squatted down and patted the young man's back. "*Gut, mein Herr. Sehr gut. Haben Sie andern Soldaten gesehen* (Have you seen other soldiers)?"

Richard thought for a moment, then nodded. With the short stick, he pointed to the left rear corner of the rectangle. "Here."

Picking up another twig, Dietrich began drawing x's. "No," Richard said and, wiping away the sergeant's marks, made one single one.

"*Danke, mein Herr.*" Straightening up, Dietrich addressed his men. "It appears there is one sentry at the rear of the building. The rest of the traitors must be inside."

"Meaning?" one of the soldiers asked.

"We either wait for them to come out, or we invade the house."

"Unless Bronstein doesn't know we're here."

"He knows, Littauer. You can bet he knows." Dietrich looked at the scratches in the dirt. "What we need to do is eliminate the sentry in the back, then we can attack on two fronts. How many men does Bronstein have left?"

"Three or four, plus the captain."

"It might be to our advantage to force them outside then, which would enable the rear flank to capture Bronstein and Bauer."

"Capture, Sergeant? Wouldn't it be better to—"

"Bronstein has supporters in Ahrweiler, and I will not have him made a martyr for his uprising. He will meet his fate soon enough."

"But what happens once the rear is secured, Sergeant? We don't know the building."

Dietrich smiled. "Our young friend will go with you. He knows the house, and more importantly, it will keep him out of the line of fire." He leaned down to Richard. *"Mein Herr, können Sie mir helfen?"*

When the only reply he got was a confused shrug, Dietrich tried another tactic. *"Kannst du mir helfen?"*

Immediately, Richard nodded. "Yes, I'll help you."

Taking the stick, the sergeant drew arrows around and inside the rectangle, indicating to the young man what he wanted him to do. Richard studied it briefly, then said, "Okay, sir. I think I got it."

*"Gut."* While his men helped Richard up, Dietrich divided the squad into two groups—the smaller to accompany Richard, the larger to set the ambush on the porch. Then after the rear flank disappeared around the side of the house, the sergeant ordered his two of his riflemen to commence firing.

\* \* \*

It wasn't until they had nearly reached the service entrance that Corporal Littauer, the patrol leader, noticed Richard was lagging behind. Silently halting the three others, he returned to where the young man stood wiping beads of perspiration off his forehead.

"*Was ist los* (What is wrong), *Mein Herr?*"

"It's my ankle, my foot," Richard answered, reading the concern in the other man's voice.

"*Komme. Ich helfe Ihnen* (Come. I'll help you)." Slipping an arm around his waist, the burly soldier braced himself under Richard's shoulder and tensed, relieving the pressure on the young man's ankle. Instinctively, Richard leaned into Littauer, and as fast as Richard could hobble, the two men rejoined the rest of the soldiers.

The corporal wasted no time. He sent two of his men on ahead to eliminate the sentry while the third, a Private Arznei, remained behind. Within minutes, one of the advance guard slipped back around the corner, signaling the all-clear, and with Richard between them, Littauer and Arznei approached the door. "Did you have much trouble?" the corporal asked.

The soldier laughed in reply. "Never heard it coming until it was too late."

"He's dead?" When the soldier nodded, Littauer turned to Arznei. "Don't let him see it, Private," he ordered, tilting his head toward Richard as Arznei shook his head in assent.

But Richard did see the dead soldier, lying just beyond the door in a pool of blood, and he had all to do to keep from retching. He had never seen a corpse, and the knowledge that this one had, just moments before, been as alive as he was almost too much for him to comprehend. Arznei, noticing the change of expression in Richard's face, said, "He would have killed us, *mein Herr*, as quickly as we killed him," and although he couldn't understand the private's words, his concern did much to help Richard overcome the revulsion he was feeling.

Once inside the kitchen, however, Richard realized he had a problem. Up until now, he had been able to communicate with

Dietrich and Littauer on a very elementary level, but to instruct the corporal on how to reach the front hall and, more importantly, which set of stairs to take, that was a different story entirely. *How am I going to tell them I can't help them anymore?* he wondered, when the alcove door swung open, and Arthur Jamison staggered out, the cannon fire having roused him from his drunken sleep.

"What's going on here?" he demanded, his words only slightly slurred.

"*Kennen Sie dieser Mann* (Do you know this man), *mein Herr?*" Littauer asked Richard, eyeing the attaché suspiciously.

"It's Mr. Jamison, Mr. Matthias's assistant," the young man answered, while in rapid German Arthur did the same, giving Richard an idea. "Mr. Jamison, can you tell the soldiers what I'm saying to them?"

"You mean, act as your interpreter? Certainly."

After a brief explanation by Arthur of what he would be doing, they got down to business. Richard quickly described their alternatives, Littauer deciding the more direct route, the stairs to the dining room, was the better option, even though the back stairs did offer the element of surprise. Giving his thanks to the two young men, the corporal directed a statement to Arthur before ordering his men to the stairs.

At once, Richard was on his feet, ignoring the searing pain in his ankle. "Wait! Wait for me!"

The four soldiers turned back as Arthur put a hand on Richard's shoulder. "Sit down, Richard. The corporal wants you to stay here, for your own safety."

"They don't understand. *They* weren't held for three days in the woods, just to be the count's scapegoat. I have as big a stake in this as they do, Mr. Jamison, only I'm fighting for my own life, not somebody else's."

"Be sensible, Richard. Think what it would do to Clarinda if you should be killed."

"I would rather die as a man than live as a coward." Richard's eyes softened. "How could Clarinda love a man without honor?"

"I'll talk to the corporal." Walking over to Littauer, Arthur said, "He insists on going with you. It's a matter of honor to him."

For the first time that evening, the soldier smiled. "Then of course he must join us."

Arthur returned to Richard. As he did, the corporal declared to his men, "Our courageous young Herr. He is a true son of Ahrweiler."

* * *

Bauer left the parlor, from where he had been watching the battle, and returned to the count. "It's useless, Excellency. Our men are all dead or dying."

"We must find the king and kill him. I refuse to admit defeat."

"And do you think Dietrich and the others will support you as regent? They'd murder you first."

"Then, Bauer, they will all hang for high treason," Bronstein laughed, pushing the girl toward the study. "This time, Fräulein, you *will* find the hidden doorway, or I shall personally take an ax to that wall."

Mutely, she nodded, praying the nightmare would end.

She was halfway inside the study when they heard the commotion in the foyer. Immediately, Bronstein sent Bauer to investigate. The captain moved closer to the stairs for a better look, returning less than a minute later.

"Well?" the count demanded. "What is it?"

"It's Dietrich and his men."

"I know *that*. I'm not a fool."

Bauer smiled villainously. "The stableboy is with them."

"You are certain, Captain?" Bronstein remarked, only the tone of his voice declaring his jubilation. He turned to Clarinda and caressed her chin with the muzzle of the revolver. "I knew I would have need of you, my dear," he said under his breath, then, his right hand over her mouth, Bronstein signaled Bauer to light the remaining sconces.

They could see the soldiers noisily congratulating each other on a successful operation, while Dietrich tried to bring their attention back to the objective of their maneuvers. "Gentlemen," he shouted above the din, "we still do not have Bronstein. We cannot claim victory for the crown until that traitor is located."

"Well then, Sergeant," Bronstein taunted, "you haven't been looking very hard for me." Stepping out further, he continued, "You have more lives than a cat, Richard, but it appears your luck has run out at last."

In the far corner of the foyer, Richard turned. The count came fully into view then, Clarinda pinioned against him with the muzzle of his weapon resting on her neck below the jaw, his thumb cocking the hammer. "Unless you give up now, *mein Herr*," he bellowed, "I'll kill her."

"All right," the young man shouted back. "Just don't hurt her."

Bronstein laughed. "That, *mein Herr*, rests entirely with you. And, Dietrich," he continued, "if you try anything, the girl is dead." Immediately, the sergeant ordered his men into the dining room, an angry Arthur following.

"Our little prince seems less formidable without his army behind him, *nicht wahr*?" he declared to Clarinda as he pressed the barrel deeper into her flesh. "Now, Richard, come toward me slowly until I tell you to stop. *This* time, I will be certain you are dead."

\* \* \*

The throbbing in Clarinda's head grew worse with each step closer Richard came, her breathing more labored. In the light from the whale-oil sconces she observed his thin cheeks and haggard eyes, his physical pain almost tangible, and wondered what kind of torment he had been through since Monday. But this Richard had a poise the one she knew lacked, a dignified strength that even Bronstein had to respect.

"*Mein Herr*, you are indeed von Kegel's grandson. Too bad no one else will ever know it." They were about five feet from each other. "That's close enough."

Richard stopped. Smiling, Bronstein removed the revolver from Clarinda's neck and pointed it at the boy.

"Not this time, Bronstein!" Joseph shouted from behind the stairs.

"Try to stop me, Steinmetz," the count answered, chuckling. He pivoted in Joseph's direction and squeezed off three shots that hit the man in the chest. Joseph staggered into the hall, bright red blood pulsing from his wounds, a grotesque smile on his lips, then his lifeless body crumpled to the floor.

Richard was already lunging forward. Grabbing Clarinda's arm, he wrested her from Bronstein. "Run!" he screamed as the dining room door flew open, and Arthur yelled, "This way, Clarinda!" Blindly, she stumbled through the foyer until she collided with the attaché, and he steered her to safety.

Richard tackled Bronstein, and the pistol flew out of the count's hand as the two men fell together. Bronstein spotted it first, lying just beyond his reach. Shoving Richard aside, he strained toward the weapon, but Richard grabbed his jacket, tearing the black serge. He lashed out with his fist, but by then, Bronstein had his large hands around Richard's neck. The young man began gagging as his breath was choked out of him. With great effort, he managed to wedge his arms between Bronstein's and force them apart. Coughing, Richard tried to clear the spots before his eyes, which gave the count time to retrieve the gun.

Once more, Richard came at him, getting his hand on the revolver. It moved in inches between them, now toward Bronstein, then Richard, neither man able to capture the advantage over the other until a muffled crack split the air. Richard's body jerked upward, then collapsed. The hall was silent, a haze of smoke partially obscuring the pair of bodies on the floor.

Bauer crawled over to where they lay and aimed his gun at the back of Richard's head. "Just to be sure," he muttered, but before he could squeeze the trigger, he was dead beside them, a tendril of smoke curling from Littauer's weapon.

Richard moaned and attempted to get up. Immediately, Littauer and Arznei were next to him, carefully lifting him to his feet. "You are safe now, *mein Herr*," Littauer told him.

The two soldiers brought him to the stairs. "Miss Clarinda?" Richard asked.

Arznei smiled broadly. "*Ja, ja. Fräulein Matthias — kommen Sie hier, bitte.*" The dining room door flew open, and Clarinda rushed into Richard's arms, her tears and kisses saying more to him than her words.

Sergeant Dietrich returned to the foyer and, seeing that Bronstein was dead, ordered Littauer to join him in the study. Several minutes later, Jack came out, his face more strained than Clarinda had ever seen it, as Dietrich's subordinate made his way down the back hall to the service entrance. "Clarinda! Are you all right?"

"Oh, Uncle Jack!" she cried, running to him.

"Thank God," he whispered, stroking her cheek with his thumb, where an ugly bruise was beginning to form. "My brave little girl. You have no idea what went through my mind when I heard you in there."

The king and queen joined them. "Where is he?" the queen asked Clarinda. "Where is my son?"

"Let me take you to him, Your Majesty."

\* \* \*

Richard sat on the stairs, his mind numb, seeing nothing but Adele grieving over Joseph's dead body. He was finally freed from the man's brutality, free to go home, but he had no idea where his home was anymore. "He should have let me die," he said to Arznei.

He became aware of a hand on his leg. "Richard?" Clarinda said.

"Not now," he replied, his voice barely a whisper.

"The king and queen want to see you;" she withdrew as they entered the foyer.

Richard refused to look up. He had always been told to keep his eyes down in the presence of his betters, but the king came over to him and raised his chin. "You do not need to fear me, Richard," he said in passable English. "My wife and I . . . we are grateful . . ." The king touched Richard's dirty, matted hair, running his hands over the boy's face before kissing his forehead.

An agonizing pain gripped the pit of Richard's stomach as he lifted his eyes and tried to swallow, the lump in his throat making it impossible. Something about the man before him sent a barely remembered quiver of yearning charging through him, and with lips that trembled uncontrollably, he wept, "Your Majesty, will you send me home? I want to go home." Then he buried his face in his hands, tears forcing their way into his eyes.

"My son, you *are* home. We are your mama and papa."

Richard looked at the queen, the diamonds in her hair glittering like the stars he always saw in his dreams. "Mama," he whispered, holding out his arms to her.

At once, she ran to him and cradled him in her arms. "It's all right now, *Liebling*, all right," she cooed. Then they cried together until, physically and emotionally exhausted, Richard fell asleep.

\* \* \*

Mary was already busy in Ralph Matthias's first floor bedroom when Littauer and Arznei entered an hour later with Richard and settled him in an easy chair, his right foot propped up on an ottoman. She began tending to the puffy, discolored ankle as Jack — his head and shoulder bandaged — came in, several items in his hand. "I realize this isn't the best time, Richard, but I have to know. What happened in the stable last Thursday?"

"Miss Clarinda came into the stable to tell me about your letter, and we started talking."

"About what?"

"Me. That's what we usually talked about. But last week, we talked about us and the way we felt about each other."

"And?"

Streaks of red began appearing on Richard's neck and under the three-day growth of beard. "I kissed her."

"Iris said you stopped when you heard her."

"Yes, sir, I did."

"Then why didn't you wait for me on Monday?"

"His Excellency said" — Richard bit his lip — "he told me Miss Clarinda wanted to see me in the stable, that she wasn't sure . . . He said he would tell you I'd be back. But it was all a trick. It wasn't Miss Clarinda in the stable, it was the soldiers."

"Do you recognize these things?" Jack put the ruby cufflink and the crumpled note in Richard's lap.

The young man stared at the jewel, then picked up the sheet of paper and read it. "I don't understand, Mr. Matthias, who wrote this? Why would I want to leave? Clar — Miss Clarinda and I didn't do anything wrong."

"What about this, Richard?" Jack continued, pointing to the cufflink.

"I've never seen it before." Richard thought a minute. "Did it belong to the count?"

"What makes you ask?"

"He accused me of stealing his jewelry earlier today. But I wouldn't do that, Mr. Matthias." He sighed. "The count had it all worked out. He must have been the one who made it look like I had run away and taken his jewelry. Did you really have the sheriff looking for me?"

"From here to Washington."

Clearing her throat, Mary addressed Jack. "I need to bind Richard's ankle, but I think he'd be more comfortable if he was cleaned up before I do."

"Yes, that would be a good idea."

She got up, returning with a basin filled with water. "Richard's going to need a bath," Jack commented.

"It's after midnight. I can't heat water now, Mr. Matthias."

Wearily, Richard sighed, "I've taken plenty of cold baths in my life. I guess I can take one more."

"I'll get the tub," Mary answered, but as she headed for the door, Jack stopped her.

"Richard is to be treated as a guest. If you could heat water for them, you are to heat it for him."

"Certainly, Mr. Matthias." She left the room.

Richard had already begun washing when Jack returned to him, the older man discerning the pain in the younger's face. "What's the matter?"

"I cut my arms breaking the window in the house in the woods. There must be glass in the cuts."

"Why on earth—"

"It was the only way I could escape the soldiers. They were getting ready to hang me."

Jack realized that there was much more to this evening than what either Clarinda or Richard had told him, and he marveled at the courage shown by his young servant. "Do you know why?"

"So it would look like I'd killed myself."

"And your ankle?"

"I fell in the woods."

The door opened. Mary reentered with a kettle of bubbling water, followed by Berthold, the king's valet, who carried the brass bathtub. Putting down his burden, the thin, elderly man bowed first to Richard, then to Jack.

While Mary added cold water to the hot in the tub, the valet removed Richard's tattered shirt, clucking with disgust when he saw the welts on the boy's back. "A horse is treated with more respect than this," he muttered, then went back to work.

The maid finished filling the tub. "Will you want me to stay, Mr. Matthias?"

Jack looked at Richard, who had begun to blush. "No, thank you, Mary, that won't be necessary."

Richard tugged on her sleeve. "Could you get a few things from my room for me, please?"

"Of course, Richard. What do you want?"

"My shaving things and my nightshirt. They're in the dresser."

"I'll find them." Patting his hand, she added, "I'm happy that you're all right," before withdrawing.

"*Ihre Hosen, mein Herr,*" Berthold requested, pointing down at Richard's legs. The young man nodded again, then bent over and began removing his left shoe.

He was stopped by Jack. "He wants your trousers, Richard, not your shoe."

"My trousers? I thought he wanted my socks." Laughing at his mistake, he undid the buttons on his pants. Finally undressed, the two soldiers carried Richard over to the bathtub.

\* \* \*

Clarinda stopped outside the room where her father had spent the last six weeks of his life and listened to Richard tell Jack of his imprisonment in the old house, the things he was describing making her ill. She stared at the small white package tied with a pink ribbon she held, then slipped it into the pocket of her dressing gown, deciding she could wait until the morning to give Richard the replica of the cipher on the blanket she had made. *His* cipher, she added to herself. After a few minutes, she headed to the parlor.

Moonlight illuminated the piano. She lifted the cover and began playing, softly at first, then, as the music took hold of her, with a passion she had not known she possessed, unaware of everything but the peace that washed over her. She paused, trying to recall the next passage of the work, when a movement from the fireplace startled her.

"Clarinda," Charles Franklin said reassuringly, "what are you doing up?"

"Oh, Grandfather," she murmured in relief. "I wasn't ready to go back to bed."

He approached her and touched her face. "You're exhausted, child. Let me take you to your room."

Shaking her head, she turned back to the instrument and ran her fingers over the keys. "I want to stay here."

"It's all over, dear. You're completely safe now." He smiled at the surprised look on her face. "I've spoken to Jack about what happened. Fortunately, your grandmother's cordial will allow her to forget the whole thing."

She began crying. "The count was going to kill me, Grandfather, and I thought he liked me. Why would he do such a thing?"

"Unfortunately, none of us saw how perverted his mind was."

"I was so scared, Grandfather. I wasn't brave at all." She felt a shiver engulf her. "I keep seeing it over and over . . . only it's Richard lying there, not the count. He was going to kill me, and I'd never have had the chance to tell Grandmother . . ." She stood up and the room began swirling around her. Catching the girl as she started to collapse, Charles swept her into his arms and carried her up the stairs.

* * *

It was still dark when Richard awoke, but the twittering of the birds outside the open window told him it would soon be light, and he stared at the unfamiliar shape of the massive four-poster he lay in. *So that much was real,* he thought, but he had trouble believing the rest of it. *Things like that don't happen to me.*

He sat up, looking at the bandages swathing his arms and hands, and he realized what he imagined a dream was all too real. He had killed a man, the recollection of it starting a surge of self-loathing impossible to control. Turning under the sheet, an intense pain shot up his right leg from the ankle, and he fell back against the bank of pillows, groaning.

There was a rustle from a chair near the bed. Richard watched the room grow brighter as the odor of whale-oil permeated the air. Then the light from the lantern flowed over the counterpane and up into the queen's face.

"Good morning, *mein* Richard," she said. "Happy birthday." She smiled at him and, resting the lamp on the nightstand, sat on the bed. "I ask Herr Matthias how to say to you."

Richard touched her hair and the tiara, which she still wore. "Mama," he whispered, "you're really here. I thought you were a dream." She nodded, not understanding a word he said, and caressed the nape of his neck, her fingers playing with the soft curls of his now-clean hair, just as she had when he was an infant.

All of a sudden, he began crying, great gulping sobs that shook the bed. Frightened, the queen went to the bell pull. Within minutes, Adele entered the room.

"What is it, Your Majesty?" the servant asked.

"Richard . . . he cries and cries, and I don't know what is the matter. He is like a baby, the way he is crying, but he rarely cried as a baby."

Adele went over to the bed. Richard lay on his stomach, moaning, but the woman knew it was not because of any physical pain that he felt. She returned to the queen, tears in her own eyes.

"He will be all right, Frau Royce?"

"With time, Your Majesty. He has not cried for twenty years, at least not in front of me. All the things we did to him, and he never shed one single tear. Now, finally, he is free to show his misery."

"But what can I do, Frau Royce, to help him?"

"Just take him home and love him. It's all he has ever really wanted." Going back to the bed, Adele laid her hand on Richard's back and whispered in German, "Good-bye, my sad little boy. Be happy." Then she ran from the room.

The queen, still in shock, sat beside him and took his hand. His crying had quieted to an occasional whimper; a few moments later, he turned over, drying his eyes with his sleeve.

"I'm sorry," he began. "It was seeing you when I woke up. I didn't mean to cry."

She kissed his hand, then leaned over and kissed his wet cheek. "Sleep now, *mein Sohn*. Your long *Heimweh* is over."

Understanding not with his mind, but with his heart, he curled around his mother the best he could and, still holding her hand, went back to sleep.

# *Epilogue*

---

## Monday, December 17, 1855

On a sunny, cold December morning, Clarinda rested her head against the blue velvet upholstery of an overstuffed settee, watching as the panorama of mountains and valleys blurred past the train's windows. It reminded her of the farmland near her boarding school at this time of year, except for the surprising lack of snow on the neatly furrowed acres and the great stone castles high above the winding river the train had just crossed. The Rhine, Count Dinsl told her. But a day of continuous rail travel had wearied her, so she turned her attention to Richard, who sat opposite, reading a collection of German folk tales.

She reflected on the changes which had occurred in him since his birthday: the dark brown hair was stylishly cut, and there wasn't a speck of dirt anywhere on his hands or under his nails, even the cuticles were clean. In the sable-colored frock coat and tailored trousers, he looked like the prince he was although, she noticed, he fidgeted from time to time with the blue brocade stock she had given him. Even his bearing was poised and confident, but when he smiled, something he did often now, she could still detect the shy stableboy.

The inner differences, however, were the most striking, as if the events of June 21 had broken through the wall he had built around himself over the preceding twenty years, and the real Richard had finally emerged. Only now did she realize, looking at his eyes, how often the shade of distrust had masked his true feelings. *Adele was right, my darling,* she thought. *You hid everything so well, especially yourself.*

"You've changed a lot too," Richard said.

She was startled. "How did you know?"

"It's not so hard to read your mind, not the way you were studying me."

"I thought you were reading your book." Another part of Richard, which had been suppressed: his thirst for knowledge and, surprisingly, the arts. "So are you going to tell me?"

"Tell you what?" he baited her, his eyes laughing.

"How I've changed."

He grew serious. "It's not as obvious with you as it was with me. I used to think you were headstrong, is that the right word, Clarinda? Not afraid of anything. The complete opposite of me. Maybe that's why I admired you."

"But you're no coward. The way you acted six months ago proved that."

"Perhaps, but I often think I'd have let them kill me if I didn't know how much you cared for me." Glancing back at his book for a minute, he continued, "What I'm trying to say is, you seem more responsible, less impulsive."

She chuckled, then leaned over and kissed him. "Well, I am eighteen and a married woman."

"Even your grandmother noticed the difference. I overheard her talking to one of your aunts at our reception."

Clarinda's face brightened. "What did she say?"

"I can't remember exactly" — he began chuckling — "yes, I can. She said, 'Leave it to that girl to toss aside all the advice I've given her these many years and still turn out better than her grandfather and I could have ever hoped for. Jane and Ralph would have been proud.'"

Count Dinsl, the official from Ahrweiler who had accompanied the two of them from Bremerhaven, entered the car from the sleeping quarters. "Your Highness," he declared, inclining his head, "we shall be arriving in Ahrweiler shortly."

"Thank you," Richard replied with a sigh, then returned to his book.

"What's wrong?" Clarinda asked.

"I'm a little nervous I guess."

"You mean worried."

"What if they don't want me back?" He stared at the curtain fringe. "Maybe we should have stayed at Landfield."

"You read your sister's letter. Everyone is thrilled about your return."

"But what if I make a mistake? I'm still not sure of myself."

"Darling, there will be plenty of people here who will be more than ready to help you. Besides, you did so well in Philadelphia, nobody could tell you hadn't spent your entire life in Germany."

"Although one woman wondered, privately she thought, why I spoke with a Boston accent." Chuckling, he continued, "I owe so much to the Groebels for what they did during the three months I lived with them and to your uncle for arranging it."

"Even Grandmother was impressed. I think that was the night she almost forgot you used to be my stableboy."

"She seemed so intent on boasting about your good fortune in marrying me, I don't think she could remember much else."

Clarinda squeezed his hand. "I realize it's difficult for you, but you'll do just fine, as in everything else you've done."

"My wise Clarinda. Always setting me straight."

"Even when it seems I'm pushing you?"

"If you didn't push me so hard, I don't think we'd be here today." Clearing his throat, he continued, "The morning your uncle asked me for the second time to be his butler, I nearly turned him down."

"What changed your mind?"

"Your confidence in me, and the way you showed me how foolish I was to do everything *he* wanted me to do." They laughed at the memory.

"I've often wondered what you found so fascinating about that awful pair of shoes of yours."

"My shoes?"

"You were always staring down at them, in the beginning anyway."

Rising, he went to the door and looked out the window. "When I was little, I remember him saying he hated my eyes because people would be able to see the truth in them, and he made me keep them down. Later on, it became a way of protecting myself so no one would know how much I hurt inside."

She joined him, slipping an arm around his waist. There was much she didn't know about this man she had married, things he still kept to himself. "We knew, Uncle Jack and I."

The train rumbled into the station. Richard looked down at Clarinda and breathed, "It's almost over."

"No, dearest, everything is just beginning." Whispering something to him, she smiled as she watched his eyes widen.

"You're sure?"

"As sure as I can be."

"What will my parents say?"

"They'll be delighted. Their son and grandson with them at last."

"It could be a girl, you know."

Clarinda snuggled his neck. "Richard von Ahrweiler, do you honestly think they'll let you have a daughter?"

"They have no choice in the matter, and come to think of it, neither do we. If I could have a dozen girls like you, I'd be perfectly happy."

"*Mein Herr?*" Richard tensed slightly, then turned to face the maid, who stood there holding their cloaks. He draped Clarinda's over her shoulders, then, after Count Dinsl helped him with his own, they left the train.

Assisted by the count into the waiting coach, Clarinda thought, *We're almost home, Richard and I.* This place that she had never seen was now her home as much as Landfield, and she knew deep down they would never leave. The two men joined her, and they began pulling away from the station.

The train whistle blew one long blast, then every bell in the area picked up the refrain. To Clarinda, it sounded like Christmas come early. Richard listened with tears in his eyes, finally asking Count Dinsl, "For me?"

"Yes, Your Highness. The king has ordered all the bells in Ahrweiler be rung to welcome you home and to convey to you our joy at your return."

All too quickly, they were drawing into the center of the city, the castle's cannon booming its welcome as the coach stopped in front of a large Gothic structure. Waiting to be helped down, Clarinda turned to Richard. "Do you have the letters?" He nodded, patting the left side of his jacket.

One of the massive bronze church doors creaked open, and the white-vested bishop of Ahrweiler descended the steps as Count Dinsl assisted Richard and Clarinda from the coach. He pronounced a brief word of greeting, then ushered them inside to a tiny anteroom off the narthex.

After the cleric withdrew, they removed their wraps and Clarinda primped in front of the room's sole mirror while Richard stared out the window at the frozen garden. A minute later, she joined him. "Will you be all right?" she asked.

"I think so. It's just everything is so—"

"New?"

"Yes." He turned and smiled at her. "It's still a bit hard for me to understand this is really happening, that it's not a dream."

Richard's musings were interrupted by the opening of the door. "*Mein Herr*," Count Dinsl said, "we are ready."

Exhaling, Richard turned and, taking Clarinda's hand, followed the official into the nave.

\* \* \*

Clarinda remembered little of the service that day, her attention drawn instead to the small white marble sepulcher which seemed to dominate the cluster of much larger tombs behind the gilded grate at the front of the church. Her imaginings had not prepared her for the sight of the pathetically few words which attempted to encompass what was believed to be an equally brief life:

*Richard, Prinz von Ahrweiler*
*Geboren* (Born)*: 22. Juni 1833*
*Gestorben* (Died)*: 25. April 1835*

and despite the fact the epitaph was untrue, she was unable to hold back the tears. She thought, too, of the hastily dug graves in Landfield's old slave burial ground, which contained the bodies of Bronstein and his confederates—for them, no mourning families or memorial markers, only the infamy of their deeds living after them—and also of Joseph, who found his honor the moment he lost his life. Glancing over at her husband, she sighed, wondering what he was thinking about as he sat there, surrounded by his family, her answer coming with a tight squeeze of her hand.

Finally, the service was over. The king stood and whispered something to his son; Richard nodded, then came over to Clarinda. "Papa wants me to go in there." He pointed to the grillwork.

"You knew what to expect, darling, what they wanted you to do."

"I know, Clarinda, but I can't do it alone. Come with me, please?"

She looked into his eyes and nodded. "Let's get it over with."

Once inside the enclosure, Richard found the mallet and chisel which the king told him would be there. Walking over to the white tomb, he studied the inscription for a long time, then positioned the chisel against the marble.

The first blow was a weak one, but as it echoed through the silent church, it released something in him, and he swung the mallet faster and harder, tears streaming down his face. Stone chips began flying in all directions, and when a particularly large one nearly struck Clarinda, she made her way over to him and grabbed his arm.

"That's enough, Richard," she insisted.

He shook off her hand. "Twenty years, Clarinda, twenty years of beatings and whippings," he replied, the sound of the mallet making contact with the chisel punctuating his words, then he paused momentarily. "Do you know when it was the worst? When I had done nothing. He hit me the hardest then, and I had absolutely no idea why." Drawing his arm across his face, he returned to defacing the tiny crypt with a ferocity neither he nor Clarinda knew he possessed.

She appealed to Richard's parents, but while they were sympathetic, they refused to stop him. "He had to destroy the demons inside him," the queen told her later. "Otherwise, he would have been the one destroyed."

Then, suddenly, the tools clattered to the floor, and Richard turned to Clarinda, his whole body sagging. Now he let her hold him, his tears falling onto her hair. "I'm sorry," he sobbed. "I couldn't stop myself."

"Oh, my darling," she murmured, then led him out to his family.

* * *

That evening, Richard and Clarinda waited outside the great hall of the palace, the buzz in the room coming to an abrupt halt when Count Dinsl entered. Tapping his long, gold-topped staff three times, he proclaimed, "*Meine Damen und Herren*! Their Highnesses, Prince Richard and Princess Clarinda!"

"I hope there's dancing," Richard whispered, a happy sparkle in his eyes, for he loved to dance.

Smiling with him, Clarinda took his arm, and they moved through the crowd of bowing and curtseying people to the raised dais where the king and queen stood with their daughters. The quiet of the hall was broken as one elderly nobleman began to clap, and soon the entire room was filled with the sound of applause. After it subsided, the king signaled to his majordomo, and twenty footmen circulated with trays of champagne. Waiting until everyone had been served, the king moved to the center of the stage.

"My dear friends and loyal subjects, this is a day which all of us believed we would never see." He glanced at his wife. "It is my unspeakable pleasure to ask you to raise your glass in tribute to my son—Richard von Ahrweiler."

The name echoed as the toast was repeated by a hundred men and women. Tears glistened in Richard's eyes as he stood alone at the front of the platform, overwhelmed by the acclaim and acceptance which he had sought for so long. His father joined him as a group of eight men walked down to the dais.

"Your Majesty!" the one in front exclaimed. "As prime minister of the Grand Council of Ahrweiler, it is my duty to declare to those present that, based upon the sworn affidavits of Frederick John Matthias III and Adele Royce, previously known as Adele Steinmetz, citizen of Ahrweiler, and other incontrovertible proofs, the decision of the inquest of 25 April, 1835 into the death of Richard Georg Artur Johann Wilhelm Franz Ludwig Peter, prince of Ahrweiler, is reversed."

A cheer rose from the assembled nobles as the king turned to his wife and said, "They read Adele and Jack's statements and looked at Richard. It was all they needed."

The prime minister signaled Count Dinsl, who once more struck the floor with his staff. When the crowd fell to silence, the aristocrat continued, "Therefore, we decree Richard Georg Artur Johann Wilhelm Franz Ludwig Peter be recognized as crown prince and sole heir to the throne of Ahrweiler."

"So say you all?" the king asked, smiling.

"So say we all."

The monarch thanked his council, then withdrew a box from his pocket. "Richard, the first time I gave you this, you tried to bite it, and I told you the day would come when you would wear it. My son, we may never fully know everything you suffered during your long separation from us, but through that and your courage, you have earned your signet." He placed the ring on Richard's left pinky and once more raised a toast. "My son and heir!"

While the second accolade rang through the hall, Richard turned around and lifted his glass to a weeping Clarinda, then motioned for her to join him. When she did, he took her in his arms and said quietly, "If it weren't for you . . . I'm home, Clarinda. I'm really home."

"Home," she repeated, her voice trembling. "Sounds wonderful, Richard."

# About the Author

Caryl C. Block has a lifelong love of reading and writing. *The Cygnet* is her first published novel. In her spare time she enjoys cooking, singing in her church choir, and doing crossword puzzles, Sudoku, counted cross stitch embroidery and crochet. Born in Englewood, NJ, she moved from her home town of Harrington Park, NJ, to Windsor, CO, in 2007.

**14 Day Loan**

**Date Due →**

Books returned after due date are subject to a fine.

Fairleigh Dickinson University Library
Teaneck, New Jersey

T001-15M
11-8-02

CPSIA information can be obtained
at www.ICGtesting.com
Printed in the USA
LVOW08s0506070917
547833LV00002B/324/P

9 781635 759419